"What is i ...
b ...

"How about the fact ... with you?"

Aiden barked out a laugh. "You don't have to sleep with me, Charlie. You just have to pretend." Just like that, all amusement was gone from his face, the intensity of his eyes leaving her breathless. He reached across the meager distance between them and captured her chin. Her heart tried to beat out of her chest as he leaned forward until his breath ghosted across his lips. "No one would believe for a second that I'd wait for marriage to have you in my bed, and so you'll be in my bed. But I won't touch you without permission."

His voice dropped an octave. "You can pretend to want me, can't you?"

She squeezed her thighs together, but the move did nothing to alleviate the ache growing between them. *Do* not *give him permission. Some things you can't come back from.*

She held perfectly still, a rabbit in a trap, and when she spoke, she was pathetically grateful that she sounded mostly unaffected. "I think I'll manage."

"Good." His lips curved a little. "Then we can begin."

are plentiful and hot!... An excellent start to a new series."

"*Romeo and Juliet* meets *The Godfather*... Unpredictable, emotionally gripping, sensual and action-packed, *The Marriage Contract* has everything you could possibly need or want in a story to grab and hold your attention."

"A definite roller coaster of intrigue, drama, pain, heartache, romance, and more. The steamy parts were super steamy, the dramatic parts delivered with a perfect amount of flair."

UNDERCOVER ATTRACTION

KATEE ROBERT

FOREVER

NEW YORK   BOSTON

Copyright © 2017 by Katee Hird
Cover design by Elizabeth Turner. Cover photography by Claudio Marinesco.
Cover copyright © 2017 by Hachette Book Group, Inc.

Forever
Hachette Book Group
1290 Avenue of the Americas, New York, NY 10104
forever-romance.com
twitter.com/foreverromance

First Edition: November 2017

Forever is an imprint of Grand Central Publishing. The Forever name and logo are trademarks of Hachette Book Group, Inc.

The publisher is not responsible for websites (or their content) that are not owned by the publisher.

The Hachette Speakers Bureau provides a wide range of authors for speaking events. To find out more, go to www.hachettespeakersbureau.com or call (866) 376-6591.

ISBNs: 978-1-4555-9707-9 (mass market), 978-1-4555-9706-2 (ebook)

Printed in the United States of America

OPM

10 9 8 7 6 5 4 3 2 1

This one's for you, dear readers.

ACKNOWLEDGMENTS

It doesn't matter if it's my first book or my twenty-eighth—the process is never the same, and some are more difficult than others. Thank you to God for making every story new and fresh and an adventure.

Endless thanks to Leah Hultenschmidt for helping to make this book shine. Aiden was a challenge to get out of his shell, and your input was invaluable. Thank you to the rest of the team at Forever for your endless support. The O'Malleys series wouldn't be half so successful without all you do behind the scenes.

Thank you to Danielle Barclay of Barclay Publicity for your support for all things promotional. I'd be lost without you.

A massive hug and thank-you to my readers. This series wouldn't be on the map if it wasn't for you, and getting to share Aiden's story has been so much fun. I hope he was worth the wait!

Last, but never least, thank you and endless love to Tim and the rest of the family. They say it takes a village to raise a kid, and it takes at least that many people to make sure life doesn't fall apart while I'm drafting a book with a rowdy toddler.

UNDERCOVER ATTRACTION

CHAPTER ONE

Something's coming.

Charlie Moreaux, formerly Charlotte Finch, tucked a strand of long white-blond hair behind her ear, narrowing her eyes. This time of night, the party should have been in full swing, everyone a little too drunk, a little too loud. Instead, people kept to their tables and talked in low voices. It created a dull roar within the faded wood-paneled walls of the bar, but nothing close to what it would have been on any other weekend night. She picked her way around the full tables, ignoring the handful of regulars who tried to catch her eye.

Jacques nodded at her. The old man had taken a liking to her from the first time she'd wandered in here, scraping rock bottom and halfway down the road to drinking herself to death. He was the one who'd pulled her back into the land of the living, who'd inadvertently put her on the path to retribution.

Charlie leaned against the bar. "Weird mood tonight."

"It's a full moon."

No one tracked full moons like ER nurses and bartenders.

Jacques poured two healthy shots of whiskey and set one on the faded wood of the bar in front of her. "You're as edgy as they are."

"Yeah, I know. No specific reason." She downed the whiskey, but the warmth curling through her stomach did nothing to battle her nerves. Intuition or superstition, she couldn't shake the feeling of fate hurtling down the tracks, pointed directly at her.

Her first clue that something had gone wrong was a hush falling in a wave through the room. Charlie didn't spin around, despite the feeling of eyes on her. Her attention fell to Jacques, as still as a rabbit facing down a wolf. He spoke low, but the words reached her easily in the new quiet of the bar. "You know I love you, girl, but you're gonna have to take this one outside."

I was right. Trouble's come, and it's here for me.

She turned slowly, still fighting against the instinct to spin, and propped her elbows on the bar as if she hadn't noticed the change in the room. Trouble stood in the doorway, his broad shoulders filling the frame. The neon lights of the bar signs didn't quite reach his face, though they highlighted his square jaw. She didn't have to see his eyes to know he was looking at her.

She could *feel* it. And the danger was just as intense as it had been a year ago when he'd first come to find her.

Aiden O'Malley.

"I'll take care of it." Charlie put enough authority into her voice that Jacques wouldn't question her. This was her problem, and she wasn't about to bring the old bartender into it. She shrugged a little, testing the weight of her holster beneath her leather jacket.

She pushed away from the bar, stalking toward Aiden. In her six-inch heels, she was almost his height, but even the fancy suit didn't hide the fact that he was *cut*. It wasn't just the size of his shoulders. It was in the way his thigh muscles pressed against his slacks when he shifted. Utterly cold and contained, he watched her watch him.

Standing across from him made her feel...vulnerable. She didn't like that. She didn't like that shit one bit. "Outside," she snapped.

He took a step back and then another, allowing her to lead him outside and down the street.

Aiden kept his hands at his sides and away from any weapon he had on him. It was designed to make her feel at ease, but it only ramped up her tension. The man had come here for her. Pretending that he wasn't dangerous just meant he wanted her to underestimate him.

Fat chance of that happening.

Charlie wrapped her arms around herself, sliding her fingers along the butt of her 9mm. The feeling of metal warmed by her body comforted her. She'd defended herself before against worse than Aiden and his bodyguard. She could do it again if she had to. "Why are you here?" *Why now? Why wait an entire year to come back around?*

"I said I'd be back for you. And now it's time. We're going to take down Romanov—together."

The old anger that she'd never quite escaped rose, threatening to drown her. She made herself let go of her gun and drop her arms to make sure she didn't do something regrettable, like shoot this damn idiot who'd decided to walk into her life to throw her past in her face. "Maybe I've gotten over it and moved on with my life."

She hadn't. She didn't think she'd ever be able to

move past what Dmitri Romanov had done. She'd spent the last twelve months poking at the few people on the force who'd actually still talk to her, but no one could—or would—answer her questions on why it was taking so long to build a case against the Russian crime lord who ruled the city.

He'd never see trial. Not for what he'd done to others, and sure as hell not for what he'd done to her.

Four years. An eternity and no time at all. Cops had long memories, and there wasn't a single one in the NYPD who thought she was innocent. How could they when the evidence was so damning?

So, no, she hadn't gotten over it.

Aiden's green eyes flicked over her face, taking in every response, though she'd long ago trained herself not to give anything away. "I don't believe it."

"I could care less what you believe." There were several reasons the head of one of Boston's Irish organized-crime families would be in a shitty little bar in New York seeking her out, and none of them were good for her. Charlie turned to him, taking in the slight tension in his shoulders that hadn't been there when he'd first shown up. *Don't like being told no, do you?*

Well, too damn bad for him. "For the last time, why are you here? Why me?"

* * *

Aiden O'Malley figured he should be grateful Charlotte hadn't pulled the gun on him that she kept touching like a security blanket. He hadn't really thought she'd fall all over herself to agree to help him—especially since she hadn't called him once during the last twelve months—but her cutting through all his bullshit didn't bode well.

He'd never had a problem getting people to do exactly what he wanted—whether he needed to force them or they only required a subtle nudge—but he couldn't do that with Charlotte Finch. He needed her to agree to help him of her own free will, or a vital part of his plan would fall to pieces.

It had taken him twelve months to get his dominoes in place and ready to knock down. The balance of power between the three Boston ruling families—the O'Malleys, the Hallorans, and the Sheridans—was as stable as it would ever be. The feds had backed off enough that he could breathe. Even Dmitri Romanov had been lulled into a false truce at the chance of bringing down a new player in the game.

The Eldridges.

They couldn't have timed their power grab better if Aiden had conjured them himself. All of it added up to a confrontation he knew he could win—if he played his cards right, he could remove the threat of both Romanov and the feds in a single strike.

But to do it, he needed Charlotte.

So he weighed his odds and, after careful consideration, decided being blunt was his best option. "You're familiar with the Eldridge operations." She'd worked the organized-crime unit in the NYPD, so there was no way she *didn't* know about them, at least in passing, but she wasn't going to trust him if he didn't slow-play this.

If she was smart, she wouldn't trust him even then.

Her step hitched almost imperceptibly. "They're run by Alethea Eldridge and her daughter, Mae. Scary, scary ladies, who have a habit of making their competition disappear, though no one has ever been able to put together enough evidence to pin anything on them. Their main income is from drugs—heroin mostly—though they dabble in gunrunning and human trafficking when it suits their purposes. They're small players in the overall New York scene."

"Not anymore. Romanov has made a deal with them— a deal he has no intention of following through on." Or so said the dossier Aiden had gotten from Jude MacNamara. Yes, he'd sold his sister Sloan for information on his enemy—a weight he'd never truly be free of. It didn't matter that Sloan had chosen Jude. If Aiden had paid better attention, she wouldn't have been put in that situation to begin with.

He wouldn't allow it to happen with his youngest sister, Keira.

He didn't trust this unexpected opportunity from Romanov any more than he trusted anything in life, but he'd be a fool to pass up the chance to put his plan into motion.

"How could you possibly know what Romanov intends?"

"It doesn't matter how. All that matters is that it's the truth." He understood her disbelief. Dmitri Romanov was about as easy to pin down as smoke. Aiden had spent the last twelve months verifying Jude's information and looking for other options, but Romanov wasn't the kind of man to leave bread crumbs that could be connected to him and his operations. Even with the sheer amount of intel Jude had on him, there was nothing concrete that could be used against him.

Or there hadn't been until Romanov himself called Aiden.

Charlotte paused, and he stopped next to her. There was a distant look in her blue eyes. "Even if it's true, I don't see how I play into it."

"You know the Eldridges. You know Romanov. You know what they will or won't do in any given situation."

"So do quite a few other people."

She wasn't saying no, so he pressed. "None of those people are as uniquely motivated as you are in seeing Dmitri Romanov taken out at the knees. The O'Malley family barely registers on your radar. You have no reason to double-cross me, because I'll be giving you what you desire above all else."

"And, pray tell, what is that?"

She didn't know it yet, but he had her—hook, line, and sinker. Aiden just had to reel her in. "Justice."

* * *

Justice.

The word rang through Charlie like a bell, and something deep inside her responded. For whatever reason, this man wanted Romanov's downfall as much as she did— possibly more, if he was scraping the bottom of the barrel for *her* help.

She knew what her dad would say. John Finch had a very low opinion of anyone even remotely connected with organized crime, and Aiden O'Malley was the head of his family. *He's as much a snake as Romanov, and getting into bed with one evil to bring down another won't solve anything.*

That didn't change the truth.

And the damn truth was that she'd been living half a life for four years. Even after Jacques saved her and gave her a purpose, no matter how small, she still hadn't bounced back. The drive she'd had ever since she was a child—the desire to be a force of good in the world and to stop bad people from doing bad things—it was gone. It'd disappeared right around the time that Romanov won.

The bad guys won.

She'd learned the hard way that life wasn't a fairy tale, and good didn't always triumph over evil. Sometimes a compelling lie was sought above a harsh truth.

"I'll do it." She didn't give herself a chance to think too hard on it. Her dad had stopped being proud of her four years ago. One more disappointment wasn't going to break him.

Probably.

He hadn't been able to salvage her reputation after she was branded a dirty cop. No one inside the law had. If Charlie couldn't fix *that*, at least she could ensure that Romanov went down in flames as retribution.

She pressed her lips together. "What, exactly, am I agreeing to do?"

Aiden moved to a dark town car that had pulled up, and opened the back door. "Get in and I'll tell you everything." When she hesitated, he gave a mirthless smile. "Look around, Charlotte. If I was up to no good, I could have hurt you at any time."

"Charlie." She'd responded without thinking, even as she did what he said. They'd wandered several blocks away from the bar. He could have cut her throat right here and no one would have sprung to assist her—and they certainly wouldn't have talked to the cops if they'd seen something. Even if Jacques had sent Billy out after her, they were too far away for him to rescue her.

Just as well. She didn't need rescuing. "I don't trust you."

"You shouldn't."

Somehow, that eased her distrust a little. His offer—whatever it entailed—wasn't too good to be true. Enemy of her enemy or not, this man was not a good man.

I'm not much of a good woman anymore, either. She'd tried—tried so damn hard it'd almost killed her—but when push came to shove, the very justice system in place to protect the innocent had worked against her.

She lost everything as a result—because of Romanov.

She climbed into the backseat and scooted over so Aiden could join her. He dominated the small space in a way he hadn't on the street, and she realized he'd been containing himself. Even now, he hadn't exactly let himself off the leash, but he'd stopped trying so hard.

Or maybe this is just another version of Aiden O'Malley—this one designed to put me at ease.

She couldn't trust the change. She couldn't trust *him*.

She took a short breath, inhaling his clean scent, which made her think of snow-topped mountains—beautiful and clear and deadly to anyone who tried to conquer them. "I won't kill anyone." She wasn't *that* far gone.

He chuckled, the sound curling through the space between them like a living thing. "Believe me, if that was my main goal, I have several people better suited." He shot her a look. "Theoretically, of course."

"Theoretically. Sure." She looked around the inside of the town car. It reeked of understated wealth. The leather seats were as soft as butter, and there was a retractable window between the backseat and the driver. With it raised, she couldn't see more than an outline of the man's head. It was entirely possible they were taking her to a secondary location for nefarious purposes, but Aiden had had a point earlier. Knowing that he could have tried to kill her several times over during their walk shouldn't have comforted her—but it did.

Charlie leaned back against the seat, rotating to face him fully. "You have me alone and at your mercy. Enough circling. What, exactly, do you want from me?"

Heat flared in his eyes, a fierce flame of interest that she'd have to be extremely naive to misinterpret. He banked it almost immediately, the cool mask back in place, but it had been there. She was sure of it.

Aiden looked out the window. "As I said, I need your information, and I need you to be a distraction."

"A *distraction*." What the hell was he talking about?

"Yes." His mouth tightened. "I need my enemies—*our* enemies—to underestimate both of us."

She tensed. "If you need a *distraction*, then you should have hired someone better suited to the job. I'm not a sideshow circus freak."

"I'm aware." He finally looked at her again, and his expression was no less intense, for all that he seemed to be trying to rein himself in. "There is no one else, Charlie. You know the players, and you know what's at risk if we fail. As a relative unknown in this game, you can move through them without raising suspicions. But you have a brain." He reached out and touched her temple.

She swatted him away, not liking the fact that she could feel his finger against her skin even after he no longer touched her.

Even as a so-called distraction, it didn't make sense that he'd need her. But she hadn't made much progress in her own investigation, though she'd had access to several decades' worth of police files. Charlie narrowed her eyes. It would be child's play for Aiden to get a hold of those files. If he didn't have ins with the NYPD, his family did with the Boston cops. All it would take was a favor asked by one of the cops on his payroll and he'd have all the information she had—more, since there had undoubtedly been new information in the last four years.

It didn't make any more sense than his supposedly needing her to be a distraction did.

There was something there, something she was missing. She crossed her legs. "Elaborate." The more she got him talking, the better chance she had of figuring out his true purpose in inviting her into his game.

"Romanov wants my baby sister. The reasons behind it are complicated, but the end result is that if I push back, he will take us to war, and both New York and Boston will bleed as a result. While there are benefits to war, our family has lost more than its fair share in casualties, and I refuse to lose another person."

It sounded quite noble... if she forgot who she was talking to.

Aiden O'Malley and Dmitri Romanov were two sides of the same coin. Aiden wasn't some white knight charging in to deliver justice to her out of the goodness of his heart. She hadn't been able to find out much about the O'Malleys, but they had a reputation for being ruthless and they'd ruled one-third of Boston's underground for a few generations, which was impressive when considering how often power changed hands in other cities. She studied his button-down shirt, taking in the cuff links glinting at his wrists. *Cuff links, for God's sake.* "I'm still missing the part where you need me."

He met her gaze directly. "You'll be my fiancée."

"Are you out of your goddamn mind? Getting *married*

is your brilliant plan? That's the stupidest thing I've ever heard."

"Calm down. I'm not actually marrying you, so you can get that look off your face. The only way you can move freely—relatively speaking—in my world is if you're mine. A girlfriend won't cut it—an engagement is required."

"Don't tell me to calm down." She made an effort to smooth out her tone. They'd been talking a grand total of ten minutes, and the fact that he'd had every emotion and reaction locked down only made her feel crazier. "I don't want to move in your world."

He didn't seem too bothered by her shock and denial. "If people think that it's a whirlwind romance, they'll believe that I'm thinking with my cock instead of my brain. The frenzy at the beginning of a relationship distracts even the most focused person, and Romanov will know it—and underestimate the situation as a result. You'll have to be convincing, of course. Not even my family can know your true purpose there."

It was an effort to pick her jaw up off the floor. She'd known he was desperate—he'd have to be to come to her twice—but she hadn't reckoned on him being insane. "No one is going to believe for a second that you fell head over heels for a *cop*—"

"Dirty cop, according to your record, and that's if anyone digs deeply enough to figure out that you aren't Charlie Moreaux."

She ignored that. "Even if they did believe that, there's still the complete fiction that we're in love. No. Absolutely not. There has to be another way." She pinched the bridge of her nose, thinking hard. "Your bodyguard. I can be your bodyguard."

"Out of the question. My family would be less likely to believe that I replaced Liam than they would be that I fell for a former dirty cop—and Romanov certainly wouldn't buy it. Not to mention, bringing in outside security is a giant red flag that would have him watching me *more* closely instead of less."

"I don't care. Figure out something else."

Aiden studied her. "What is it about being my fiancée that bothers you so much?"

She didn't even know where to start, so she went with the first thing to pop into her head. "How about the fact that I'm not going to sleep with you?"

He barked out a laugh. "You don't have to sleep with me, Charlie. You just have to pretend." Just like that, all amusement was gone from his face, the intensity of his eyes leaving her breathless. He reached across the meager distance between them and captured her chin. Her heart tried to beat out of her chest as he leaned forward until his breath ghosted across her lips. "No one would believe for a second that I'd wait for marriage to have you in my bed, and so you'll be in my bed. But I won't touch you without permission."

She licked her lips, her skin too tight, her nipples pebbling until they almost hurt. If he'd looked down, he would have seen them pressing against the thin fabric of her shirt. But Aiden didn't look down, didn't drag his gaze away from her lips. His voice dropped to something akin to a growl. "It's just pretend, Charlie. You can pretend to want me, can't you?"

She squeezed her thighs together, but the move did nothing to alleviate the ache growing between them. *Oh God.* She tried counting to ten, but lost her place halfway through. There was only Aiden and his clear mountain scent filling the back of the town car.

He won't touch me without permission. Do not *give him permission. Some things you can't come back from.*

She held perfectly still, a rabbit in a trap, and when she spoke, she was pathetically grateful that she sounded mostly unaffected. "I think I'll manage."

"Good." His lips curved a little. "Then we can begin."

CHAPTER TWO

The next day, the first order of business was getting Charlie clothed appropriately. Aiden had dispatched Liam to take her shopping, which was a chore on multiple levels. He'd seen the hesitance in her face at the thought of spending his money, but he'd argued that she had to present a particular look if she was going to play in his world. Liam would ensure that she spent enough and didn't try to take the easy way out. Aiden would have asked for his sister Carrigan's assistance, but they were barely on speaking terms at this point. He couldn't quite forgive her for being the reason the family was in this precarious position with Romanov in the first place, even if he was happy she'd found love.

A family of traitors. That's all we are.

Cillian caught him as he walked through the front door. His youngest brother was dressed in his usual three-piece suit, tattoos peeking out at his neck and wrists. "Where have you been? You were supposed to be back last night—"

"I got caught up." Aiden nodded to the man at Cillian's back—Mark Neale, one of their hired men. "Bring Keira to the office immediately."

Cillian stopped short, horror suffusing his face. "No. Aiden, you didn't. Tell me you didn't."

It stung that his brother had immediately jumped to the worst-case scenario, even if that was exactly what Aiden wanted him to believe. *Always so willing to cast me as a knockoff version of our father.* He couldn't let the opinion of his siblings affect his plans, though. They'd see the truth when the time came—and not a second before.

"Office. Now." He injected a bit of the forbidding tone their father had always used to get immediate obedience. He'd be damned before he let Cillian contradict him in the middle of the foyer. His brother didn't mean it as a way of undermining Aiden's tenuous hold on power, but there were men who worked for them who might interpret it that way. A unified front was the only thing that would see them through this until the threats of Romanov and the Eldridges were removed.

Cillian barely waited for the office door to close before he was in Aiden's face. "I have done everything you asked of me and more, and never once did we agree on giving Keira to that monster. Christ, Aiden, she's a kid. He'll eat her alive."

He won't have her.

He couldn't say it, couldn't tip his hand in the least. Cillian was as trustworthy as they came, but he was well on his way to being married to Dmitri Romanov's half sister. Olivia claimed she wanted nothing to do with Dmitri, but she still allowed him access to her two-year-old daughter, Hadley, on a regular basis. Aiden didn't think his brother or future sister-in-law would betray him...but he couldn't risk it.

Not with the number of lives at stake.

So he let his face fall into the familiar cold lines, the mask of the new leader of the O'Malley family. "You aren't the one who makes that decision."

Cillian fell back a step. "You're fucking kidding me. What the hell did Dmitri say in that meeting that was tantalizing enough to get you to agree to *this*? Why now, when you've held him off for a goddamn year?"

I got an opportunity that I couldn't pass up.

He couldn't say it aloud. Every part of this plan depended on a precarious balance that anything could upset. Dmitri needed to believe the lie, so that meant Aiden's family needed to believe the lie as well. "Keira is an adult. She's more than capable of meeting the demands of the family." *As if I'd actually ask that of her.* Aiden had seen all too clearly the pain and suffering that came from arranged marriages, and he had no intention of subjecting his baby sister to it.

"Sure. Whatever the hell you say—because that's worked out so well for the rest of our sisters." Cillian shook his head. "You're going to lose her, too, Aiden. *We're* going to lose her."

Not if I can help it. He slid his hands into his pockets, the very picture of polite disinterest. "She'll be here shortly. Can you contain yourself, or do I need to ask you to wait outside?"

The look his brother gave him was filled to the brim with disgust and disappointment, the twin judgments lodging in Aiden's throat like a blade.

"I'll keep my mouth shut like a good boy." Cillian dropped into one of the chairs in front of the desk.

"Good." It didn't matter what Cillian thought of him. All that mattered was the end goal. If his remaining family despised him by the time that came around . . . so be it. At least they'd be alive to hate him.

The door opened, and Keira stumbled in. She looked like shit, dark circles beneath her eyes, her face drawn from losing weight that she couldn't afford to lose, her hair wild and uncombed. She blinked dilated eyes at him, none of her usual arrogance present. "I take it my time is up."

"Sit." He motioned to the empty chair.

Some of the customary fire sparked in her eyes. "I'll stand."

There was no delicate way to put this, and she wouldn't thank him for trying to sugarcoat it. "We're in talks regarding you marrying Dmitri Romanov. Negotiations will begin shortly for the wedding itself and the living arrangements. I suspect, having waited this long, Romanov will want to expedite things."

He watched her, fully expecting a meltdown. Keira wasn't exactly the most even-keeled and obedient of his siblings. It would have been so easy to pull her aside, to tell her that he had no intention of letting Romanov lay his filthy hands on her, but he needed her and everyone else in his family to respond authentically every step of the way. That meant no one could know the truth.

But his baby sister just shrugged, like this was exactly what she'd expected. "Okay."

He exchanged a look with Cillian, and the fury his brother was directing at him was stifling. Aiden took a deep breath. "Good. You're under house arrest until this is ironed out."

That got a response. Her chin jerked up, her shoulders going back. "Fuck that."

"It's nonnegotiable. You're putting yourself in danger every time you go to one of those goddamn parties, and it ends now." Frankly, he was a little surprised that Romanov hadn't just taken Keira. He could have last year when he'd delivered her to their front door, a warning no one dared ignore. That he hadn't taken her indicated he was playing a deeper game than any of them could begin to guess.

After that little incident, Aiden had put Mark on Keira's detail. They'd never lost her again, and since he always knew where she was, he hadn't been required to curtail her nighttime wanderings.

Things had changed. "I'll nail your window shut myself if I have to, but you're not leaving this house without an escort."

Something like panic bled into her voice. "Don't put me on house arrest, Aiden. Please."

He remembered all too well what she'd threatened to do the last time he'd issued the same command. Aiden crossed to her and put his hands on her shoulders. She felt so terrifyingly frail, like she might shatter into a million pieces if he hugged her too hard. "It's only for a little while—and only at night. Take an escort and you can go wherever you damn well please during the day. But Keira"—he waited for her to meet his eyes before he continued—"the second you ditch your protection duty, that privilege is gone. This is not a game, and I'm not making idle threats."

Her hazel eyes filled with tears, making him feel like the biggest asshole in existence. He didn't let that sway him, though. Her safety was more important than her freedom. Finally, she jerked out of his hold. "I hate you."

"I know." He'd do more to deserve that hate before this thing was through.

* * *

Charlie tried very, very hard not to think about the sheer amount of money she'd spent that day. Every time she'd balked, that bastard Liam had all but dragged her into another store and thrown her to the mercy of the salespeople there.

And they'd had none.

She ran her hand down her thigh, a small, stupid part of her thrilled at how soft the fabric of her dress felt. It was a deep purple, a simple sheath that she'd been assured was the height of fashion right now. She didn't know much about that, but the price tag would have paid her rent for a month. *Who the hell had that kind of money to spend on* clothes?

Criminals.

Like the one who had her panting after him like some kind of fool. He hadn't taken advantage of it last night, but that was more about his restraint than her morals. *If he'd kissed me…*

Her body flushed hot at the thought, and she had to fight not to squirm. This wasn't her. Sex had a place, and she indulged whenever her hormones got too out of control, but it was always with appropriate men. *Safe* men.

Aiden O'Malley was many things, but appropriate didn't begin to enter into the equation, and safe wasn't even in the same universe. He was dangerous in ways that had nothing to do with the family he was born into, and everything to do what how he frayed her control without even trying. He was a man who inspired the kind of lust that left nothing but ash in its wake.

She had no intention of letting this devil's bargain put her in the ground.

No, the only reason she was doing this was to see justice done when it came to Dmitri Romanov.

Justice sounds a whole lot like revenge.

She shoved the thought away. She'd deal with it when she was finally face-to-face with that monster. In the meantime, she had other things to worry about—like the fact that she was about to meet her fake fiancé's family.

"We're here."

She jumped. The town house they'd pulled in front of was a monster. It reeked of money and pretentiousness, the massive front door sending a very clear message to people like her: You are not welcome. She didn't come from money, but she'd encountered it enough to recognize it on sight.

I've a feeling we're not in Kansas anymore.

Charlie climbed out of the town car, fighting the urge to throw herself into the backseat and demand that Liam take her back to New York. No matter what her former brothers in the NYPD thought of her, she wasn't a coward. She could walk into this situation and be cool and collected, and not lose her head and do something stupid. She *would*.

Taking down Dmitri Romanov wouldn't restore her good name, regain her father's respect, or give her life back, but it was better than the alternative. Wasting her life away playing poker.

Before she could reconsider, she strode across the sidewalk and up the stairs. She hesitated for half a second, wondering if she should knock, but if she was supposedly Aiden O'Malley's fiancée, this would be her home. She would rule at his side. Her stomach fluttered, but she wasn't sure if it was nerves or flat-out fear.

This isn't for real. I'm playing a part, not diving head-first into the dark side. Dad would—

But she couldn't think about her father without her chest twisting into knots. There wasn't a more by-the-book man than John Finch. For her father, there were no shades of gray—there was only black and white, right and wrong. He wouldn't approve of this plan, and if he found out she was "engaged" to Aiden O'Malley, he might arrest her himself. She didn't know what he'd charge her with, but her dad could be a genius when it came to the law.

"Charlotte?"

She realized she was standing on the top step, staring blankly at the massive door before her. *Get it together.* She dredged up a smile for Liam. "Charlie. Please. No one calls me Charlotte unless I'm in trouble."

He nodded, but he studied her like she was a bug under a microscope. "You don't have to do this, you know. He'd find another way if you changed your mind."

She hadn't known him long, but she recognized the words as the truth. Whatever Aiden's endgame, he wouldn't let a little speed bump like her bolting affect his plan. In reality, though, it wasn't about him. It came down to her— her and Dmitri Romanov. She may have never met the man face-to-face, but she'd seen his dirty work the few short years she'd worked as a cop. She'd seen how he'd benefited from cops turning against everything they were supposed to stand for.

They chose that. Those cops compromised their honor of their own free will.

She knew that. Romanov hadn't put a gun to their heads and forced them into anything—he'd just offered a truly outstanding amount of money for them to look the other way when it suited him.

It made her sick to think about.

"I know." She gave Liam a weak smile. Then she took a deep breath, opened the door, and walked into the O'Malley home.

* * *

Keira O'Malley froze at the bottom of the stairs as the woman walked into their house like she owned the place. She was pretty in an alternative sort of way, her long white-blond hair pulled back to reveal that her temple was shaved on one side, and though she wore a designer dress, she didn't look comfortable in it. More than that, though, she was a fucking *stranger*. "Who the hell are you?"

That was when she caught sight of Liam at the woman's back. Keira waited, sure that he'd toss this chick out on her ass, but he just followed her inside and shut the door behind him. He shot Keira a look like *she* was the one out of line. "Keira, meet Charlotte—Charlie. This is Aiden's fiancée. Charlie, this is Keira, Aiden's youngest sister."

Keira clutched at the banister to keep from toppling over. She searched Liam's face, but there wasn't any amusement to indicate that this was a goddamn joke. She shook her head, but it didn't do a single thing to stop the rushing in her ears. *Aiden's fiancée?* When had her brother found time to get engaged? *Does everyone know about this except me?*

She turned without another word and marched up the stairs. Every single fucking person in her family was looking out for themselves first. If Aiden thought she was going to sit here like a good girl until he shipped her off to be the slave-bride of Dmitri Romanov...

Her traitorous body warmed at the thought of what, exactly, would be required of her if she married Dmitri. He was beautiful in the way of fallen angels, even if he was an evil bastard. God had really broken the mold with that one—or he would have, if she believed in God anymore.

Something terrifyingly like a sob lurched in her chest, and she broke into a run the rest of the way to her room. No one called after her, no one chased her down to see if she was okay. It wasn't self-pity that drove her to the window of her room and had her wrenching it open. It *wasn't*.

That's always been my problem. I feel too damn much.

Sometimes she feared all the feelings would suck her under and she'd never see the light again. The only thing that kept the sea at bay was the drugs and alcohol. She'd dialed it back a little—she'd had to because Aiden had cut off her money and she wasn't desperate enough to trade other things for coke. But getting through the day stone-cold sober?

Out of the question.

Keira shimmied out the window, ripping her jeans in the process, but she managed to climb onto the fire escape that ran down the building a few feet over. It groaned beneath her weight, but it held, just like it always had. Through it all, one word drummed through her head in time with her heart. *Free, free, free.* It was a lie. Everything in that house was a lie these days.

Maybe it always had been.

She slowed her pace as she rounded the corner, keeping her head down, determined not to bring attention to herself. Despite what Aiden thought, she knew how to fly beneath notice when it suited her. Keira brought out her phone and scrolled through the handful of texted invitations tonight, and picked the closest one. She wasn't trying to endanger herself, but staying in that house a second longer than necessary was more than she could bear.

It won't be my house for much longer.

Marriage. She'd always known that was the role she would be required to play. She'd gone so far as to offer it last year when she'd witnessed Dmitri's ultimatum. A small, dark part of her figured being a wife to that man was nothing more than she deserved. An even smaller part of her had flickered to life when she had gotten close to him those two times, but that flame had died when she realized that he wasn't coming around for *her*. He was sending a message to her brother.

He didn't want her. Not really. He needed her to secure his position—and to put her family in their place.

"Enough. I'm so goddamn tired of feeling sorry for myself." Feeling anything at all, really.

She made good time walking to the party, slipping through the door and moving into the crowd that had already gathered. It was being held in the basement of an old club. She recognized about half the people there, though she'd never go so far as to call them friends. They were here for the same reason she was—to forget their shitty lives for a little bit.

A guy she'd seen around often enough that she should know his name approached, a broad grin on his face. "If it isn't my favorite bitch."

She accepted the vodka bottle he passed over, pausing to check the seal. It hadn't been tampered with. *That's something, at least.* She peeled off the plastic around the cap and nodded. "Thanks."

"I know your rules." He grinned, his gaze skating over her in a way that made her skin crawl. A year ago, maybe she would have taken him up on the nonverbal offer, but now she couldn't trust that whoever she went home with wasn't working for an enemy. And besides, after she'd gotten tangled up with Dmitri, no one had sparked her interest enough to risk it.

Keira wove through the crowd to the couches lining the wall. There were people fucking on most of them, but one was empty. She dropped onto the thin cushion and took a long pull off the bottle. Blessed burning shot down her throat and warmed her stomach in a way nothing else seemed to be able to. She took her first full breath since Aiden had called her into his office. But she hadn't come here to think about that. She took another longer drink, her need to breathe battling with her need to forget.

"Keira O'Malley."

She eyed the man who appeared at her side as she took another swig of vodka. He didn't fit here. He was too still, too watchful. That would have given him away, even if his Russian accent hadn't. She slowly lowered the bottle, barely resisting the urge to scan the room to see if *he* had come. *It doesn't matter. I hate him, remember?*

Sure she did.

The man crossed his arms over his chest, and a flash of metal showed beneath his jacket. "Mr. Romanov would like to speak to you."

"No."

He gave a slow blink, like he wasn't sure he'd heard her right. "That wasn't a request."

"I don't care." She studied the label on the vodka. It was cheap shit, tasting more like rubbing alcohol than the stuff her brother had in their liquor cabinet. When it was clear the man was about to threaten her, she pinned him with a look. "From what I understand, I'll be marrying that Russian bastard. So let's start this correctly. If he wants my presence, he can damn well tell me himself instead of sending one of his butchers to summon me like a naughty child." Her words started slurring toward the end, but she bore down, forcing clarity for a few moments more. "You can pass that along— and tell him if he really wants my attention, he should bring some of the good stuff." She motioned to the bottle. "Now get the fuck out of here. I'm tired of looking at your face."

Dmitri Romanov might have tempted her once upon a time, but he was just another shade of O'Malley or Sheridan or Halloran. They were all the same, and she was so god-damn done with the petty power games.

There wasn't a single thing he could do to her that hadn't already been done.

She had nothing left to lose.

CHAPTER THREE

Charlie should have known how things were going to go after she met Aiden's sister on the stairs. She might have taken a page from Keira's book and fled, if Liam hadn't been a wall at her back. His silence and strength were strangely comforting. He, at least, knew this thing for a fraud, and he was playing along. She'd do the same.

"Third door on the right."

She followed his low instructions, her heels clicking on the tiled floor as she walked down the hall to the room he'd indicated. A fortifying breath did nothing to fortify her, so she walked through the door before she could talk herself out of it.

Aiden leaned on the edge of a giant desk that was almost perfectly clean. She'd have thought the lack of clutter meant he didn't do work there, but Charlie suspected it was because Aiden was a control freak of epic proportions. She'd seen his type around the poker table—the man who uses masks to manipulate the people around him. He was the best buddy, the overwhelmed newbie, the blustering idiot, all depending on what would serve him best.

But the pros she knew looked like children playing pretend compared to Aiden O'Malley. The main skill Charlie had developed after she'd been so horrifyingly wrong about her brothers in blue was people-reading...and she couldn't begin to guess what the real Aiden was like.

At the moment, he looked slightly rumpled, a few buttons of his shirt undone, his hair not quite perfect, as if he'd been running his hands through it. He went still as she walked toward him. "Charlie." She heard the door shut behind her, but she had eyes only for him.

Pretend. It's just pretend.

It didn't feel very fake when he held a hand out to her and she crossed the room to take it. She had a vague impression of masculine colors on the wall and sturdy furniture, but she couldn't take her gaze from him.

He took in her dress with a quick look, the heat in his green eyes banking just as quickly as it had last night. "I like it."

"Thanks." This felt too weird, especially considering why she was really here. Charlie looked around. "I met your sister when I walked through the door."

"Keira." He said her name on a sigh, the very picture of the beleaguered brother.

Real or pretend?

"She's pissed at me right now, and I don't expect that to change anytime soon." Aiden motioned her closer and took her hand again, running his thumb over her knuckles as he examined the manicure she'd gotten today.

She didn't ask what he'd done to make his sister angry.

It was none of her business. She wasn't here to get to know him—something she desperately needed to remember. "What's the plan?"

"Dinner." He saw her confusion and explained. "Before we can convince our enemies that we're madly in love, we need to convince my family. Their belief will lend the whole thing credence. Some of them are terrible liars."

She doubted that very much. Charlie looked down at their joined hands, the contact so innocent and yet branding her all the same. "Well, then let's make it convincing. This holding hands makes me feel like I'm back in seventh grade and awkward as hell."

"What are you proposing?" His tone gave nothing away, not anticipation, not condemnation.

"The only way they'll believe you proposed marriage so fast is if the sex was off the charts." *Idiot, idiot, idiot.* She was on dangerous ground, and she knew it, but she wasn't going to risk what little she had left to lose on a plan destined to fail because they half-assed it.

Charlie took a deep breath and stepped into him. He felt good, all long lines and hidden strength, but she was about to jump out of her skin just being this close. Seductress she was not. "We have to be all over each other, have to constantly look like we're about to fuck or have just fucked—or a combination of both."

His hands came to rest on her hips, not pulling her closer or pushing her away, just touching her. "It would make the charade more convincing. I can't argue that.'"

"Then let's…" She ran her hands up his chest and looped them around his neck. The move pressed her breasts more firmly against him, and his fingers flexed on her hips. It was a slight movement, but it was the first physical indication he'd given since that moment in the car that he wanted her. *We're both the problem here. Too cold. Too contained.* "Let's mix things up a bit."

"You're playing with fire, Charlie." The words came out in a rumble. "I promised I wouldn't touch you unless you asked me to, but make no mistake, if you want to play this close to the line, then we'll be crossing that line. Repeatedly."

"I know." Her body tingled, but she couldn't be sure if it was in fear or anticipation.

"Be sure."

He was giving her an out, which was kind of sweet, but she was right and she knew it. They had to cross this line, and cross it before they encountered any more of his family. The reasoning felt flimsy, but she pushed away her doubt. She was an adult, and she was well aware of the risks that came with taking things to this level. "I'm sure."

He didn't ask again. Aiden let go of her hip with one hand, and slid it up her side to bracket her throat. There was no pressure, no pain, just a startling possessive gesture that seared her to the core. "Take off your panties. Now."

She swallowed hard, the move dragging his calluses against her sensitive skin. "I'm not wearing any."

The look he sent her nearly had her on her knees, her legs shaking, her breath already coming in short gasps. "Good girl."

* * *

Aiden knew he should put the brakes on this insanity. It was a bad idea, a distraction neither of them could afford. He stared at Charlie's fuck-me-red lips telling him she wasn't wearing any panties and reacted. "I'm not fucking you. Not today, not like this."

Was there disappointment in those blue eyes of hers? He thought so. Aiden tightened his grip on her throat, just a little, claiming her even though he had no right to. "Make no mistake—I *am* going to fuck you, Charlie. I will spread your thighs, rip off your panties, and drive into you until your eyes roll back in your head and you see the face of God. But I will do it when I'm damn well ready." He dipped his hand beneath the hem of her dress, slowly skating up the outside of her leg to her hip, taking the fabric with him until she was partially bared.

She shivered a little. "I don't know that I put sex on the table."

"It's not on the table." He turned, putting himself between her and the door, and backed her up against the desk. "Not today." It was a mistake, but he couldn't stop as he lifted her onto the desk.

You knew this was going to happen. Fuck, you even planned on it.

Not like this. He'd fully intended on seducing Charlie, but on his own terms. Control was vital for every aspect of his plan, including taking her to bed. He fought against the need to spread her legs and do exactly as he'd promised, right then and there. *Not the time. You need her panting for it so she doesn't start thinking too hard about why you picked her.*

She braced her hands behind her, looking a little nervous. The fact that this woman had almost pulled a gun on him during their first encounter and was looking nervous *now* made him feel...He wasn't sure how to put it into words. He wanted to reassure her, to pull them back onto safe ground. It was too damn bad there was no such thing as safe ground.

And it was all his doing.

"I'm going to touch you now." *Just touch. Not fuck.* He needed the reminder as much as she did.

He leaned back and looked down her body. Her thighs were lean and muscled, showcasing God alone knew how many hours of hard work. And her pussy...His mouth watered at the sight. He tore his gaze away to look her in the face. "Unless you changed your mind."

Charlie licked her lips, and he nearly groaned. "The argument still stands. Trial by fire and all that."

He smiled a little at the comparison. "This will feel better than walking through fire." He stroked her, gauging her reaction. He was already hard, but at her tiny little whimper, he damn near split his pants. "Tell me how you like it." He paused, fighting for distance. Doing his best not to be swept away by the fact that she looked vulnerable for the first time since he'd met her. "Show me."

"Right now?"

"Is there a better time?" He took her hand and pressed it against her lower abdomen. "Show me how to drive you crazy."

She touched herself, hesitantly at first, but when he stroked her thighs, her eyes slitted and her movements smoothed out. Aiden waited until he knew what she wanted, and then he took over. He rubbed her clit with the same little movements she'd done, watching her face. "Like that."

"Yes." Charlie nodded, letting her head fall back and her eyes slide shut.

He wanted to demand that she open her eyes and *look* at him, to acknowledge that she was teetering on the edge because of what *he* was doing to her, but there was no room for being possessive. It wouldn't do either of them any favors.

He kept control through sheer force of will, but Aiden cursed aloud when he pushed a finger into her and she clamped down around him. "Fuck. You've been neglecting yourself, haven't you?" He stroked her, keeping up the motion against her clit as he explored her from the inside. "You don't have to answer that. I can tell. You wouldn't be so tightly strung if you were fucking someone regularly."

"Guess what?" She lifted her head and pinned him with a look. "The only thing I need from you is to make me come so we can get past this ridiculous roadblock. If I want to be psychoanalyzed, I'll hire a shrink."

There you are.

She'd been almost hesitant since she got into the car with him. He'd started to wonder if she couldn't hold her own, if this was a mistake. "Then come, Charlie." He pushed a second finger into her, feeling around until he found her sensitive spot. He crooked his finger against it, sheer masculine satisfaction rolling through him at her gasp. "Let go."

Her back bowed, and her lips opened in a cry that he wanted to eat. Aiden heard the office door open, but he didn't stop, finishing her off and cursing himself for having a goddamn plan that didn't involve sinking into her. Not yet.

A throat cleared behind them, and he shrugged out of his jacket and draped it over her lap before turning to find Liam standing there. "Yes?"

"Teague and Callista are in the dining room with Moira." He hesitated. "There was no mistaking the sounds coming out of this office as they walked past."

That was the goal, but Aiden still glanced at Charlie to

see if it bothered hcr. In the fifteen seconds it had taken Liam to deliver his report, she'd managed to fix her dress and stand. The only indication of what they'd just been doing was a flush to her cheeks and chest that hadn't been there before, and her nipples pressing against her dress.

And his rock-hard cockstand.

"Good." She passed back his jacket and adjusted her hair. "Then I suppose it's time for me to meet the family."

Liam's gaze jumped between them, but he just nodded. Aiden would hear what he thought of this mess later, he had no doubt—but his man wouldn't question him while they had an audience. "I'll let them know you're on the way."

"Do that." Aiden waited for the door to shut to turn and face Charlie. "Most of my siblings won't believe us."

She arched her eyebrows. He kind of hated that she'd put herself together so quickly, even if that was a valuable skill to have. "That's to be expected, I'd think."

"Yeah, well, my sister Carrigan is the sole exception." He'd gone back and forth about inviting Carrigan to this dinner. Her husband, James Halloran, was still more enemy than ally, and she never went to any of these types of things without him. His presence could very well agitate the issue, and that wasn't even taking into account that Carrigan could go for Charlie's throat.

He ran a hand over his mouth. "She's overprotective, even if we rarely see eye to eye these days."

"She's going to label me a gold digger and a whore, then."

"My sister doesn't slut-shame." He didn't know why he was defending her. If Carrigan had married Dmitri Romanov like their father had arranged in the first place, he'd be their ally instead of their enemy . . .

Aiden shuddered a little at the thought of Carrigan at Dmitri's side. The wild and fiery part of her that came to life in James's presence would have died as a result of that marriage.

But he doubted his sister's vengeance for being forced in that relationship would have spared her own family. She would've helped Romanov take over the entire eastern seaboard inside of five years—Boston included.

"Bully for her." Charlie gave a mirthless smile, drawing him back to the present. "I can handle it."

"I know." It was why he'd recruited Charlie in the first place.

That, and because of her father.

The same FBI agent his brother Teague had been supplying with information for years.

Aiden smothered his rage. Both at his brother and John Finch.

Keep it locked down.

He offered Charlie his arm. "Shall we?"

She nodded, no evidence of anything but calm confidence on her face. *She would have made one hell of an undercover cop.* She smiled. "Let's do this."

CHAPTER FOUR

Charlie braced herself, nearly overwhelmed when Aiden led her into a room with eight other people—three couples and two little girls. They were talking, though tension ran through the space like fault lines.

And the power.

Good God, the power.

She'd once read a book that described one of the characters as wearing a mantle of power. Back then, it had been impossible to wrap her head around. Now, standing in this room, she understood.

Liam had given her a brief rundown of the family tree while they were shopping today, so she could put names with faces without too much trouble. The blond woman sitting at the table was Callista Sheridan, newly appointed head of the Sheridan clan. Her husband, Teague, was Aiden's middle brother, and the small child in his lap with a head full of curls was Teague and Callista's daughter, Moira. Callista was pregnant again, far enough along to show. They should have looked like just another American family—and they did, until Charlie looked into the woman's blue eyes.

If she thought I was a threat to her family, Callista Sheridan would kill me without a second thought and bury my body where it would never be found.

The thought left Charlie cold. Rationally, she'd compared Aiden to Romanov and she knew he wasn't some good man who just happened to run one of the three crime families who ruled Boston. But now that she was standing in a room with both him and the other two-thirds of that power wheel, it was clear... Aiden was ruthless.

Another couple sat at the far end of the table, as far from the rest of them as they could get. The man was like a blond lion lazing in a chair with his woman on his knee, but there was a coiled tension in his body that spoke of violence ready to be unleashed. For all his surface attitude, it was clear he didn't want to be here and didn't trust any of them. This had to be James Halloran—which made the woman perched on his lap in a borderline indecent dress Carrigan. She, at least, wasn't pretending to be anything other than what she was—powerful and dangerous.

God, Charlie could barely breathe.

Her gaze skated to the middle couple. This man was dressed in a three-piece suit and had tattoos peeking out at throat and wrists—that would be Aiden's brother Cillian. He was in charge of the O'Malleys' accounting and cyber-security, and though he didn't have the level of power that some of the other people did, the way he hovered over the woman and child at his side... Another person not to cross.

She started to dismiss his wife—a pretty Middle Eastern woman with a wild mane of hair—but froze. Charlie knew that face. Olivia Rashidi and her daughter were Dmitri Romanov's last remaining family, though Olivia was only his half sister via their late father's mistress.

Liam had left out *that* little piece of information.

Charlie shot a look at Aiden to silently tell him that he'd be answering her questions later, but found his attention focused on James and Carrigan.

I am in the room with the most dangerous people in Boston. Who thought this was a good idea?

She'd gotten through the last four years by flying under the radar and biding her time. Now she was about to be thrust into the limelight, such as it was, and Charlie suddenly wanting nothing more than to turn around and walk out of the room. Only the fact that Aiden promised to bring about the justice she desperately wanted kept her feet planted and her chin up as every eye turned to her.

Aiden, at least, didn't seem the least bit bothered by the attention. But then, he'd grown up in this world. This was his natural habitat. He guided Charlie to a chair and pulled it out for her. Her instinct screamed at her to remain standing with a clear path to the nearest exit, but she managed to sink into the seat all the same.

He stood at her back, likely knowing that she was half a second from bolting. "Thank you for coming."

Carrigan uncoiled herself, though she didn't move away from James. "I'd be tickled pink over the invite if I thought for a second this was a friendly family gathering. Except I know the O'Malleys don't have those, and, even if we did, I wouldn't be invited." She made a show of looking around. "Where *is* our darling father? He's been missing in action for well over a year now." She raked her gaze over Charlie. "And who the hell is *this*?"

Charlie wasn't going to touch *that* with a ten-foot pole. The only thing Aiden had told her before leading her in here was to let him do the talking, and she was more than happy for him to field the hostility.

No one seemed particularly thrilled to be here—herself included.

"You know damn well that Seamus is in Connecticut," Teague snapped. "I'd think you'd be as grateful as the rest of us for his absence."

"It's not like I see him when he is in town. That's your burden to bear, obedient son that you are." Carrigan smoothed back her hair. "Though I much prefer dealing with Aiden to Seamus. At least *you* aren't pretending I'm dead and buried."

There were so many undercurrents that Charlie felt adrift in shark-infested waters. These people had been playing dangerous political games long before she showed up—long before Dmitri Romanov was on their radar, too, she'd wager.

Aiden ignored his siblings' bickering and looked around the room before nodding at Liam. The man detached himself from the wall he'd been leaning against and moved to stand next to them. Aiden spoke low enough that Charlie doubted anyone else could hear him. "Where is Keira?"

"Mark's on her, but I don't have the exact location. I'll look into it." Liam walked through the door, and if she hadn't been watching him so closely, she would have missed the flicker of worry in Aiden's green eyes.

Carrigan clapped. "You've lost Keira. Again. Congratulations." Apparently, Aiden *hadn't* spoken softly enough. His oldest sister's upper lip curled into a truly impressive sneer. "You really know how to treat your sisters, don't you?"

There was too much history in that question for Charlie to fully understand. She knew there was another sister, Sloan, but Liam hadn't said much about her other than that she wasn't currently in Boston. *Maybe I should have been taking notes when he was bringing me up to date.*

A muscle jumped in Aiden's jaw, but he didn't give any other sign of agitation. His mask had slipped into place the second they walked out of his office, and now he was the picture of the formidable family leader. "That's not why I asked you here."

"Then do tell us, dear brother. Why *are* we here?" Carrigan's smile was downright vicious. She looked like she was ready to take a chunk out of him, and only James putting his hand on her hip kept her from doing so.

"As my family, I want you to be the first to meet my fiancée." He kept speaking over several sounds of disbelief. "Charlie Moreaux, this is my family."

And then all hell broke loose.

* * *

Aiden regretted calling this dinner almost as soon as he walked into the room. It would have been smarter to meet with each of his siblings individually and break the news in a controlled environment where he had the advantage— or what passed for an advantage in this family. As it was, Cillian was demanding to know what the hell was going on, Carrigan was calling him seven kinds of a fool, and Teague was staring at Charlie as if he had met her before but couldn't place where. *Time to shut it down.*

"Enough!" He had to roar it to get them to shut the hell up, but it worked. His life would have been so much easier if his siblings were content to follow orders like good little soldiers instead of striving for their individual independence every step of the way. He wouldn't have to play the hard-ass and could be a brother instead of the head of the damn family that they seemed to resent as much as they loved.

But that wasn't how things were. He'd had to sacrifice bits and pieces of his relationships with them—especially Carrigan—for the bottom line. The family's safety lay in its power—to threaten one was to threaten the other—and he'd do whatever it took to ensure that their enemies detected no weakness.

He was about to sacrifice even more. "I'm not asking for your permission or your goddamn blessing. I'm telling you that I'm marrying this woman, and I expect you to fall in line and accept it." He didn't actually expect anything of the sort. That wasn't who his siblings were. But if he acted in any other way, they'd be suspicious.

Carrigan snorted, but it was Callie who rose to her feet, still graceful despite being over halfway into her pregnancy. Her smile didn't quite reach her eyes, but it never did when she spoke to him. "Congratulations." She crossed to look down at Charlie. "It's a pleasure to meet you. I look forward to getting to know you better."

And that right there was what made Callie one of the biggest threats in the room.

Teague followed her, Moira on his hip, though he didn't lie as well as his wife did. "Welcome to the family."

"If you knew what was good for you, you'd run screaming out of this room." This from Carrigan, who hadn't moved. She shook her head. "God, Aiden, I never pegged you for the biggest drama queen out of all of us. A surprise fiancée? *Really?*"

"Oh for fuck's sake, shut up, Carrigan." Cillian stood, looking at Aiden like he'd never seen him before. "This is a mistake, and I'm telling you that now." He nodded at Charlie. "No offense. I'm sure you're a great person, but I've never heard of you. You marry my brother and it's as good as painting a target on your chest. I don't care how good the sex is, it's not worth it."

Aiden tensed, ready to step in—the last thing he needed was his brother scaring her off—but Charlie reached up and covered his hand where he'd set it on her shoulder. "Your concern is touching, but I'm well aware of what I'm getting into." She sounded cool and in control despite the relative chaos going on around them.

Just another confirmation that Aiden had been right to choose her.

Cillian didn't look like he believed her, but he finally shrugged. "Then welcome to the family. Hope you survive it."

Satisfied, Aiden looked at Carrigan. Of them all, she was the one he'd been closest to, the one who understood the stakes of the games they played. Maybe that was why her betrayal hurt so fucking much. He didn't know. He didn't spend a ton of time reflecting on it—personal feelings had no place in a situation where so many people depended on him to maintain the stable power structure that kept them safe.

They'd avoided all-out warfare so far. He'd do everything in his ability to ensure that they continued to do so.

Up to, and including, lying to his family so he could remove enemy number one.

Carrigan's green eyes, so like their mother's, condemned him. "Whatever it is that you're doing, it's a mistake, Aiden. You're going to get her killed."

"*Her* is sitting right here." Charlie stood, moving to Aiden's side. Her fingers laced through his as if they'd held hands a thousand times. "While your concern is appreciated, it's as unnecessary as his." She nodded to Cillian. "Now, I don't know about you, but I'm starving, and I hear the staff has put together an excellent dinner for us. So why don't we all play nice and enjoy it?" If Aiden didn't know better, he'd think that she wrangled with mob families on a regular basis. Her hand didn't so much as shake in his, and her blue eyes showcased an icy calm that he admired even as he analyzed it.

Thrives under pressure and in dangerous situations. Good to know.

"I've lost my appetite." Carrigan stood, James following her. He hadn't once spoken, just watched the whole circus. Aiden didn't like to admit it, but the Halloran territory was in good hands with this man—and so was his sister. Those two had already made some big changes, creating a nonprofit organization to help victims of sex trafficking, and quietly bringing down the perpetrators of the slave trade by means both legal and illegal. As a brother, he was proud of his sister and happy that she was happy.

As the head of the O'Malley family? Her actions had put every single person under his care in danger, and she'd do it all over again in a heartbeat. James Halloran might not be the worst choice for a husband, but it didn't change the fact that he and Aiden would never be friends. There was too much history between their families—too many betrayals.

Too many deaths.

Aiden couldn't help thinking of Devlin, his youngest brother, who'd been gunned down three years ago. Back then, the O'Malley siblings had been more friends than enemies. Devlin had been good and kind, but Aiden couldn't help thinking that his youngest brother's relative innocence would have disappeared over time. That if alive, Devlin would have been as much a stranger to him now as the rest of his family.

For the first time in a very long time, Aiden felt well and truly alone.

Charlie squeezed his hand, bringing him back to the situation at hand. He'd anticipated Carrigan's reaction, but it wasn't her that he needed to convince. It was Teague and Cillian. Teague had never been stupid—his idiot decision to become an FBI informant aside—and he was still looking at Charlie like he recognized her. She had only superficial similarities to her father—the line of their nose, the shape of their eyes—but Aiden wouldn't put it past his brother to connect the dots if given the opportunity.

So he wouldn't give him the opportunity. He stroked Charlie's shoulder again. "We're setting the wedding for November."

If anything, Cillian looked *more* aghast. "In two months?"

"No reason to wait." *And every reason to rush this along so no one has too much time to do more than react.* Their pending nuptials would distract the rest of the family from what he was doing with Keira and Dmitri, at least for a little while. Cillian knew about the deal with Romanov. He *had* to know. But Teague and Carrigan would revolt, and it would put them all in a precarious position of fighting each other when they should be fighting Romanov.

"Is she pregnant?"

"*Cillian!*" Olivia broke her silence to smack his arm. "You're being rude."

"No surprise pregnancy." One of those in the family was more than enough. His managed a grin. "Just true love."

Liam appeared in the doorway, and the look on his face sent Aiden's every instinct on high alert. He kept his expression neutral. "Excuse me."

Liam barely waited until they had the door shut to pull Aiden aside. "Keira went out her window and down the fire escape. She gave Mark the slip, but he's checking her usual haunts, and I've sent men to help him search. We'll bring her back."

The last time she'd escaped them so thoroughly, *Romanov* had been the one to retrieve her. He'd deposited her at the front door without harming her—or that was what she said. Keira had been pale and shaken and downright vicious when he tried to question her, so he'd found his answers in a more roundabout way.

Interrogating idiot druggies wasn't his idea of a good time, but the answers he'd discovered supported Keira's claim that Romanov hadn't hurt her—at least not physically.

After that, Aiden stopped taking chances with his youngest sister's safety. He'd put Mark on her detail, with a secondary perimeter when they knew she was leaving, so that she wouldn't be taken again.

But it was impossible to ensure that if he didn't know where the fuck she was.

While there was no reason for Romanov to strike now, when Aiden had agreed to help him, he didn't trust the Russian for a second—and that wasn't even taking into account *other* enemies who may see her as a weak link to be exploited. Fear rose, the one emotion he never allowed himself. He wrestled it back and locked it down deep. Fear would get him and the people he cared about killed. What he needed was cold, hard logic.

"Find her."

Liam nodded once and was gone, striding away at a pace that was almost running. Keira was as much little sister to him as she was to Aiden. He'd never forgive himself if something happened to her on his watch.

Neither of them would.

CHAPTER FIVE

Dmitri Romanov studied the man in front of him. He'd sent Mikhail on an errand, and the man had come back empty-handed. "Explain."

Mikhail seemed to shrink in on himself, a feat since he was built slightly to begin with. "I'm sorry, Mr. Romanov. If she was anyone else, I would have taken her regardless of her wishes, but she's to marry you, and..."

And once he married Keira O'Malley, she would outrank every one of his men. None of them were sure what that meant exactly or how Dmitri would implement his marriage within the power structure, and it made them all jumpy. If Mikhail crossed Keira now and she held it against him later...

Dmitri understood why he was hesitant to take that step. It didn't mean he forgave it.

"Mikhail, did I or did I not give you an order?"

His shoulders slumped a second before he got control of himself and straightened. "You did." He managed to meet

Dmitri's gaze. "And with all due respect, sir, she would have caused a scene, and I judged that to be worse than to deliver her message."

Ah yes, her message. If he wanted her, he was to come get her himself.

Despite everything, the challenge sent a thrill through Dmitri. He was a man who liked things in their place. He read people well enough that he could anticipate their moves with ease. There had been setbacks along the way, but he hadn't been wrong yet.

Except when it came to Keira O'Malley.

The woman had surprised him at every turn, had pushed him to the limits of his control seemingly without effort. He wanted her—in a number of ways—and he had no business wanting her, future wife or no.

Then the rest of what Mikhail had told him penetrated. "You left her there alone."

Mikhail gave a sharp shake of his head. "I left one of our men to watch her. To keep her safe."

She had an uncanny ability to avoid her brother's men and slip out unnoticed. It wasn't in Dmitri's interest to have her harmed, though he hadn't yet fully dealt with the fact that the one most likely to harm Keira was Keira herself.

Her brother had cut her funds and threatened her cocaine dealers into blacklisting her, but Dmitri didn't trust people who could be compromised for the sake of money. All it took for Dmitri to get things under control was making an example of the first one who defied O'Malley's command and the others were too terrified to even go near her. She thought O'Malley was behind it, and Dmitri was content to let her keep believing that.

Other than ensuring that she wasn't touched while drinking

herself into oblivion, there wasn't much either he or O'Malley could do about the alcohol abuse currently. That would change the moment she and Dmitri were married.

It was nothing more than guarding a future investment.

He ignored the way the thought felt like a lie and refocused on the man in front of him. "I suppose I'll have to pay her a personal visit." Now.

Wasn't that why I came to Boston tonight in the first place?

He found her exactly where Mikhail said she would be, holding court in the midst of what looked to be an orgy. Dmitri counted six couples in the immediate area around her, all in varying stages of fucking. Through it all, Keira stared off into the distance, untouchable. She lifted her head and looked at him as he stopped a few feet in front of her, as if she could sense his presence. "You."

At least the music was several levels below deafening at this particular party. It wasn't always the rule with the places she frequented. "You requested my presence."

She arched her eyebrows. "And do you always come when you're called? Like a good dog?" Her words were slightly slurred, courtesy of the vodka bottle dangling from her fingertips. Judging from its current level, she was well on her way to blacking out.

Irritation rose, as unwelcome as his attraction to this waif. If Keira would stop turning the blade on herself long enough, she might realize what a weapon she could be. He still hadn't decided if he wanted to encourage that revelation or stifle it.

Dmitri had the unsettling thought that he might not be in control of which way that realization would swing. And he liked that he couldn't begin to guess which way it would go.

He held out a hand. "Come with me."

"Sorry, but that ship has sailed." She looked at the bottle of vodka as if just registering that she was holding it. "You had your shot—twice, in fact—and passed. Third time might be a charm, but there's not enough alcohol in this place to convince me to make a fool of myself over you—again."

"You're going to be my wife." The words felt strange to say aloud to her, as if he were claiming her. He'd told Aiden that he'd allow Keira to make her own choice—and he would—but he'd never given his word that he wouldn't orchestrate events to drive her to the altar at his side.

She shrugged. "That's what I hear. No one asked me."

Dmitri crooked a finger at her. "Come with me, Keira. Yours and mine is not a marriage that starts with bended knee and declarations of devotion. You know that."

For a moment, she looked so incredibly sad, then she made a visible effort to wipe all expression from her face. She did an admirable job, until only a hint of it lingered in her hazel eyes. She stood, bracing as if going to battle.

Movement at the edge of his vision caught his attention, and he turned to find Mikhail. One look at the man's face and Dmitri knew the O'Malley men had found Keira. Time to leave. He captured her hand and pressed a kiss to her knuckles. "It seems I'm being called away. Until next time, *moya koroleva*."

She gave him a grin that was downright lethal. "Dmitri Romanov, marrying me is going to be the worst decision you ever made."

* * *

With the chaos that had erupted around Aiden's missing sister, dinner ended as soon as it started. Charlie was almost pathetically grateful to be escorted up to a room and left out of the whole damn thing. She'd signed on for this, but there had been an overwhelming amount of information to absorb in twenty-four hours.

She needed time to adjust.

She was tempted to call her dad and use him as a sounding board the same way she'd done all through her childhood and most of her adult life. *Not anymore.* Not since she was branded a dirty cop. That closeness with her dad—that *trust*—was something she mourned almost more than anything else she'd lost as a result of what Romanov had done.

Not just Romanov.

She yanked off her dress, wishing she could yank out her memories as easily. She'd been naive, maybe, for thinking that all cops were good cops—that the NYPD would fulfill her deep-seated desire for a real family. Oh, rationally she'd been aware that some of them crossed the line, but she hadn't really thought that when push came to shove, they would turn on her like rabid dogs because she didn't fall in line and take the bribe money.

The things they'd done after she lost her badge...

Charlie headed for the shower, needing the stinging spray to clear her thoughts. She kept thinking she wanted justice, but that wasn't strictly the truth. The truth was that she wanted the ones who'd hurt her to pay. Getting a cop indicted was damn near impossible—something she'd been glad of when she wore the badge. It was very easy for civilians to only see the bad cops, the ones who couldn't be trusted. It was even easier for them to paint all cops in the same light.

They didn't know how goddamn *hard* it was to go out

into the streets night after night and hold on to her honor. How difficult it was to trust the law to do what was right—and to see the times when the law failed. Theirs wasn't a perfect system, but it worked more often than it didn't.

Until she got on the wrong side of it.

She scrubbed harder with the sponge. Sometimes it felt like there were two people living in her skin—the one who still had stars in her eyes, believing that the good guys always won, and the one who saw the world for what it really was. The good guys didn't always win. They didn't even *usually* win.

The ones with power did.

She stepped out of the shower and dried off, looking around the room for the first time since she'd been led here. *This is what power looks like.* There was nothing overtly proclaiming that the person who lived here had more money than God, but the knowledge was there just the same. It was in the high-end furniture stained a delicious dark brown, and in the thick carpet beneath her bare feet, and in the insanely high thread count of the blankets she ran her hands over. There was the old saying that if you couldn't beat them, you should join them.

Well, she'd done more than join them.

She'd gone and gotten into bed with them.

Her phone rang as she pulled a ridiculously expensive pair of pajamas out of one of the many bags that had mysteriously appeared in the room while she was in the shower.

Charlie's chest tightened at the sight of her dad's number, despite the fact that she'd considered calling him earlier. The last thing she wanted to do was fake a smile and pretend everything was fine. *But then, that's what I've been doing for years. What's one more time?* She smiled—it was so much easier to fake a happy tone if she was grinning—and answered. "Hey, Dad."

"Is everything okay?"

He knows. She fought down the impulse to confess. He'd used that trick on her more times than she could count while she was in high school. Finally, she'd caught on to the fact that he often didn't know a damn thing until *she* told him. *Confess nothing* became her mantra after that. "Sure. Why wouldn't it be?" How closely did he keep watch on the O'Malleys and the other families in Boston?

Her dad laughed, but it was as fake as her cheery tone. "No reason. I just worry about you, you know."

He just lied to me.

"I know." Bitterness threatened to choke her. Her fall from grace wasn't her dad's fault. He should have been in her corner, though—the one person who would back her up no matter what. She'd known one of John Finch's unforgivable sins was being a dirty cop. She just hadn't expected him to turn on *her* because of it.

The truth was he'd always loved his job more than he'd loved anything—anyone. Including her. Any chance she'd had of changing that disappeared with her career in law enforcement. These days, all she had was their regular dinners, complete with strained conversation and quiet judgment.

When she was branded a dirty cop, she'd lost two families.

Maybe she hadn't even had them to begin with.

She cleared her throat, not liking the way her thoughts were headed. "I'm fine."

"I stopped by the bar, but Jacques said you were on vacation."

She frowned. "You were checking up on me." In the years she'd worked for Jacques, he'd never *once* gone there. Even before she was kicked out of the force, she and her dad had led separate lives. They'd had their dinners, but that was it. And after...Well, there wasn't much to talk about without a mutual career in law enforcement. Anyone sane would have stopped trying after the first few months, but if the Finches had nothing else in common these days, they had sheer stubbornness.

To have him suddenly showing up at the bar the day after she agreed to help Aiden...

Charlie didn't believe in coincidences.

"I'm your father. I was worried about you, so I dropped by."

She hated his high-and-mighty tone, the one that said he had no intention of explaining himself. He was always so damn sure he knew best, and he thought that gave him permission to do whatever he pleased. Getting him to admit that maybe he'd been wrong was a lesson in impossibility.

Charlie forced the tension out of her voice, though it was a struggle. "It's been several years. I needed a vacation, so I took one."

"Spur-of-the-moment, without sending so much as a text to tell me where you've gone." The suspicion in his voice was so thick, it was a wonder he could speak at all.

He definitely knows.

Maybe he had someone watching her, or maybe one of his contacts who monitored the O'Malleys had reported back— but her dad knew exactly where she was. She could keep pretending that everything was peachy, or she could drop the veil and hope he did the same. Even though she knew better, she said, "This is the only way, Dad."

"Walk out of that house right now, baby. Just walk out. I'll see that you're protected."

Like he'd seen that she was protected from her former brothers-in-arms? *No, that's not fair. What happened to me wasn't his fault.* She paced from one side of the room to the other. It was one thing to suspect that he knew where she was and what she was up to—it was entirely another to know for certain. *He'll never forgive me for this.*

Then again, it's not like our relationship can get more *strained and distant.*

She'd gone too far. There was no turning back now. She didn't want to. "No."

"Charlotte, you listen to me. You're in over your head and you don't even know it. He's using you to get to me."

She'd suspected her father's identity had something to do with Aiden choosing her, but she'd let herself put that aside because their purposes aligned for the time being. She'd gone into his scheme with her eyes wide open, even if her dad was determined to see her as an innocent who'd lost her way. And maybe there was a petty part of her that had known that the second her dad found out about this he'd lose his damn mind. "This is something I need to do."

Maybe if she could see Romanov find justice, she could stop living the half life she'd condemned herself to.

Maybe she could finally move on.

"Baby, you don't know who these people are."

She laughed, the sound raw and jagged in her throat. "I know as well as you do." She'd seen the worst the world could offer, and Aiden wasn't it. She might be giving him too much credit because her attraction to him was clouding her thoughts...It didn't matter. He'd help her see her vengeance come to fruition. And after...

There was no point in thinking about after. There was only the here and now.

"I can't protect you if you stay there."

"You never could protect me, Dad. I love you...but you need to stay out of my way." She hung up before either of them could say something they'd both regret. She hadn't done anything illegal yet, but there was no telling where she'd end up now that she had chosen her path.

Charlie couldn't bring herself to care.

CHAPTER SIX

W hat the fuck were you thinking?" Aiden knew he was losing his temper, but he couldn't get his control back into place. He wanted to shake Keira until she saw sense, but he knew all too well that it wouldn't make a damn bit of difference. Carrigan would be laughing her ass off if she could see him now, in the midst of a battle of wills with their baby sister.

Then again, maybe she'd be as pissed as I am.

He took a deep breath that did nothing to help him get a leash on his anger. "Answer me."

Keira twined a lock of hair around her finger. "I don't know why you care. I won't be your problem much longer, since you're marrying me off to Dmitri Romanov."

Over my dead body. He couldn't say it, couldn't show the least bit of wavering resolve. No one except Charlie and Liam knew the depth of the game he played, and even those two were a risk.

Liam wouldn't turn. Aiden had trusted him with his life countless times.

Charlie was something else altogether. Aiden might have picked her initially because of who her father was, but since he'd met her, every instinct he had said that she wanted justice—vengeance—more than she wanted anything else. She was a woman who was intimately acquainted with rock bottom, and she'd been living a life apart until he'd shown up and offered her something she hadn't dared take for herself.

As long as he didn't do anything that forced her to confront exactly how similar the O'Malleys and Romanovs were, she would fall in line.

Aiden looked at his baby sister. He hadn't handled things well with Carrigan and Sloan when it came to their personal lives. He couldn't afford to make the same mistakes with Keira. He needed her to stop fighting him long enough for him to free her from Romanov.

It took effort to soften his tone, but yelling at Keira would only make her plant her feet and refuse to yield. "Did you ever stop to think that Romanov has as many enemies as we do? More, even. The second the news that you're marrying him gets out, you'll be a target."

"What? Like I'm not a target now?" She tossed her hair over her shoulder. "Lock me up or throw me in the basement or do whatever you're going to do. I don't give a fuck anymore." The tremor in her voice gave lie to her bold words.

"Keira, come here." He stood and pulled her into a hug. She was so damn frail in his arms, and he called himself seven kinds of a bastard for putting her in this position. *It's only for a little while longer.* "I wouldn't ask anything that I didn't think you were capable of handling."

"That's a comfort." She lifted her head and glared at him.

While Aiden had no intention of letting his sister marry Romanov, he wasn't above using her as bait and a distraction. His endgame involved layers upon layers, and he couldn't afford to let wanting to protect Keira from a little hurt be the reason she ended up married to that bastard. He set his hands on her shoulders. "Trust me. Please. Just…trust me." Everything he did, he did for the love of his family. He'd do everything in his power to keep her safe, and Aiden tried to convey that truth with his gaze.

She pressed her lips together, her hazel eyes holding too much pain for a woman her age. "I trust you to take care of the family. I don't trust you to take care of *me*."

He took a step back, keeping his hands on her shoulders. Trying to browbeat her into submission wasn't working—hadn't been working for a long time—so it was time to try a new tactic. "We're in a precarious position with negotiating, and I need you to be on your A game. I can't have you doing anything to jeopardize my negotiations with Romanov."

Her eyes shone, though she blinked back the tears before they fell. "You're a real asshole, you know that?"

Damn it, she *would* take it as criticism instead of as an olive branch. "I'm better than our father. At least I'm giving you a seat at the table. He would have locked you up, and you damn well know it."

Keira laughed. "So I should be grateful? You're two sides of the same fucking coin. Just because you pretty it up doesn't mean anything. I'm still being sold like a cow to the slaughter." She shoved to her feet. "Don't worry, Aiden. I'll be a good little puppet. God forbid someone shoot me like a dog in the street the way they did Devlin, because I didn't listen to my older brother who thinks he knows everything."

She gave a mock gasp. "How would you live with yourself then?" Keira strode out of the room before he could come up with a fitting reply.

Not that he had one.

Some days it was like dragging his naked body over hot coals to stand here and appear unaffected while the seas of change raged around him. One wrong step and they could lose everything.

He wouldn't let it happen.

Not on his watch.

Aiden glanced at the clock on the wall and cursed. It was damn near midnight, and he'd left Charlie unattended. If she wanted, she could have spent the last few hours exploring the house to her heart's content. There wasn't much in the way of incriminating evidence left sitting around in the open—even their files were digitized and encrypted thanks to Cillian—but that didn't mean the thought sat well with him. He rolled his shoulders to relieve some of the tension.

Liam met him at the door. "You need to sleep."

"Speak for yourself. You're running on just as little as I am."

Liam fell into step beside him as they headed down the hall. "Mark will take over for tonight. We don't expect trouble, but with the new face in the house, I'm not taking any chances."

Aiden wanted to ask Liam what he thought of all this. Once upon a time, they'd been good friends—they were *still* friends, he thought. But when he'd made the changeover from heir to the head of the O'Malley family, a new distance had cropped up between them. He didn't know how to fix it or even if it should be fixed. Too many lives rested on Aiden's shoulders, Liam's included, and he was required to play his cards close to his chest.

So all he said was, "Good."

He headed upstairs, not stopping to think about the fact that Charlie would be sleeping in *his* room until he was through the door, and nearly tripped over a massive pile of shopping bags on the floor. A light was on next to the bed, bathing the room in a golden glow, but Aiden had eyes only for her.

She looked so deliciously rumpled, her blue eyes hazy with sleep, her hair less than perfect for the first time since they'd met. Charlie frowned. "What are you doing?" She shook her head as soon as the words were out of her mouth. "Silly question. Of course you're sleeping here. We're engaged after all." Her lips twisted into something vaguely resembling a smile.

It was the first time they'd been alone since he brought her to orgasm in the office, and he didn't know what to say. Explaining what he'd been doing was out of the question—sharing his concerns over Keira even more so.

She seemed as at a loss as he was. "I don't know what side of the bed you slept on. I just chose one at random."

"It's fine." It struck him that he'd never had a woman in this bed. He'd been in serious relationships, but they'd always played second to his family, and so he'd never brought the girls home. That was ultimately why each relationship failed—no woman wanted to be with someone whose top priority wasn't them.

This isn't a relationship. It's an alliance.

That didn't stop him from liking the picture of Charlie in his bed, or keep the possessive instinct he'd fought so hard to subdue from raging to the forefront. He wanted her naked and beneath him and coming on his cock with his name on her lips.

He had no business wanting those things from her.

Sex was on the table. She'd put it there.

Possession was not. He wouldn't allow it to be. Aiden realized he was staring at her, and cleared his throat. "I'm going to take a shower." Maybe that would give him back a modicum of control.

"It doesn't have to be weird." She made a face. "Okay, so this is the very definition of 'weird.' But we're both adults—adults who have a healthy attraction to each other. There's nothing wrong with you fucking my brains out while I'm here. I won't let it be a distraction."

He went rock-hard at her words, and it was everything he could do not to fall on her there and then. Aiden took one step back and then another. "You're playing with fire, Charlie."

"Maybe I like the burn." She slipped out from under the covers, and he saw she was wearing an artfully slouchy shirt with only a pair of panties. "The truth is that I'm feeling out of sorts and twitchy." She crossed her arms and pulled her shirt over her head, dropping it on the floor as she kept walking toward him. Gone was the strange hesitance he'd seen in her earlier today. There was nothing but lust in her blue eyes. "I don't want to think about tomorrow or what I'm risking by being here with you, and you look about half a second from trashing the room because you can't risk showing any of that pent-up emotion to them."

She went to her knees in front of him, as graceful as a dancer. "Let me make you feel good. Let me make us *both* feel good." She gave a tentative smile. "If you let that ice-king facade slip, I promise not to tell a soul."

He allowed her to undo the front of his slacks, stifling the voice that said this was a mistake—just like earlier in his office had been. She stroked him though his boxer-briefs, licking her lips, but he laced one hand through her hair and held her immobile until she looked at him. "If we're doing this, Charlie, there are two things you need to know."

"Yes?"

A man could drown in the blue of her eyes. He tightened his hold on her hair as much to ground himself as to hold her back. "You put my cock in your mouth and you had damn well better suck it like you mean it."

"As if I would do anything else." Her smile gained a bold edge. "And the other?"

"If you think this is going to result in me fucking you tonight—it's not." He gentled his grip, smoothing her hair back. "But, Charlie, I'm going to make you feel so good, you're going to beg me to let you ride my cock. You're not going to be able to help it. It won't make a goddamn bit of difference—we fuck when I say, how I say. Do you understand?"

* * *

Charlie was in over her head and sinking fast. If she was smart, she'd beg off and go to bed without tempting fate. All her assumptions about Aiden O'Malley being cold and freakishly controlled completely changed as she knelt before him, looking up into his green eyes. The man was an inferno. One wrong step and he'd incinerate her.

Say no. Leave this alone.

But those weren't the words that came out of her mouth. "Yes. I understand."

His expression was every bit the patient wolf. He had her exactly where he wanted her, and she'd just agreed to his terms. There was no way to convince herself that she had the advantage in this situation—in any of it.

She didn't.

Aiden unbuttoned his shirt with quick, efficient movements, and her mouth went dry at the slice of his chest revealed. This wasn't a man who left anything to chance. He would see his body as a weapon at his disposal, to keep as finely honed as his wits.

"You're staring."

Yes, she was. "Just appreciating the view." She reached up and ran a single finger along the light trail of hair that ran south from his belly button, disappearing into his boxer-briefs. His stomach flexed beneath her touch, but his expression didn't change. He was devouring her the same way she was currently devouring him.

"You'll keep the panties on tonight." His gaze lingered there, heating her straight through. "I like the look of black lace on you."

"You should see me in red." Not knowing how this first night would go, she hadn't been willing to whip out the red lingerie. Red was a blatant invitation, and if that encounter in the office was the exception to the rule, she didn't want to feel like a fool...But if he was going to delve into power games in the bedroom, she'd meet him every step.

It made sense in a way. Aiden had put together an insanely detailed plan to take out one of his enemies. All evidence pointed to the fact that this wasn't the first time he'd orchestrated someone's downfall, either.

She'd seen more than a few control freaks in her time, and he put them all to shame. The man had his emotions in a stranglehold, and it stood to reason that he'd bring that same attitude to the bedroom. She had a feeling Aiden wouldn't know vulnerable if it bit him in the ass, let alone how to bring down his walls enough to enjoy himself.

What does he look like when he loses control?

Am I brave enough to push his buttons and find out?

She grinned. *Bring it.*

For the first time in a very long time, a thrill went through her. Getting involved with Aiden might put her heart in danger, at least in theory, but she just didn't see it. She wasn't even sure she had a heart left to lose—though the organ in her chest was beating hard enough to leave her breathless.

Aiden slid out of his slacks and stood before her, gloriously naked. His fingers laced through her hair, the movement strangely soothing even as it made her body tighten. "Second thoughts?"

It struck her that her silence could be misconstrued as regret or wanting a way out. Charlie gave a sharp shake of her head. "Not in the least. Just contemplating my plan of action."

His dark chuckle curled her toes. "Charlie, you're not coming out on top of this encounter." He pulled lightly on her hair, and she had to bite back a moan. "But you will be coming. Now, bright eyes, if you're going to suck my cock, stop wasting time. I crave the taste of you and I'm not a patient man."

"Liar." She wrapped her fist around his length, giving him a quick but thorough exploration, and then licked the head of his cock. She flicked a glance to his face. The man watched her like he was glimpsing heaven, seeming to enjoy the view as much as he enjoyed the act.

Next time I'll wear red lipstick.

That would give him the show of a lifetime.

Charlie held his gaze as she took him deep, exploring him with her mouth the same way she had with her hand. There were times when a hard-and-fast blow job was the name of the game. This wasn't one of those. She wanted to push him to the edge of his legendary control.

And then she wanted to push him a little further.

His cock bumped the back of her throat, and she made an effort to relax and take him deeper. His muttered curse was reward in and of itself. Aiden's grip tightened on her hair. "Enough. You've had your fun."

She released his cock reluctantly. "I'm just getting started."

"Not tonight."

Because it's too good.

The truth was written across his tense body and the deep lines bracketing his mouth as he watched her. He'd told her that she would be the one begging tonight, but he looked in danger of doing exactly that if she kept going.

Next time.

"Bossy, bossy." She allowed him to guide her to her feet and ran her nails lightly over his chest. "It's sounding like the game is rigged. How am I supposed to convince you to change your mind if you take away all the tools at my disposal?"

Aiden laughed again, the sound just as dark as it had been the first time. "You try my control just by standing there looking like you do right now, your body aching for me and your lips wet from sucking my cock. I'm doing my damnedest not to throw you down on the bed and sink between those sweet thighs of yours. You're ready for me, aren't you?"

"Yes." There was no point in lying, and she liked the way he talked to her. Right now, he wasn't the head of Boston's most powerful family. He was just a man who wanted a woman—who wanted *her*. She still couldn't believe this was happening, but she'd do anything to avoid putting on the brakes.

She grabbed his hand and pressed it between her legs. "Feel me."

"I feel you." He stroked her through her panties, toying with the edges of the lace.

"I won't be begging tonight." It felt like a lie when she said it—especially given the way he watched her. *He likes a challenge.* Charlie would do her best to give him exactly that. She rolled her hips. "But you're welcome to try."

He took his hand back. "The bed—on your back with your legs spread."

"And if I don't?"

"Then the game ends. You want this, I want this, but it will be on *my* terms."

Charlie took a half a second to consider disobeying, just for the sake of seeing the look on his face and knowing he'd spend the night with an epic case of blue balls.

But she wanted the pleasure his green eyes promised more than she wanted to push back. For now. She crawled onto the bed and lay down, arching her back and slowly spreading her legs. It had nothing to do with modesty and everything to do with dragging out the show for him.

He stood at the edge of the bed, every muscle straining as if he was holding himself back. "Your tattoos are exquisite." Aiden coasted his hand up her body. He didn't touch her, maintaining a bare breadth of distance between them. He traced the ink that wound up from her ankle to her hip, and over her ribs to her sternum.

She quivered, shaking with the need to move enough to

press against his touch but held in place by the forbidding expression on his face. There was no mistaking who was in charge of this encounter.

As if she was in any danger of forgetting.

"We'll talk about the ink. Later." He didn't request the information. He demanded it. So damn sure of his power that he had no doubts she would fall in line like a good little soldier.

That snapped her out of her haze of lust and allowed her to think a little beyond when he'd actually *touch* her. "I might be letting you call the shots right now, but that doesn't extend outside the bedroom door."

"Wrong." His index finger ghosted over her nipple. She sucked in a harsh breath, not sure if he'd actually touched her or if she'd imagined it. Aiden did the same thing to the other nipple. "I'm going to keep us both alive, bright eyes, and that means I call the shots and you obey, no matter how much taking orders from me chafes."

He moved back down her body. Every muscle shook as she fought to keep still, even as a small voice in the back of her mind called her a fool seven times over. Aiden reached the band of her panties again and dragged his fingers over the lace. "We'll fight about it tomorrow."

"Fine." She tried to snap out the word, but it emerged breathy. Irritation rose. "Touch me or let me go to sleep. I'm tired of these games."

"No, you're not."

She got no warning. One second, she was seriously considering telling him to fuck off, and the next, he grabbed her hips and dragged her to the edge of the bed. Aiden went to his knees and pulled her panties to the side. "As pretty here as everywhere else."

And then all she knew was his mouth.

Aiden went after her clit like it was his favorite candy. He sucked and licked and nibbled, emitting these little growls as he did. Charlie stopped trying to hold back after two seconds, giving herself to the sensation of pleasure rising and falling, pushing her closer and closer to the edge. Every time she teetered too close, he drew back, gentling his kisses or diverting himself to worshiping her thighs.

She managed to hold it together until the fourth denied orgasm. "Aiden, *please*."

"Please what?"

"Stop teasing me."

He dragged his mouth over her and, for one eternal second, she was sure he'd give her what she needed. Then the bastard laughed. "No."

She lifted her head and glared. "If you don't let me come, I'm going to do it myself."

Those green eyes were so bright, they could have been on fire. "You even try and I'm going to tie you down and make you wait longer. You agreed to the terms, Charlie." His grin was downright feral. "Unless you want to stop?"

She shot a look to the bathroom door. She could tell him she was done and go to the bathroom. She was so primed, it would take a flick, maybe two, and she'd orgasm.

Aiden, the bastard, knew exactly what she was thinking. "If you changed your mind, I'll respect it, and that will be the end of things between us."

"What?" She shook her head, trying to think. "Maybe I just changed my mind for tonight."

"Or maybe you're trying to cheat me out of your orgasm." He held her thighs in a grip just shy of bruising. "This is what it means to go to bed with me, Charlie. Either you can handle it or you can't, but I won't have you crying foul every single fucking time. So what will it be? Are we done?"

She slammed her hands on the mattress, twisting against his hold. "That's not fair."

"It's the very essence of fair. Decide."

She ran her hands over her face. Aiden just waited, not touching her further but not letting her move, either. Charlie looked down her body at him. "I want to come, Aiden, please." She tried a sweet and cajoling tone, and got icy silence in response. *Damn it.* She flopped back onto the bed. "I must be a masochist, because I don't want this to stop."

"I know." He didn't give her a chance to curse him. She was too busy moaning as he fucked her with his tongue. Charlie slapped a hand over her mouth to keep from screaming. Aiden lifted his head long enough to say, "No, bright eyes. Let them hear you."

Because of the plan, because we're pretending…

But as she looked at his expression, she wasn't sure that was the truth. He looked like a man who wanted everyone within hearing distance to know that he was pleasing his woman and pleasing her well.

I'm not his woman.

It didn't matter as he sucked her clit into his mouth, stroking her with his tongue with the exact same motions she'd shown him earlier in the office. That was all it took. Her back bowed, his name a cry on her lips as she came hard enough to tilt the world off its axis. Her orgasm rolled over her, cresting again and again, hours' worth of pent-up pleasure taking her to a place beyond thought, beyond worry, beyond mere mortal things.

She slowly came back to herself to find Aiden lying next

to her on his side, with his head propped in his hand. He ran one hand over her body as if memorizing every detail. She blinked. "Hey."

"How do you feel?"

She gave the question entirely too much consideration. "I'm thinking being a masochist might not be such a bad thing."

Aiden grinned. "It's a fleeting feeling." He cupped first one breast and then the other. "We're not done."

"You're joking." She shook her head. "You have to be joking. I just came harder than I've ever come in my life. I can't do it again." She wasn't even sure she wanted to.

He cupped her chin, his thumb tracing over her jaw. "Yes, you can. And you will—until I'm done with you."

"But..." She hadn't signed on for this.

Except, yes, I did.

She just hadn't thought that he'd be able to follow through on his promises. *I really should have known better. Aiden doesn't make false promises.* Charlie huffed out a breath. "What about you?"

"What about me?"

She waved a hand at his cock, still gloriously hard and straining as if it knew the kind of pleasure that awaited if he'd stop with his games. "You keep playing with me, you're going to be sporting a truly impressive set of blue balls."

He guided her leg that was closest to him up and over his hip, opening her completely. "If it makes you feel better, once I'm done with you, if you still want to suck me off, you're more than welcome to."

She frowned at him, sensing a trap but unable to discern the shape of it. "That sounds...fair."

"I'm glad you think so." He pushed a finger into her, pumping a few times. "Now, remember what I said before—the more you beg for me to fuck you, the more punishment you'll receive."

"I won't beg."

"Aw, bright eyes, yes, you really will."

And, God help her but she did.

CHAPTER SEVEN

Y ou look tired."

Aiden ignored Cillian's pointed statement—and the implication behind it. He'd known what he was doing when he told Charlie not to stifle her cries, though it wasn't solely to make everyone believe that they were madly in love. He'd liked hearing his name on her lips and being the reason she lost control again and again.

When he'd finished with her last night, she'd passed out before managing to give him that blow job she was so determined to deliver. Knowing he was responsible for her being in his bed, exhausted from pleasure *he'd* given her, had satisfied a primal part of him he hadn't even been aware of before last night.

I'm a goddamn savage in a three-thousand-dollar suit.

He drank down his coffee, though he was wired even before his first cup. Everything was finally falling into place.

The end was in sight. He just had to hold it together long enough to see the plan through.

The next stage started now.

He pulled out his phone, earning a frustrated curse from his brother. Aiden spoke to Cillian without looking up, keeping his tone even and disinterested. "I'm ignoring you because you know damn well why I'm tired and you're fishing for information that you won't get. We have work to do."

"Work that involves selling our baby sister to a monster."

"If you want to look at it that way." He hated the expression of betrayal on Cillian's face, hated how little his brother trusted him. There was no help for it. He dialed Romanov.

The man himself answered the phone. "*Da?*"

"Before we do anything official regarding Keira, you need to understand that there will be negotiations required."

Romanov sighed. "And *you* need to understand you have no rights to be making demands of me."

"Oh, my mistake. I didn't realize that you'd already dealt with the Eldridges and didn't need my help."

The silence stretched for a beat, and then two. "Explain these demands."

Interesting. He'd expected more pushback. Romanov might need some assistance with the Eldridges, but he could have potentially called in favors with his extended family back in Russia. There were politics there, and he wouldn't do it lightly, but it *was* an option.

He hadn't. Instead, he'd come to the O'Malleys.

Because he wanted Keira.

Romanov wouldn't still be pressing for a marriage alliance if he didn't need it desperately. Being spurned by Carrigan had hurt his reputation, a hurt that was only aggravated when his half sister, Olivia, fled the Romanov home and name, into the arms of the O'Malleys. In his world, reputation was everything. Demanding the only remaining O'Malley daughter would repair his damaged status and reinforce his power base.

Maybe he can't ask for assistance from his extended family, because they think he's weak. That would explain a lot.

"We will announce the engagement at a party." A distraction in the carefully planned circus he had put into motion. He needed Romanov focused on Keira and everyone else focused on Charlie so he could make his next move.

The thought that he could be sentencing his sister to an actual marriage with that monster made him sick to his stomach. *Not real. I won't let it get that far. Romanov gave his word, and she'd never choose him.* He didn't let any of his inner feelings into his voice. "I'll put together something and issue the appropriate invitations."

"How considerate." Romanov didn't sound like he found it considerate in the least. "Don't think to cross me, Aiden." He hung up, his words ringing in Aiden's head for several minutes afterward.

Aiden couldn't shake the feeling that, despite his plan, he was playing right into Romanov's hands.

He set down his phone and looked at Cillian. "If you have something to say, say it now. We'll move forward as a single unit, so I won't have you questioning me every step of the way."

His brother gave him a long look and sank into the seat across the desk. "I don't know what game you're playing, but I don't like it. You're putting our baby sister on the line, and if you don't manage to do whatever it is you're trying to do, she'll be the one to pay the price." Cillian huffed out a breath. "I know the world we live in. I get that you're do-ing what you think is best—truly, I do. But how about we stop pretending that you fell so deeply in love with some stranger that you brought her in here and plan to marry her. Maybe Teague and Carrigan—and even Keira—will fall for that. They aren't here, day in and day out. I am. And I know you'd never let your heart get the best of you."

His brother was right, even if he'd never admit it. Ai-den's heart didn't even come into the equation when the O'Malleys were on the line. He managed a brief smile. "Al-ways damning me with faint praise."

"It's the truth."

Cillian had always been too smart by half. He'd covered it up when he was a kid with a reckless streak a mile wide and a string of shitty decisions, and these days he put that brilliant brain of his to use spinning numbers, doing the books for their operations, and managing anything that re-quired the hacking skills he'd been developing since he took over the job. He'd never bothered to analyze *Aiden*, though.

He met his brother's gaze directly. This wasn't the time for softness or kid gloves. He spoke to Cillian as leader of the O'Malleys to a subordinate. "I don't care what you think of the situation—or of Charlie. You will fall in line."

"Consider me the very picture of a loyal soldier." Cillian rose. "But you had damn well keep Keira safe, Aiden. She stopped painting. Did you know that?"

Aiden sat back in his chair, the sheer weight of everything he carried threatening to drive him into the ground. There were a million ways to kill a person that had nothing to do with stopping their heart. He might have scared off his sis-ter's dealers, but it seemed like he'd been doing a shitty job taking care of her otherwise. In the last few years, she'd gone from being a snarky, flourishing artist to a shell of the woman she was supposed to become. "This will all be over soon."

Cillian shook his head. "Save the bullshit, Aiden. It will never be over. Even Sloan didn't escape it, and she ran halfway across the world."

She hadn't escaped, but she'd carved out a little slice of happiness for herself, despite everything.

And the information her man provided had been instrumental in Aiden finding the right pressure points to bring Romanov to his knees.

He stared at the desk, the wood polished so thoroughly that it gleamed. Knowing that Sloan's relationship had strengthened the O'Malleys should have brought him satisfaction, even if she'd gone back into hiding to avoid living in their world. There was no satisfaction to be had, though. He couldn't bring himself to admit it to anyone out loud, but he missed his little sister.

He missed *all* of his sisters.

Cillian watched him too closely. "She's doing well, in case you were wondering. We have a nephew to go along with our nieces. They named him Grady."

Named for Jude's dead father, the same way Teague and Callie's daughter was named for her mother. They were all haunted by the sins of the past and the losses they never got quite over.

It was up to him to ensure that they didn't have any more names to be added to the list of beloved dead.

* * *

Charlie woke late, her body still aching from what Aiden had done to her through the early hours of the morning.

She rolled over and stretched, luxuriating in the feel of the silken sheets against her bare skin. It would be too easy to let herself get used to this. To forget that this was all a ruse to bring down their mutual enemy.

Aiden might want her body, but he was focused on the endgame. She'd be a fool to do anything else.

She sat up. Through all the plans he'd shared with her, he'd left one thing out—what she was supposed to do with her free time. When she'd agreed to this, she hadn't really thought about much beyond bringing Romanov to justice. It never occurred to her that it would take *time*. Charlie had never been much good with idle hands, and she didn't imagine she'd learned that skill overnight.

She usually worked from nine to two at Jacques's, and then woke late and hit the gym for an hour or two, where she went through her regular Krav Maga training, then worked with newbies, assisting as necessary. There was always a need of sparring partners and she was more than happy to help out. Anything to make sure the person across from her had the skills necessary to ensure that they never ended up as helpless as she'd been when she was attacked.

But she hadn't had time to research gyms in Boston—or talk to Aiden about what he expected of her while they played out this scenario.

After showering and throwing on a pair of ridiculously expensive jeans and a flowy tank top, she padded out of the room on bare feet. No guard stood outside the door, so she wandered down the hall, taking it all in.

Last night she'd been too overwhelmed and exhausted to really notice the space she moved through. There was something strange about the hallway, but it wasn't until she was halfway to the stairs that she realized what it was. Charlie

stopped and looked back the way she'd come. *No photos.*
There weren't any in the rooms she'd been in downstairs,
either, now that she thought about it.

Downstairs, she could understand. Her dad might have a
scattering of photos from the last twenty-nine years on the
fridge, but the few framed ones were in the upstairs hallway.
He didn't take meetings in their house, but some habits die
hard, and displaying his weakness—Charlie—went against
the grain.

But to have no photos at all?

That spoke volumes about the family that lived in this
place.

She turned back to the stairs. *What else will I find if I
do some snooping?* Aiden and the O'Malleys weren't tech-
nically the enemy, but she'd have to be an idiot twice over
to take whatever information he decided to feed her without questioning it. Meeting his siblings last night had only
driven home what the stakes were—and the fact that the
knife in the darkness coming for her might not be held by a
Romanov but an O'Malley. Or a Halloran. Or a Sheridan.

Charlie didn't want to admit that her dad was right and
that she was in over her head, but it was sure as hell starting
to feel that way.

She walked to the stairs and peered over the railing.
Raised voices—Aiden and Cillian—but they were muffled
enough that she couldn't pick out the words. She doubted
she could make it down the stairs and to the office door to
eavesdrop without their realizing she was there and turning the conversation to safe topics, so she headed toward
the back of the house. There had to be a second stairwell
around here somewhere.

The temptation to explore the closed doors lining the

hallway rose, but she held back. There were two doors—Aiden's and another—on this leg of the hallway, before it took a hard right turn. Charlie walked to the corner and counted another three doors before the hallway turned again, creating a U shape. Seven rooms...for seven children?

She looked at the room across from Aiden's and opened the door before she could talk herself out of it. She stopped just inside the doorframe, inhaling a spicy feminine scent. The décor was the very definition of luxury, the big white bed looking soft enough to swallow a person whole, and the dresser along the opposite wall scattered with expensive-looking jewelry and perfume bottles.

The decorations were too...understated to belong to Keira. She didn't know much about the other sister—Sloan—but Charlie bet this room had belonged to Carrigan. From Liam's brief family history, the woman hadn't lived here in almost two years. And yet her room looked as fresh as it would have if she'd just stepped out this morning.

"What are you doing?"

Charlie didn't jump, but it was a near thing. She glanced over her shoulder at Aiden, noting that he stared at her and pointedly didn't look around the room she stood in. It didn't matter that he gave nothing away with his expression or body language—the information was as clear in what he *didn't* do as what he did. *So much baggage there.* "I was curious."

"Curiosity killed the cat."

She snorted. "And satisfaction brought him back—which isn't quite the same kind of warning."

"Funny." His tone said he found her anything but. He stepped backward, a clear demand for her to join him in the hallway. That was all she needed to confirm the room had belonged to Carrigan.

Charlie closed the door softly behind her. The move left her close enough to touch Aiden, but she hesitated, not sure where they stood after last night. He'd driven her to ecstasy more times than she could count...but he'd never kissed her.

Makes sense. Kissing is far more intimate than sex when it comes right down to it.

Being logical did nothing to dull the sting—and neither did knowing she had no right to be hurt. He wanted her body. He didn't want *her*. Which should suit her just fine. She liked the way Aiden filled out a suit, but she couldn't pretend there was a path that ended with them together. Dishonored or not, she was a cop in a long line of cops, and he was a mob boss who wasn't suddenly going to go straight.

She needed to remember that.

"Snooping?"

She shrugged, doing her best not to stare at his mouth. *Just sex...Right.* "I got bored. I'm not used to sitting on my hands."

His green eyes softened, just a little. "I have just the thing."

Or maybe she was imagining things.

"Oh? More shopping?" She didn't need or want more, and if he suggested such a blatantly bullshit activity, she'd have to start some trouble on principle.

"Hardly." Aiden shook his head and turned, waiting for her to fall into step next to him before he walked down the hallway in the opposite direction from the stairs. "You met my sister last night."

"Which one?" But she knew which one he meant as they took first one turn and then the next. "Keira."

The youngest sister, the one who'd fled at the sight of her. *Promising.*

Then again, she was preferable to Carrigan, who seemed inclined to go for her throat. Charlie had a significant amount of training, but she couldn't say beyond a shadow of a doubt that she'd walk away from a violent encounter with *that* woman. Carrigan had the feel of someone who fought dirty and fought to win.

"Yes. Keira." Aiden paused in front of the last door. It faced the front of the house, and Charlie nearly rolled her eyes. The window opened to *both* a tree and a fire escape. Convenient way for the twenty-one-year-old woman to escape whenever she saw fit.

"Why don't you move her room if she's causing such issues?"

His mouth thinned, the slightest of tells. She'd bet a ton of money that his little sister followed the tradition of little sisters everywhere—giving their older brothers no end of trouble. "It's complicated."

Obviously, he wasn't going to bend over backward to explain things to Charlie. *Fine.* She didn't need to know about the inner workings of the O'Malley family or details about the wounds than ran so deep they seemed to be splintering the siblings apart. She wasn't really engaged to Aiden. It wasn't her job to fix the broken people in this house.

She wouldn't be here long enough to try, even if she was interested.

Charlie knew what it was like to have a family fall apart, but it still seemed like such a waste. She'd never had siblings—she'd never had anyone but her dad. Aiden had *five* living siblings and he seemed to only have regular contact with two of them. She couldn't help comparing their situations. Even with the limited information she had, it was clear Teague, Carrigan, and Sloan had more or less fled the O'Malleys because of their father.

Aiden could mend those fences. Carrigan, especially, wouldn't have been so furious about his getting "engaged" to Charlie if she didn't still care about him.

But he didn't seem interested in even trying.

She just didn't get it.

"So what is it that you need from me?" There. That made her sound just as perfectly polite and disinterested as he was acting.

From the sharp look he sent her, it wasn't quite what she was aiming for. "My sister is a key part of keeping Romanov occupied while we get the other pieces into place. She can't do that if she's trying to sneak off every time I turn around."

Comprehension dawned. "You want me to babysit your self-destructive sister?" She wasn't sure what she found more irritating—that he wanted her to play babysitter or that he hadn't just come out and asked her in the first place.

He sighed. "I want you to talk to her, to spend time with her and, yes, to keep her from getting in over her head in the meantime."

"You know, you don't have to handle me. I'm not one of your siblings, or an employee. We're in this together." She turned so she wouldn't give in to the temptation to watch his face for a flicker of the man beneath the mask. The door looked like every other one in the hallway, except for the punk music coming through loud enough to shake the walls. She counted to ten, but Aiden didn't seem all that inclined to jump in. "And what about after?"

"After."

It wasn't quite a question, but she still glanced at him. Or maybe she was just weak and he was a pretty puzzle that fascinated her far more than he had a right to. "What about after we take down Romanov? What happens to Keira then?"

"It won't matter, because you won't be here to see it." He turned on his heel and stalked away, leaving her staring after him, her stomach in knots.

Not going to be here. Just pretend. God, Charlie, stop forgetting that.

One day and she was already having trouble telling reality from pretend. It was like she'd tumbled into the twilight zone, and up was down and down was up. Nothing made sense anymore. She shouldn't care what Aiden thought of her or if he was as eager to see the back of her as he was to see his enemy brought down.

It *shouldn't* matter.

But it kind of did.

CHAPTER EIGHT

Keira's room was a mess. No, calling it a mess was too kind. Charlie couldn't take a single step without fear of trampling on piles of clothes and empty bottles and discarded magazines. Aiden's sister sat on the bed, a joint dangling between her fingers with the ease of someone who smoked often. "What the fuck are you doing here?"

The music was so loud, Charlie had to read her lips. *Aiden owes me for this.* She carefully made her way to the stereo and shut it off, the silence as deafening as the music had been. "We weren't properly introduced yesterday."

"That's because I don't care who you are." Keira took a long inhale from the joint, the end shining a bright orange. She exhaled a cloud of noxious smoke. "You won't last. Your pussy might have my brother acting temporarily insane, but he's too smart to actually marry you."

Charlie stared at her for a long moment and then burst out laughing. After all the careful verbal circling with

Aiden, Keira was a hurricane blast of fresh air. "Cute. Really cute. You kiss your mother with that mouth?"

"Please. My mother is one of the most vicious members of this family." She grimaced. "Though she'd kick my ass for saying 'pussy.'"

Charlie tried to picture the woman responsible for bringing seven O'Malleys into the world, and failed. The ones she'd met were such strong characters. She didn't know if she should be terrified of their mother or pity the woman.

Since Keira didn't seem inclined to move from her spot, Charlie waded through the clothes to the single chair next to the bed. "Here's the deal—I won't insult your intelligence by pussyfooting around."

The woman arched her eyebrows. "I see what you did there."

That was almost amusement. She'd take what she could get. Charlie sat cross-legged on the chair, not wanting to have any more contact with the floor and its mystery contents than necessary. "Regardless of whether you agree with it or not, your brother is marrying me." *Liar.* But she had to play this as if it was real or Keira would see right through her. If Charlie was *really* marrying Aiden, she wouldn't put up with this bullshit for a second.

Which meant she couldn't now. It wasn't fair to take out her aggravation at Aiden on his sister, but she'd known the woman a grand total of two minutes and it couldn't be clearer that what Keira needed most was a kick in the ass by someone who had nothing to gain from her. Charlie had no problem being the one providing that.

"You can play nice and try to get to know me, or you can keep stomping around like a petulant teenager and end up with one of Aiden's men shadowing your every move."

Keira took another pull off the joint. "I take it this means you're playing good cop. Is Aiden going to come in here and yell at me again if I tell you to fuck right off?"

"Have it your way." Charlie gritted her teeth and stood. "You want to turn down a chance to get the hell out of here for a while just to piss off your brother, that's your call. If you change your mind, I'll be in the library." Liam had mentioned it in passing during their shopping spree, so that was one room she was reasonably sure she could spend time in without someone calling foul.

She made it to the door before Keira said, "Oh for fuck's sake, don't leave in a huff. I know coming in here wasn't your idea." When Charlie turned around, she held up the joint. "Want some?"

"I don't smoke."

She shrugged. "There's a bottle of vodka in the desk."

It was nine in the morning, but Charlie made her way to the desk and opened the drawer to find that there was, indeed, a bottle of vodka stashed there. She uncapped it and took a hefty swig, conscious of the younger woman's gaze on her.

Keira huffed. "No holier-than-thou shit about drinking before noon? Maybe you'll actually be entertaining. Okay, Charlie, why don't you tell me how you and my brother met?"

It didn't pass her notice that Keira had remembered her name from their brief introduction before. If Charlie guess was correct, there was a sharp mind behind those glazed eyes, though it was a toss-up if it would be put to good use.

Did it bother Aiden that Keira was spending all her time blitzed out of her mind? The family had enough money for rehab, though it would be a challenge to keep Keira there if she was as adept at sneaking out as she seemed to be. But...

She was his little sister. She was obviously drowning, and just as obviously desperate for something—anything—to save her. She wouldn't have latched on so quickly to Charlie if she was actually intent on destruction, which only made the whole situation more tragic.

Charlie took another, smaller drink. It wasn't her problem. Aiden might need her help with Dmitri, but he couldn't have made it clearer that he had no interest in her meddling with the family. She had to remember that.

Focus. Keira asked you a question. She and Aiden had come up with an origin story that seemed plausible enough. Now it was just a matter of selling it. As off-center as she felt after crossing the line with Aiden last night, the fact that he'd had his hands and mouth all over her body would only help legitimize the whole thing. "I run a backroom poker game—high-stakes."

Keira studied the smoke swirling from the end of the almost-depleted joint. "Is there any other kind of backroom poker game?"

She laughed. "No, I guess there isn't. Your brother attended a few times, and the second time, he stuck around and we had a few drinks." Keira's hazel eyes started to glaze over in a way that had nothing to do with the pot she was smoking. Charlie raised her eyebrows. "And then we fucked on the poker table."

"Magical pussy." Keira snapped her fingers. "I knew it. It's a very rags-to-riches story, because, God knows, you didn't buy those clothes with your money."

She'd expected this, which was part of the reason she'd

resisted the shopping in the first place. Aiden had turned around and argued that being a gold digger was a motivation people would understand more than love at first sight. "What we have works for us."

"I'll just bet it does." Keira shot her a look. "You're nuts for voluntarily coming into this life, and I think you have no idea what you signed on for, great sex or no. But I get it."

There was something there, something beneath the words. Charlie studied her, wondering where she'd come across a man who'd turned her head enough to make her question everything. *If she runs off with him… it would be a disaster.*

But telling her that—reminding her of her duty—was just going to spur Keira into actions she might not have otherwise done. She seemed contrary like that.

Her thoughts must have shown on Charlie's face, because Keira rolled her eyes. "Trust me—I'm not going to break rank. I'm destined to marry the monster in the castle, except I'm not beautiful or virginal enough to tame him, and this isn't a fairy tale, where my wit and charm are going to see me into a happily ever after." She sounded so defeated, Charlie had the insane urge to hug her.

"It'll be okay." She said it out of habit, but the truth was that no one—not Aiden, or Charlie, or Keira—could guarantee that it was the truth.

"You keep telling yourself that. You're the only one in the room with a magic pussy that makes men lose their minds." Keira rolled onto her side and took another puff of her joint, finishing it off and tossing it into the ashtray perched precariously on her nightstand. "But I'm tired of talking about me and my pathetic life. You said you run a poker game—teach me to play."

* * *

"You can't be serious."

Aiden looped the tie around his neck. "It's the best opportunity we'll have." He watched Charlie in the mirror as he tied the knot. It was strange getting dressed while talking to her. He'd stayed away from her as much as possible the last few days, though they were required to put on a good show during dinner for whoever attended.

But he hadn't let things get intimate since that first night.

"You want to talk to the Eldridges at a party you're throwing for Dmitri and Keira? That's insane. Do you know what those women are capable of? Not to insult your manliness, but they make the O'Malleys look like schoolgirls by comparison."

"It's important to the greater plan." Romanov thought the Eldridges would ascribe to the theory that the enemy of their enemy was their friend—or if not a friend, at least a useful tool. Aiden wouldn't have to fake his hatred of the Russian, and they both believed that Alethea would approach him as a result.

Charlie crossed one long leg over the other and cocked her head. The move sent her hair, pinned to one side, cascading over her shoulder. "You're playing a dangerous game."

"I know." He finished with his tie and shrugged into his jacket. "Desperate times."

"Very." Charlie rose, and he caught his breath all over again at the sight of her. She wore a silver dress that just about hit the floor, a slight flare in the fabric drawing attention to her hips and narrow waist and how well her breasts filled out the beaded bodice. As she turned to the door, he staggered to a stop. The dress dipped down to just below the small of her back. Any lower and it'd be indecent, and he couldn't stop staring, anticipating the fabric shifting just a bit.

She looked over her shoulder. "Marvelous, isn't it?"

"That's one word." He cleared his throat, tamping down the need to tell her to put on a wrap or, even better, change. She wasn't his. Walking into that room and drawing every male gaze was the intention. If the men were so busy thinking about her, they wouldn't be watching their words as closely as they should.

Knowing that still didn't dampen his desire to toss her on the bed and fuck her until his scent clung to her skin, so that every man she'd come into contact with tonight would have no doubt as to who she belonged to.

"Aiden?"

He blinked, finding her watching him with concern in her blue eyes. "I'm fine."

"Are you sure?" She took a half step toward him before she seemed to remember their relationship wasn't the kind that allowed for comforting. She gave a faint smile, something melancholy flitting across her expression before she shut it down. "If it's any consolation, I have a large amount of respect for the lengths you're willing to go for your family."

John Finch had failed her horribly if she thought what Aiden was doing was admirable. *Probably after she was labeled a dirty cop.* In the research he'd done on the man, the FBI agent didn't seem like the type to allow for gray area. Either a person was a criminal or they weren't. To have his daughter labeled as one of the people he hunted had to have shaken him to the core.

Anger rose, threatening to melt the cold wall he kept around himself. It shouldn't fucking matter if Charlie *was* a dirty cop. She was the last living member of Finch's immediate family—his *daughter*. It wasn't like she'd been accused of murder. The charge had been accepting a bribe, which was the very definition of petty shit. For her to be turned out after that...

It made him want to orchestrate a private conversation with John Finch that had nothing to do with the O'Malleys, and everything to do with the daughter he'd hurt so spectacularly with his callousness.

Aiden shifted, not liking the turn of his thoughts. Charlie was a means to an end. She'd have to fight her own battles—Aiden had enough people to watch over without adding a former cop who would never understand that his life wasn't the same as most people's and he could give two fucks how many laws he broke in the pursuit of protecting his family.

As much to remind himself as to remind her, he asked, "Does your father know where you are right now?"

Charlie frowned. "My father is no concern of yours."

She didn't ask how he knew enough about her father to ask, and he didn't offer. Admitting that her role as John Finch's daughter was a large reason why he'd singled her out might be enough to make her bolt, and Aiden had put too much time and money into this plan to change gears now.

No one but Charlie would do.

So he allowed her to change the subject.

She walked to the mirror and fixed her brilliant red lipstick, close enough that her shoulder brushed his. "Your sister is drowning. I think half the reason she's been sneaking out is so someone will pay attention to her."

He didn't particularly want to hear about the ways he was failing Keira. He knew. He had been for years. "She's not happy when I pay attention to her. She claims I'm stifling her."

"And you just listen to her?" Charlie snorted, but the amusement fled as soon as it'd appeared. "Those ruined paintings in her room, the ones that have been ripped to shreds or smeared with black... those were hers, weren't they? It's not my place to say it—"

"Then don't." He spoke too harshly, but he couldn't stop himself. Aiden put his hands on her hips and leaned against her back, pressing her against the counter and meeting her gaze in the mirror. "Leave it alone."

She glared. "Don't ask too many questions, don't try to fix things. Am I allowed to piss without your permission, or should I check in with you first?"

This was what he needed—a fight or a fuck to burn off some energy before he had to get his mask firmly in place. "Don't be pissy."

"*I'm* not the one being pissy." She pushed back against him, but he didn't give her an inch. "Back off."

"Why are you really angry, Charlie? Because I'm telling you not to meddle with my family? Or because I haven't touched that pretty pussy of yours in days?" He ignored her gasp of outrage and reached around to press the heel of his hand against the junction of her thighs. "Do you ache for me?"

She laughed softly, the sound hoarse as she pressed back against him again. "Who said I need you?" Red haze filtered across his vision, and her next words did little to calm it. "I'm quite capable of taking care of that myself." She covered his hand with her own, digging her nails in a little. "In fact, I fingered myself while you were in the shower."

It was all too easy to paint the picture in his head, of her on her back on the bed, her eyes closed and her fingers working between her thighs. He removed his hand, ignoring the way she allowed her nails to rake across the back of it. "Let's get one thing clear—"

"*One* thing? I have a goddamn list."

He bracketed her throat, putting just enough pressure there to stop her words. "Did you change your mind?"

She narrowed her eyes but didn't try to pretend she had no idea what he was talking about. "You play your game your way. I'll play it mine."

Disobedient and willful to the very end. He couldn't decide if she was trying to provoke a response or if she was just that opposed to being locked down in any way. In the end, it didn't matter. "I should bend you over this counter and fuck you into submission."

"Don't think for a second it would work." Charlie rolled her eyes. "And beyond that, we're already going to be late, so unless you're looking for a quickie, fucking me in any way is out of the question."

The irrational side of him, which always seemed to come into play around her, rose to demand he throw caution to the wind and prove her wrong. He reined it in, but only barely. Every time she pushed him, intentionally or not, he slid a little closer to the edge. It was only a matter of time before he went over—and took her with him.

Aiden let go of her and stepped back. He didn't like the confusion on her face—or the flicker of hurt that rose as he moved to the dresser across the room. For all her spikes, there was something fragile about Charlie, and he'd have to be a special kind of bastard to want to shatter her, no matter who her father was.

He opened the drawer at the bottom that had been empty until a week ago. "Take off your panties."

"I'm sorry, what?"

He gave her a look. "You heard me."

"I'm waiting for you to explain."

Aiden shook his head slowly. "There aren't two separate games—there's only *my* game. Either play along or deal with the consequences." He picked an item out of the drawer and held it up. "Here's your first punishment."

"I didn't do anything wrong." But her eyes lit with interest at the small blue vibe in his hand.

He motioned her forward, giving her plenty of time to tell him to go to hell.

But she didn't.

Charlie moved to stand directly in front of him. He lifted her dress to the tops of her thighs, bunching the shimmering fabric. "Hold this," he ordered.

"You are aggravating in the extreme."

"So I've been told." He pulled her panties down to her thighs. It was tempting to kiss her there, but he forced himself to stay on task. Aiden held the small vibe against her clit as he shifted the lace back into place. It took a few seconds to maneuver it to exactly where he wanted, but then he sat back on his heels. "You can let go now."

"This is an important night, Aiden." She shifted, a frown on her face. "We don't have time for your sex games to distract me."

He pulled out his phone and brought up the app he'd downloaded when he bought the sex toy. A flick of his finger and her entire body tensed. Aiden didn't bother to hide his satisfied smile. It fell away when he touched his pocket and the little box it held. "One more thing."

"I swear to God, I draw the line at anal plugs, so don't even think about it."

That surprised a laugh out of him. What surprised him even more was how good it felt. When was the last time he'd laughed freely in a way that wasn't calculated?

Aiden couldn't remember.

He stood and pulled out the ring box. "I'd go down on one knee, but that isn't the kind of relationship we have."

"No, it's not." She looked a little sick, but she held out her hand so he could slide the ring onto it. "Aiden, it's beautiful."

"It was my grandmother's." It had taken some shady work to figure out Charlie's ring size after he'd first met her, so that he could get the ring resized. He hadn't told anyone about it. Though he'd been as sure of her as he could be of a near-stranger, he hadn't wanted to admit the lengths he'd gone through, in case things didn't pan out.

If anything, she looked even more horrified. "I can't wear your grandmother's ring. It's not right."

"You have to. As oldest son and heir, that ring rightfully belongs to my future wife. It would be more than a little suspicious if I *didn't* give it to you."

She touched the massive diamond. It was in the same setting as when his grandfather had proposed, little rubies and garnets surrounding the diamond, to represent colors in the O'Malley crest.

It felt a whole lot like he'd just branded Charlie.

It didn't bother him nearly as much as it should.

CHAPTER NINE

Charlie was going to kill Aiden. He didn't let up on that goddamn vibrator for a second during the ride over to the party. Between that and the giant diamond ring that she swore was weighing her hand down, she didn't feel like herself anymore. She *wasn't* herself anymore.

By the time the car pulled to a stop, she was panting a little, her body so primed for him, she was putting serious consideration into breaking her own rule and begging.

And then the vibrations between her legs...stopped.

She took a breath, and then another. "I hate this."

"No, you don't." Aiden glanced out the window and then at the expensive watch at his wrist. "We have a little time."

"What—*oh*." She found herself in his lap, her back against his chest.

"You might think this is a mercy." He pulled her dress up and slid his hand into her panties. "It's not."

She didn't care. All that mattered was his hand working

between her thighs, taking up where the vibrator had left off. Charlie let her head rest on his shoulder as he fucked her with his fingers. "God, Aiden."

"Tonight, bright eyes. If you make it through this dinner without sticking a fork in my jugular or embarrassing us both, I'm going to be inside you tonight."

And just like that, she was coming, his free hand over her mouth to muffle her cries. He didn't gentle his touch, ruthlessly driving her over the edge again, until all she knew was the man at her back, his fingers buried inside her.

He adjusted her panties, and she sobbed out a breath as the vibrator came into contact with her oversensitive clit. She was aching from the orgasm, and the sheer deviousness of what he'd just done struck her.

Charlie pushed off him, cursing. "Maybe I don't want that cocktease of yours." She couldn't catch her breath. He wasn't doing this. He couldn't. When he made a move to get out of the car, she grabbed his arm. "Aiden."

The desperation in her voice was clear. She didn't even try to hide it.

He stopped, closed the door that he'd just opened, and turned to look at her. She could almost feel his attention sliding over her, and she saw the exact moment he realized this wasn't just a game of protesting for the fun of it. "You don't want this."

"This?" She motioned between them. "This is fine." But now wasn't the time for bravado—not when she was about to climb out of this car and face down the man who'd been instrumental in her being branded a dirty cop. Charlie took a deep breath and muscled past her pride. "I like the games—when it's between you and me. You can't honestly expect me to go out there with a goddamn vibrator in my panties."

He was so still, she wasn't sure he was breathing. Finally, Aiden smiled. "I don't."

"What?" She pressed her hand to her chest to hide the relief that made her shake. "What are you talking about?"

He had her dress up and the vibe removed before she had a chance to tell him she could do it herself. Then Aiden pulled her back into his lap and rested his chin on the top of her head.

Charlie stared blindly into the shadows of the town car while Aiden...comforted her. She'd be lying if she called it anything else. He didn't say anything, and she didn't know what to say, so they sat there in silence as he rubbed her back and held her. The shift happened so fast, she was surprised she didn't have whiplash.

I don't even know what's happening right now.

Movement on the outside of the car drew her attention. People were walking through the front doors, each dressed glitzier than the next. "What are we doing, Aiden?"

"You were worried about meeting Romanov tonight. Now you're not."

Charlie froze. All this was a distraction? For *her*? To put her mind at ease because he knew how nervous she was to finally face the man behind her downfall?

She didn't know what to think of that—of any of this. Just when she thought she had his number down, he went and did something to make her question everything she thought she knew about him. She wasn't fool enough to believe that he had a soft gooey center beneath all those barriers and masks, but maybe he wasn't as much of a cold bastard as she'd originally assumed. "Thank you."

Aiden shifted her off his lap so he could climb out of the car. He adjusted his slacks before bending to offer her his hand. "If you get overwhelmed and need a break, just take my hand and I'll get you out of there."

"I can handle it." Her body still hummed from pleasure, but she felt much more in control now. Like she might actually be able to do this.

Because of him.

"I know." He looped a possessive arm around her waist, a clear signal to anyone who looked that she was his and his alone, and headed into the building.

Charlie didn't look to the right or the left as they made their way into what was probably a very impressive ballroom. It might as well been a shack, for all she cared. The location didn't matter—the act did. She let herself lean a bit more into Aiden, telling herself that she was selling the lie, rather than taking comfort from his being so close.

"Brace yourself, bright eyes."

There was no mistaking his meaning as he guided her toward the dark-haired man standing on the other side of the room, his people flanking him. He was attractive, though not in the flashy way that Aiden and his brothers were. This man had an earthier handsomeness that screamed violence even though he looked perfectly at home in his suit. His men, on the other hand, were almost caricatures of bad guys—all dead eyes and poorly concealed weapons. As a group, they looked out of place in the finery of the ballroom—wolves among sheep.

Except the O'Malleys are wolves in their own right.

"Romanov." Aiden's arm tightened around her. "You made it."

And there he was, the object of so much of her hatred. Charlie had seen pictures of Dmitri Romanov before, and he had always seemed so completely unremarkable. Tall,

dark, and handsome, sure, but there was nothing there to indicate he was one of the most dangerous men on the eastern
seaboard.

Standing here in front of him, she suddenly understood
all too well.

"I prefer to be punctual." He turned those inky eyes on
her. "Who's your..." His gaze flicked to her left hand,
where the ring felt like a line of fire against her skin. It
didn't matter that it was all in her head. She was suddenly
half-sure that Dmitri could see how uncomfortable the piece
of jewelry made her.

He arched his brows. "A fiancée. Aiden, I didn't think
you capable of surprising me, but I stand corrected. De-
lighted to meet you..."

"Charlie." She could barely get her name past her lips,
couldn't do anything but stand there like a statue as he lifted
her right hand and kissed her knuckles. It wasn't anything
like what Aiden had done that one time—it was perfectly
polite and without the slightest bit of heat.

That didn't stop her from wanting to bolt to the nearest
restroom and scrub at her skin to remove any trace of him.

"I can see why you've turned our mutual friend's head."
He took in everything in a single sweep, and she realized with
horror that he'd noted every indication of her arousal before
he turned back to Aiden. "Now, where is *my* fiancée? I have
something I'd like to give her before this circus begins."

"Romanov." The steel in Aiden's voice had the other
man looking at him with polite disinterest. But he *was* looking. "You might be planning on marrying my sister, but if
you touch her before the ceremony, I'll skin you alive."

The Russian smiled, and the sight chilled Charlie despite
the warmth of the room. Dmitri picked a phantom piece of lint

off his jacket sleeve. "I can't be responsible for her actions. They *are* her choice, after all." He must have seen something on Aiden's face, because his shark's smile widened. "Your request is noted." And then he was gone, moving through the growing crowd, two men trailing behind him.

"I'm going to kill him."

It was only then that she noted the tension in Aiden's body. He was holding himself like he was half a second from chasing the Russian down and beating the shit out of him. She stepped in front of him and looped her arms around his neck. To anyone watching, it would appear she just couldn't get enough of her man. No one was close enough to hear her murmur. "He's trying to provoke you."

"It's working." His hands on her hips held her tightly enough to bruise, but they relaxed as he took one breath, and then another. "Sorry. That asshole gets under my skin."

"I understand." *He did it on purpose.* She leaned back enough to look at his face.

"I suppose you do." His slow smile was confirmation enough. "You did pull a gun on me the first time we met."

"You deserved it." He'd scared her half to death and chased her through the streets. For all she knew, he'd been sent by Romanov to tie up the loose end she represented.

"I did." He exhaled, the last of the tension bleeding from his body. "Thank you. I won't lose control again."

Wouldn't he? She didn't think anyone—least of all Aiden—realized how close to the edge he stood. Words she had no business saying rose to crowd against her lips. *You can lean on me. Trust me. Let me help you bear the burdens you carry.* She didn't say any of it. He'd told her to back off earlier, and she'd be a fool not to do exactly that.

Charlie was only an interloper in Aiden's life—there for

a short time and then gone again. She couldn't try to force him to lean on her just because it bothered her to see him struggling.

So she smiled and took a step back, pausing to adjust his tie. "Don't worry. I know you won't." But she wasn't going to leave his side for the duration of the night.

Just in case.

* * *

Keira had tried to sneak out for a smoke break, only to find every exit blocked by O'Malley men. None of them were too thrilled at the idea of her leaving the room. Her constant disappearing acts had created more work for them, which was something she suspected she'd be paying for until she was shipped off to Dmitri.

At least his *men won't know to lock me down so tightly.*

Wouldn't they, though? Dmitri was the one who kept finding her, even when she thought she'd done a good job of slipping away unnoticed.

It didn't matter. Nothing mattered anymore.

Keira walked into the ladies' room, leaving a frustrated-looking Liam at the door, and hopped onto the counter. She wouldn't crawl out a window, no matter how much she wanted to. Tonight was too important to her brother. She didn't like being traded like chattel, but if she left now, Aiden would catch heat for it.

So Keira didn't run. She just pulled a joint out of her clutch and lit it. The first inhale burned her throat like a hot poker, and she luxuriated in the feeling, even as her thoughts slowed down. One toke wasn't enough to blitz her out—or even half the damn joint—but she wouldn't smoke the whole thing. All she wanted was some much-needed distance to get through the night.

The door opened, and she spoke without looking up. "Bathroom is occupied."

"There are several stalls. Greedy of you to deny them to ladies in need."

She jerked her head up so fast, she almost fell off the counter. "What are you doing here?"

Dmitri closed the door behind him and flicked the lock. "Your brother and his men are aggravating in their zealous desire to protect you." He crossed to stand in front of her. "Should I tell them exactly how many times you've been in my tender care and walked away unscathed?"

"Three." She held up the appropriate number of fingers. "You talk like it happens on the regular. It doesn't."

He moved closer, and she didn't realize his intent until his hand flashed out and snagged the joint from her. Keira grabbed for it, but Dmitri was too fast, flipping on the faucet and dousing it. "What the fuck?"

"Nasty habit of yours. Tell me something, Keira—when was the last time you spent an entire day sober?"

How dare he sit there and judge her. She started to hop off the counter, but Dmitri was there, his body between her knees. He braced his hands on either side of her, not quite touching her but leaving her feeling exposed all the same. "Answer the question."

She froze, torn between the need to fight her way out and the traitorous desire to spread her legs a little more and invite him in. She already knew how the latter would play out. Dmitri might want her, at least in part, but he had turned her down too many times for her pride to allow her to keep throwing herself at him.

She tossed her hair over her shoulder and glared. "That's none of your goddamn business."

"Maybe not yet. But it will be." His gaze raked over her, a heat like she'd never seen before kindling in his gray eyes. He seemed to realize he'd given her a glimpse of it, because he took a careful step back. "I got something for you."

"I don't want anything from you."

"Liar." There was the heat again, just as quickly smothered. "But that's not what I'm offering at the moment."

Of course it wasn't. She refused to feel disappointed. Keira crossed her arms over her chest and waited. "Fine. Give it to me."

He pulled a box out of his jacket pocket and opened it. Despite everything, she gasped. It was a huge diamond set in a platinum band with smaller pink diamonds framing it. It looked like something a duchess would wear. Or what she imagined a duchess would wear. "I thought this would suit you."

It was the most beautiful thing she'd ever seen.

It actually made her heart lurch to turn her face away. "I don't want it."

"That's the second time you've lied to me during this conversation." Dmitri took her hand, the heat of his skin against hers sparking things low in her stomach. "Truth between us—that's all I demand of you." He chuckled at the arch look she sent him. "You're right. That wasn't the full truth. We can come to terms later, but in the meantime—truth."

Terms.

Such a cold word to encompass all that marriage should be. Then again, what did she know? Her parents seemed to like each other just fine, but her mother had essentially been sold to her father in a political marriage the same way Keira was being sold to Dmitri. She knew it was for peace. That was the only thing that would keep her here when all she wanted to do was follow in Sloan's footsteps and flee to a far corner of the world.

Liar. The voice in her head sounded so much like Dmitri that she blinked.

Okay, there are a few reasons I'm staying.

She watched him slide the massive ring onto her finger, half-surprised the weight of it didn't drag her off the counter. "I suppose after I pop out the requisite heir and a spare, you'll let me come back to Boston." It was the same deal he had offered Carrigan. She wasn't sure what she thought about that.

"Hardly. Once we exchange those vows, *moya koroleva*, you're *mine*." He waited for her to meet his gaze, and then he dropped the mask. There was no ice, no pleasant gentleman-murderer there. No, there was only the monster beneath.

And that monster wanted *her*.

CHAPTER TEN

Aiden kept his hand on the small of Charlie's back while he guided her through the crowd to where the Eldridge women had staked out the northern corner of the room, directly opposite the Romanov men. Romanov had been certain they would show, but Aiden still breathed a slight sigh of relief to see the matriarch of the Eldridge clan, Alethea, sitting surrounded by her men. Her daughters were nowhere to be seen, with the exception of her heir, Mae, who sat poised at her mother's right elbow.

Alethea didn't rise as he came to a stop in front of her, but she inclined her head slightly. "Aiden O'Malley."

"I hope you're enjoying your evening." He nodded to Mae. "Both of you." Neither woman was beautiful in the traditionally accepted way, their features too strong, their bodies built for strength rather than model-thin, but they were striking. He'd caught several of his men giving Mae long looks earlier, and he had made a point to tell Liam to keep them the hell away from her.

Alethea had made her fortune in the world dealing with the people even he avoided, and her daughter was no damsel in distress. When he'd asked Cillian to get him information on the family, it had come out that sadistic didn't begin to cover Mae's proclivities.

Mae was staring at Charlie like a lioness considering its next meal. "Who's your date?"

"Mae, Alethea . . . I'd like you to meet my fiancée, Charlie Moreaux." He was every inch the welcoming host, even as he mentally cursed at the situation he'd created. In all his careful planning, he'd never once stopped and considered what would happen if Alethea's daughter looked at Charlie and saw competition. *I just put a fucking target on her chest.* He'd known it was a possibility, going into this, but the reality of it had changed the second he got her into his bed. It made him want her safe and as far away from the Eldridges as humanly possible.

It was his fault she was in danger to begin with.

Charlie didn't seem to be suffering from the same distraction he was. She moved forward with a smile. "Pleasure to meet you."

Mae glared at her outstretched hand, but Alethea beamed. "We hadn't realized you were engaged, Aiden, but I can see why you've hidden her away. Look at you, girl, you're so tiny and breakable. A woman like you doesn't have to try hard to twist a man around her little finger."

"Oh, I wouldn't say that." Charlie's smile didn't waver as she extracted her hand. "I had to play dirty to get his attention in the first place."

Tension rose, which was the exact opposite of what he'd wanted to accomplish. It was vital to his and their plan that the Eldridges see Aiden as a potential ally and act accordingly. If they were checking out the O'Malleys, they wouldn't be looking over their shoulder at Romanov. If Aiden and Charlie didn't play this initial interaction correctly, all his plans would go up in smoke. Antagonizing Alethea Eldridge was *not* on the agenda.

But he underestimated Charlie.

She laughed. "You know how these things are, though— easy come, easy go."

Did she just… He shot her a look, but now wasn't the time to haul her ass somewhere private to talk about how he felt about her changing the story without talking to him. "I wouldn't have proposed if I wasn't serious, Charlie."

"I know." She waved it away like he was an annoying gnat and winked at Mae. "I bet you know a thing or two about getting what you want. You don't seem the type who takes no as a final answer." She injected admiration into her tone, and the other woman relaxed, just a bit.

Mae examined her maroon nails. "I can be very convincing when provoked."

"Oh, I'll bet." Charlie *giggled*.

What the hell is she up to?

Alethea cleared her throat, her eyes on something over Aiden's shoulder. "Do you let your youngest sister wander unattended regularly?"

He turned in time to find Keira walking out of the women's bathroom. He was about to comment on the fact that the restroom was the one place he didn't demand his men follow his sister when the door opened behind her and motherfucking Dmitri Romanov walked out, looking as pleased as the cat that ate the canary. *Fuck.* That was *not* part of the goddamn plan. "Ladies, excuse me."

"Aiden." All warmth had disappeared from Alethea's

voice, leaving no doubt that this woman had more than earned her reputation as one of the scariest players in the underground game in New York.

The fact that Romanov had the balls to cross her baffled Aiden. The Russian didn't seem the type to act without a reason, but hell if he could figure out what it was—even while working with the man, and with all Cillian's hacking skills.

Alethea's blue eyes were just as cold as her voice. "It seems we may have an interest or two in common."

This was exactly what he'd hoped to accomplish, but he felt no victory at getting into bed with the Eldridges. Even if it was a lie. "It would seem so."

"Come see me soon. We'll discuss things in private." Her gaze flicked to Charlie. "Bring your fiancée. My Mae has taken a charm to her."

That only served to make him want to haul Charlie's ass as far away from these two as possible. He smiled instead. "It would be my pleasure. Enjoy the rest of the party, ladies." He looped his arm around Charlie's waist as they walked away, and he could actually feel both the Eldridge women's gazes pinned between his shoulder blades. He pulled Charlie closer. "What the fuck was that?"

"Playing a part, Aiden." She sounded as sweet as pie. "That's what we're doing. I got you what you wanted."

Before he could respond, she waved at Keira and stepped away from him to go talk to her. He surveyed his sister, looking for signs of shakiness or fear or something that a normal person would feel after having been cornered by Dmitri Romanov in the bathroom. She lifted her hand to brush back her long, dark hair, and Aiden froze. A giant-ass diamond glinted on her ring finger, and that sure as fuck hadn't been there earlier.

Cillian stepped up next to him and crossed his arms over his chest. "Tell me something."

He didn't look over. "Now isn't the time."

They both spoke so low, someone would have had to practically be on top of them to eavesdrop. "I think it's the perfect time."

Obviously, his brother wasn't going to let it go. He clenched his jaw. Was *anyone* going to do what they were supposed to tonight? "What?"

"If you're so determined to marry Keira off to Romanov... why the hell are you so pissed that she's wearing his ring?"

Aiden finally looked at his brother, finding too much knowledge on his face. So he'd figured it out. *Damn.* "We'll talk about it tomorrow."

Cillian gave a short nod. "Excuse me. Dmitri wants to see Hadley before it's her bedtime." He never let the other man near Olivia and his stepdaughter without being there. Aiden didn't blame him, though one of the few good things he could say about Romanov was that he seemed to genuinely care about his niece.

Then again, he *seemed* to do and say a lot of things. None of it could be trusted.

Olivia might claim that her half brother always kept his word, but Aiden couldn't risk believing that. His only job was to provide for the O'Malleys and expand their power. He couldn't do any of those things with Romanov in his way. He'd crossed the O'Malleys too many times, and now he had to be removed as a threat.

Aiden sat at an empty table and monitored the interaction between Cillian and Romanov. Olivia was tense, but the year and a half she'd been living with the O'Malleys had gone a long way to repair her relationship with Romanov.

She still didn't like him, but he hadn't crossed the line she'd drawn in the sand when it came to her daughter.

Romanov went down on one knee, bending his head to speak at Hadley's level. The little girl was the spitting image of her mother, her skin hinting of the Middle Eastern descent she'd inherited by way of her maternal grandmother, her hair a wild riot of dark curls. She was a solemn child, and she was serious in the extreme as she spoke to her uncle until he pulled a floppy bunny from his jacket. He couldn't have had the thing the entire time, but he managed to make it look like a magic trick. Hadley's trill of delight could be heard even halfway across the room.

"Cute." Charlie sank into the chair to his left, her attention following his.

"Yes, it is." He looked at her, searching for any signs of doubt or softening. "Still on board?"

She frowned. "Why wouldn't I be? Even monsters have soft spots. That doesn't make them less monstrous. He could cuddle his niece and turn around and order a person's death without blinking." She shook her head. "No. The kid's young enough. She's got a good mom. She'll be fine if her uncle disappears off the face of the earth."

Aiden didn't ask whether she was looking for Romanov to end up in prison or six feet under. He didn't have it in him for a fight—not here, not now. "It's almost time for food—and toasts."

"Toasts?"

He shrugged. "It's part of the process. We'll have a meeting to hash out the details and argue to a standstill about which ceremony will be performed."

She stared. "You're serious."

"The Romanov family is Eastern Orthodox. We're

Catholic. They might not seem that different to an outsider, but they are—and neither family will be happy about compromise."

Charlie didn't look any more convinced. "You're not actually planning on letting Keira marry that piece of shit, so why does it matter?"

He glanced around, but there was no one particularly close. That didn't stop him from hooking a hand under her chair and towing her over to his side, the move putting her half in his lap. "What is it with people wanting to discuss state secrets while we're in a room with fifty other fucking people."

"That's the best time to discuss secrets," she murmured.

To anyone looking on, they were a couple in love—or at least in lust—so entwined with each other that the rest of the room didn't matter. With Charlie's citrus scent teasing him, it wasn't a hard part to play. He kissed her neck. "Romanov is many things—stupid isn't one of them. If I don't fight and argue and bitch the same way I would in reality, he'll know something is up. Ultimately, it's Keira's choice, but until she makes it, we have to proceed accordingly." *Until the deal with the Eldridges is done and she knows she has a choice at all.*

"Makes sense." She inhaled sharply as he nipped her shoulder.

"You going to tell me what the fuck was up with that game you were playing with Mae?"

"Now's not the time."

He growled, which only seemed to amuse the infuriating woman. She grinned at him. "But I'm more than willing to be persuaded."

"Oh, bright eyes, I'll persuade the fuck out of you."

* * *

Charlie did her best to focus, but it was a lost cause. All she could feel was Aiden's attention heavy on her, the promise of *persuasion* in her future. There was no mistaking what that meant—not when he'd spelled it out in the car earlier. Sex. He'd made her beg, something she'd thought was impossible. Charlie was hardly a virgin, but she liked her sex like she liked everything else since her life had gone down the shitter—without fuss. Why bother with romance when the only thing both partners were after was a pair of mutually satisfying orgasms?

Not that she could call what had happened between them in his bed *romantic*.

"Charlie."

She turned, her breath coming a little too short to be totally at ease. Seeing how smug Aiden looked made her want to set him on his ass. That was her problem, though. Not his. He'd been mostly consistent up to this point. *She* was the one who was in danger of changing the rules. *Hard to take the high ground when I don't have a ledge to stand on.* "What?"

"It's time."

She looked around, a little panicked at the realization that the room had emptied while she was obsessing over the thought of having sex with Aiden. *You're trained better than that, distracted to high hell or not.* She tried for a smile and failed miserably. "Great." All she wanted to do was get the hell away from here. The night had left her feeling raw and exposed in a way that had nothing to do with the physical.

She'd thought she was prepared for everything that working with Aiden would entail.

She was wrong.

She brushed past him and headed for the doors they'd come in through. She could feel him at her back, but Aiden didn't say anything as they climbed into the waiting town car and then rode back to the O'Malley house. She stared through the window, not feeling any more welcome than she had the first time. This wasn't her place. She'd be worse than a fool to believe otherwise, even for a second.

Aiden took her hand at the front door, the contact shocking her out of her funk. It hadn't skipped her notice that he barely touched her unless he was looking to prove a point or there were orgasms involved. And he hadn't come close to kissing her. Not once. *That's very* Pretty Woman *of him.* The joke fell flat, even in her head. She knew better than to get caught up in this bullshit. She did.

But she still followed him into his room and shut the door behind her.

And her traitorous body was still primed and aching for him.

It didn't seem to matter that she wasn't even sure she *liked* Aiden—how could she when the only parts of him she knew were the ones he allowed her to see?

She wanted him despite that.

For now, that was enough.

"Take off your dress."

She unzipped the side and let the heavy fabric fall to her feet. The only thing she wore beneath it was her panties, and she wasted no time sliding those off as well. Only then did she dare look at Aiden.

He'd taken a seat on the edge of the bed, and he watched her with an unreadable expression on his face. "How are you doing?"

"What?" She'd expected more games, or at least some kind of command. She hadn't anticipated him asking her a frank question that she didn't have an answer to.

"Tonight couldn't have been easy for you."

She stared at him. If she didn't know better, she would think he was offering an olive branch and inviting her to talk with him. Maybe to share actual honest-to-God emotions.

But this was Aiden O'Malley, so she had to be misreading the situation.

Exhaustion rolled over her in a wave that had her eyeing the bed for purposes that had nothing to do with sex. She could jump through his hoops tomorrow. Tonight she was just done. "Aiden, we've been talking on and off all night. If you're going to fuck me, fuck me. If not, I'm going to bed." Charlie hadn't anticipated how draining it would be to be constantly on guard and worrying about staying in character—or how twisted up she'd be about her fake fiancé in the process. *Should have run faster that first night.*

Something crossed his face, something she couldn't put into words. Aiden exhaled harshly and stood. "I haven't been doing a good job with you."

"Uh, what?" He'd switched tracks so fast, her head spun as she tried to take the mental jump with him. "What are you talking about?"

He walked to the phone on the dresser. "Did you manage to eat anything during that shit show of a party?"

Now she was *really* confused. "No..." She'd been too nervous—and even if she'd wanted to, there were so many people drifting up to talk to her, she wouldn't have had a chance.

"It's late, so there won't be any fancy options, but I know for a fact that Mark makes a mean turkey club."

Her stomach chose that moment to grumble, and she pressed her hand there, as if the contact could tell it to shut the hell up. As attractive as sleep sounded, her mouth watered at the thought of a sandwich. "I could eat."

"Thought so." He motioned toward the bathroom without looking up from where he was dialing. "Take a shower, bright eyes. By the time you're done, there will be food. Then we'll talk."

More talking.

She didn't know if she was disappointed or relieved, but she padded into the bathroom all the same. A shower sounded like heaven, and so she wasn't going to think too hard about the fact that they apparently weren't going to have sex tonight. Stepping beneath the stinging spray made her gasp a little, but she welcomed the shock to her system. She gritted her teeth and scrubbed herself down, washing her hair until it was no longer stiff from the liberal amount of hair spray needed to tame it. And then she just stood there, her head ducked beneath the running water, letting it course over her until she felt a little more in control.

It took far longer than she would have liked.

She finally shut off the faucet when it became apparent that peace wasn't in the cards for her. She was too aware of Aiden in the next room over, and the rest of the night hanging over their heads. Talking was all well and good, but she was all talked out. Sex was even better, but she was exhausted.

Right now, she was just one big mess.

Charlie hadn't had the foresight to bring in a change of clothes, so she walked out of the bathroom as naked as she walked in. *It's not like Aiden hasn't seen every inch of me.*

He held up a shirt and then tossed it to her. "Wear this.

I can't focus with you sitting there looking so downright fuckable."

"Sounds like a personal problem." But she pulled on the shirt, belatedly realizing it was far too big to belong to her, so long it hit the tops of her thighs. She frowned down at it. "I'm wearing your shirt." It didn't look like anything she'd seen Aiden in to date. It was a normal T-shirt with faded writing across the chest. "Boston University?"

"Even mob families go to college, Charlie." He gave a mirthless smile. "Business major."

It made sense. If the O'Malleys were anything like the Romanovs, they had a carefully balanced array of businesses—a good portion of which were on the up-and-up. It was possible to delegate some of that, but the more the boss handed off, the higher the chance of someone sneaking in and undercutting him because he didn't understand the business side of things. She looked at Aiden with new eyes, feeling a little like a layer had been peeled back. "Nice."

"It was a huge pain in the ass, but necessary. Most of us have college degrees of one sort or another." He sighed. "Not Keira, though. She dropped out of art school two years ago, and she doesn't seem interested in going back."

"You're . . . really worried about her." She moved to sit on the edge of the bed, taking in the tray with sandwiches sitting beside him. "She's a good kid."

"You were right before. She's lost and hurting." He pushed one of the sandwiches toward her. "And I'm partly to blame for that, for a number of reasons. It's been a rough couple of years for our family, and I was so focused on getting us through it without more losses that I didn't realize she was slipping away until it was almost too late. Now she won't talk to me even when I try to reach out."

"And your other sisters?" The ones who had left the family behind in pursuit of... Well, Charlie couldn't say for sure what they were in pursuit of. She still didn't know the full story behind Sloan, and Carrigan seemed to fit in just fine with the mob life, even if she'd chosen a rival family over her own.

Aiden stared at something she couldn't see. "I've kept things under control, and kept our business prospects from suffering too much during this time of uncertainty."

It sounded a whole lot like a rehearsed speech—or someone else's words coming out of his mouth.

He seemed to realize the same thing. He shook his head. "But, yeah, I've mishandled all three of my sisters. Repeatedly. The problem with putting the family first is that the individuals sometimes get lost in the shuffle."

"I'm new to the scene, so I might not be reading things right, but it sure looks like you have a powerhouse of alliances going on in Boston." Carrigan linked them to the Hallorans, even if there was tension there. Teague had married Callista Sheridan, which finished off the trifecta. Charlie might not support the illegal aspects of their lives, but she didn't see how any of that was a bad thing.

"Yes and no. If Romanov wasn't a threat, it would be true that the family is as powerful as it's ever been, and a good portion of that is because of the events of the last few years." He didn't look particularly happy about it.

"I sense a 'but' coming."

Aiden gave a tight smile. "But even if business is flourishing, the personal relationships have suffered. I'm sure you noticed the tension."

"I did. I also noticed that all of your siblings jumped to your defense when they thought you were marrying a gold digger." She shrugged, even though she still hated that aspect of their lie.

"Yes, I suppose they did." His smile softened a little. "Families are complicated. We all grew up knowing what was expected of us, but some of us were more at peace with it than others."

Strangely enough, she understood. Being raised in a family full of cops meant that everyone expected her to follow in their footsteps. But that was where the similarities ended. She'd wanted to be a cop, wanted it more than anything else in the world. She'd run cross-country and lifted weights in high school almost religiously because she wanted to be at the top of her game when she went into the police academy. All with her dad's approval. There had never been another path available, because that was the only one she wanted.

She wasn't sure what her dad would have done if she'd dreamed of running off and joining the ballet or becoming a doctor, but she couldn't really picture him taking any other field of work as seriously as he took law enforcement.

She studied him. Aiden O'Malley had layers upon layers. Even now, when it seemed like he was being perfectly honest, she wasn't 100 percent sure this wasn't another of his masks. He had so many.

That didn't stop her from asking, "And were you at peace with it?"

"Mostly." He shrugged. "It never occurred to me to want something different. Even if it had...Teague is occupied with the Sheridans, and Carrigan with the Hallorans. Sloan is gone with Jude MacNamara, and I'd never force her back to Boston. Devlin is dead. Cillian has a brilliant head for numbers but no interest in leading. He probably could do it if something happened to me, but I'd never ask him to pay that price just because I didn't feel like taking the responsibility. No, bright eyes, there's no one else."

This isn't a mask. I'm sure of it.

She was equally sure that he hadn't meant to reveal so much of himself—and would instantly backtrack if she commented on it. Charlie picked up half of her sandwich. "Thank you for the food." She had a lot to think about. Too much. Every time she thought she had his number down, he went and threw her a curveball.

Who is the real Aiden O'Malley?

CHAPTER ELEVEN

They ate in silence until the food was gone, but Aiden was no more settled than he had been when they left the party. He should just fuck Charlie and be done with it, but he couldn't get her words about his sister out of his head. Or the fact that there had been understanding on her face when she asked about his role as heir.

Who could have guessed that he'd actually have something in common with a cop's daughter, besides smoking-hot chemistry?

He knew about Charlie. He'd done his research before he'd approached her. He'd looked even deeper into her after that initial encounter. Her record for the short time she'd been a cop was truly impressive. She'd been on the fast track to be detective—or at least she had before she refused to roll over and play dead for Romanov. She'd never been formally charged with taking bribes, but she'd been tossed out on her ass and, for all intents and purposes, she'd disappeared off the face of the earth for several months after that. The next time he could find her, she was running the poker games in that shitty bar.

"Where were you?"

He didn't realize he'd spoken aloud until she cocked her head. "What? When?"

If he was smart, he'd change the subject and get them back to what they were good at—sex—but he genuinely wanted to know. "After you were kicked off the force. Where did you go? The next time I found you was months later." Maybe she'd been lying low at her father's house. That was the most logical explanation he could come up with.

She looked him dead in the eyes. "I was in the hospital for a week, and after that I was drinking myself into oblivion."

He couldn't get past the first few words to focus on the rest. "The hospital?" But even as he said it, he knew exactly what had happened. "Those cops on his payroll didn't like it that you tried to rock the boat."

"That's a wild understatement." She didn't look away, didn't try to hide the pain still lurking it the depths of her blue eyes.

"How bad was it?"

"How bad would it be if one of your own betrayed you?" *Another thing we have in common.*

He still hadn't dealt with Teague becoming an informant for the FBI. Truth be told, Aiden had left that conversation alone for far too long. It was a loose end in desperate need of tying, but admitting the sheer depth of his brother's betrayal wasn't something Aiden was eager to do.

He was supposed to be in control at all times. It should have been nothing to face down his little brother. But therein lay the problem—Teague was his little brother. The same kid who'd followed him around for years when they were in grade school. The one he'd maintained the best relationship with through high school and beyond. Aiden knew Teague was struggling with everything being an O'Malley entailed, but never in a million years would he guess that he'd turn to the feds.

"It's the worst thing in the world."

"Yes, it is."

He didn't resist the urge to pull her into his lap. Charlie went tense but slowly relaxed into his arms, allowing him to prop his chin on her shoulder. He didn't have a simple solution to offer her any more than he had one to deal with his own betrayal. Life was rarely neat and easy.

Offering to kill those pieces of shit would be an insult to the injury she'd suffered. He still made a mental note to find out their names and pay them a visit. Telling her that he was glad she survived was so damn inadequate. He had a hard time imagining a situation that would put her down permanently—would break her—but that had to have come close.

He didn't know what to say. There wasn't anything *to* say.

So he kissed her.

She twisted in his lap, her hands coming to rest on his chest. Aiden had every intention of keeping the kiss light and short, but his good intentions went up in smoke the second her lips parted to allow him in. He should have pulled back, or should have kept them on comfortable territory and just fucked her brains out. That was a whole hell of a lot safer than sitting here exploring her mouth while she wore nothing but his shirt.

Giving her that shirt was a statement.

He'd known that. He'd still given it to her.

Charlie shifted, moving back so she could straddle him. She gave him a strange look, but he kissed her again. It was easier than answering the questions in her eyes. And the truth was that he enjoyed the hell out of kissing her. Aiden skimmed his hands up her thighs to cup her ass, bringing her more firmly against him. "Feel how much I want you."

"I do." She rolled her hips, and then her mouth was on his again, her tongue slipping out to stroke his bottom lip.

He lost himself in the feel of her, in how the taste of her drove every thought out of his head. Aiden lay back on the bed, taking her with him, and then rolled to settle between her thighs. The move had her shirt hiking up around her hips, something he couldn't take full advantage of with his slacks still on. He pulled away enough to say, "I'm fucking you tonight."

"Thank Christ."

He climbed off the bed and stripped, staring at her all the while. She didn't try to cover up, just propped herself onto her elbows so she could watch him as closely as he was watching her. The sight of her with just that shirt on— *his* shirt—and bare from the waist down...Aiden moved faster, shucking off his pants and kicking them away. He took a step toward her but stopped, then retrieved a handful of condoms from where he'd stashed them in his dresser and tossed them onto the bed next to Charlie. She raised her eyebrows but, for once, didn't comment.

"Those are for later. Right now?" Aiden went to his knees next to the bed and grabbed her hips, dragging her within reach of his mouth. "I'm starving for you, bright eyes."

* * *

Charlie cried out, her voice hoarse from all the things Aiden had done to her. Time ceased to have meaning, awash as she was in the unbearable pleasure of his mouth. Finally, desperate for more, she jerked away and stopped him from closing the distance with a foot on the center of his chest. Her pink toes looked absolutely ridiculous against his tanned muscles.

Aiden glanced down at her foot. "I'm not done with you yet."

"No, you're not." She pushed a little, forcing him further back. "But I want you."

He knocked her foot to the side and surged up, taking her mouth as if he couldn't help himself. He tasted of smoky whiskey and her, the combination making her moan. She wrapped her legs around his waist, needing as much of him against as much of her as possible.

Aiden went to reach between her legs, and she cursed. "Nope." Charlie shoved him, twisting until he landed on his back, with her across his chest. "You're a sadist, and while I kind of dig that, I want you inside me."

His green eyes went dark. "Careful there. That was almost begging."

"Not even close." She palmed him, hissing out a breath at the feel of his cock in her hand. A couple strokes was enough to give her a good feel for every inch of him, and she grabbed the closest condom. "Now be a good mob lord and let me have my way with you."

"There's only one person who will be having their way, bright eyes."

Maybe it was the prolonged pleasure from earlier or the

fact that she was finally going to get to have sex with him,
but she felt downright punch-drunk. "You're right. Me." She
rolled the condom on and gave him another stroke for good
measure. "Now, shh. You talk too much." She adjusted her
angle and sank onto his length.

The feel of him stretching her was almost too much. She
gasped, wiggling her hips a little to adjust to the new sensation. "God, Aiden."

"God doesn't even enter into the equation." He gripped
her hips, guiding her lower a little at a time until he was
sheathed to the hilt. "Fuck. Just...fuck."

She braced her hands on his chest and began to move,
slowly at first and then finding a good rhythm. She watched
Aiden's face, unable to look away. A person shouldn't be
able to brand someone with a single look, but she felt it all
the way down to her soul. She shivered, suddenly sure that
they'd passed the point of no return.

Charlie straightened a little and went to pull off her shirt,
but Aiden stopped her. "Keep it on."

Because it was *his*.

Her breath caught in her chest, fluttering there like a
trapped bird. Slowly, oh so slowly, she lifted the fabric just
enough that he could look down and see where they were
joined. The tightening in his jaw was reward enough, but
she didn't stop there. Through every interaction they'd had,
Aiden had kept firmly in control. She didn't want control.
She wanted the wildness she could feel calling to her, just
beneath the surface. "Do you like seeing me wearing your
shirt while I'm riding you?"

"You know I do." He couldn't seem to tear his gaze away
from where she slid up and down his cock.

"I know why." She rolled her hips, lifting her arms over

her head so that her breasts pressed more firmly against the thin fabric, her nipples blatantly visible. "Because it marks me as yours." His fingers tightened on her hips, and she kept going, driven as much by the pressure building inside of her as by the look on his face. "Because you love knowing that you can do damn near anything you want to me and I'll beg you for more."

She palmed her breasts, pinching her nipples, so turned on she could barely stand it. "Tonight was your perfect fantasy, wasn't it? To have me ready and wanting, soaked and aching for you." He finally managed to drag his gaze up to her face, his expression making her moan. "I'll tell you a secret. You could have shoved up my dress and bent me over one of those ridiculously decorated tables, and I would have let you fuck me right there in front of everyone."

Something changed on his face, and the next thing she knew, she was on her back.

Charlie blinked. "That's one way to go about it."

Aiden gripped her neck with one hand, not restricting her breathing at all, but there was no mistake that it was a claim of dominance. *Ownership.* "You enjoy testing my patience, don't you?" He used his other hand to hitch her leg higher, allowing him deeper inside her. "And what if I had done what you described, bright eyes? Would you have moaned so sweetly for me? Come harder than you ever have before?"

She pictured the scene and clenched tighter around him. "Maybe."

"There's no maybe about it." He kissed her, quick and brutal. "There's a club in Boston that I think you'd like. I'm going to take you there sometime. Soon." He pulled almost all the way out of her and shoved in. "I think you're harboring some exhibitionist tendencies. Would you like me to fuck you in front of a room full of strangers? Let them see how you get off on what I do to you—on knowing they can see every single inch of you. Every response..."

Charlie came, screaming, her orgasm a tidal wave she couldn't avoid even if she'd wanted to. Aiden kept up his pace, prolonging her pleasure until it was almost pain. Only then did his strokes become more irregular, his curses music to her ears.

She stared at the ceiling, wondering where her life had taken a hard right turn. It was one thing to want revenge against Dmitri Romanov. One thing to want Aiden O'Malley in a way she had no business wanting someone who ran a mob family. It was entirely another to get off on the mere thought of him doing filthy things to her in a room full of people. She shivered.

He lifted his head. "My thoughts exactly." Aiden slid to lie next to her.

As much as she wanted to let it go, she couldn't just sit here and soak up the postcoital bliss. Charlie rolled on her side to face him. "That club you talked about..." She wasn't sure what she was going to say. That she wanted to go? That she most definitely did *not* want to go?

He saved her from having to decide. Aiden gave her a downright rakish grin. "It doesn't exist."

Her jaw dropped. "You...I can't...*You*..." Charlie smacked his shoulder. Then she smacked him again for good measure. "I can't believe you. I..." At a complete loss for words, she did the only thing she could think of. She threw herself at him and kissed him for all she was worth.

CHAPTER TWELVE

Aiden woke up early. He watched Charlie for a few minutes, marveling at how different she looked with her face relaxed in sleep, one arm flung over her head as she breathed evenly. It was almost enough to draw him back to bed to lose himself in her for a few more hours.

Last night had been a reprieve—a welcome one that he had every intention of revisiting—but now there was business to attend to.

He showered and dressed, and then headed downstairs to take care of any complications that had arisen overnight, before the rest of the household was up and about. Business had been quiet for the last year as they'd engaged in their cold war with Romanov. Aiden hadn't wanted to pull the trigger on full-out war, and the Russian seemed just as hesitant for reasons unknown. In the meantime, the O'Malleys were pulling in as much from their legit businesses as they were from the darker side of things.

He reached the bottom of the stairs, and stopped short. Liam blocked his way. The man looked downright worried.

Cause for worry was a problem, but if there was immediate danger, they wouldn't be standing there staring at each other. He waited, but Liam didn't seem all that inclined to break the silence. Finally, Aiden sighed. "What's going on?"

Liam cleared his throat. "You should go to your office. Immediately."

That had been his intention, but now it seemed that was the last place he wanted to be. He gave himself a mental shake. Whatever was waiting for him there couldn't be worse than he'd faced in the last few years. Still... "You're very cryptic this morning."

His man hesitated and then muttered, "Seamus is back."

He froze. *No.* But there was nothing joking on Liam's face. Which meant his father was, in fact, behind the office door, waiting for him. At six in the morning. "How long has he been here?"

"He got in last night." Liam held up his hands and took a step back. "I was under command not to disturb you. He's been in the office since he got here."

"What time last night?"

"Around eleven."

Which meant someone had called him about the party, and he'd left the house in Connecticut almost immediately to drive here. The only reason Seamus O'Malley would be back and snooping was because he expected to catch Aiden doing something he shouldn't be doing.

Considering the plan he'd already put into motion, there was quite a bit for his father to find.

I don't have to explain anything to him. He took himself out of the equation when he left and never came back.

The thought wasn't comforting in the least. He shot a look at Liam. "Is my mother here?"

"Yes."

Then shit was *definitely* going to be hitting the fan.

The only thing worse than dealing with his father was having his mother sniffing around Charlie. She'd more than proven she could hold her own, but it was one thing to face down his enemies and his siblings. His mother was a different animal altogether.

One thing at a time.

Aiden took a steadying breath that did nothing to steady him, and headed for the office. There was no point in delaying this coming confrontation—because it would be a confrontation. He'd worked too damn hard to get all the pieces in motion to have his father step in and fuck it up. No matter how much Seamus O'Malley liked power.

Aiden stepped through the door and closed it softly behind him. "Hello, Father."

Seamus didn't look up from the desk, where he had several stacks of paper scattered. "You sure as hell made a mess of things while I was away, didn't you?"

"Actually—"

"Sit down and shut up. I'm speaking."

Aiden instinctively moved for the chair before he caught himself. He straightened, working hard to keep his voice calm and controlled. "With all due respect, you don't have the full story."

"Don't I? In the last year, you lost your sister Sloan, handing her off to none other than Jude MacNamara, one of the deadliest hit men out there, in addition to being a sworn enemy to our closest allies, the Sheridans. You also reached out to yet *another* enemy and offered your baby sister to him in marriage to keep your cowardly hide safe—feel free to step in if you think I've got it wrong—*and* you've hooked up with some gold digger and put my mother's ring on her finger. It sure as hell sounds like you're so busy thinking with your cock that you're not doing what is required of you." Seamus sat back. "So I've come to resume control."

Absolutely not.

Aiden wrangled back his instinctive response—but only barely. "We're in a delicate position currently—"

"Because of *your* actions." His father's dark eyes were steely. Unforgiving. "All your current problems are a direct result of steps you've taken."

Aiden crossed his arms over his chest, and then abandoned the stance because it made him look defensive, and looks mattered when it came to going toe to toe with his father. He couldn't let his temper off its leash, because any display of emotion would confirm the impression he didn't want—that he was out of control. "We need to remove Dmitri Romanov from the equation."

"Then maybe you should have paid Sloan's new man to do exactly that." Seamus steepled his fingers. "You want a chance to explain yourself? Now's the time. Because I have half a mind to remove *you* from the situation."

Aiden froze and did his damnedest to smother the instinctive fear that had been drilled into his head from the time he was a kid. Fear wasn't driving him. He refused to allow it.

He dropped into the seat and stared his father down, keeping his words clipped. "You want to throw around accusations? Fine. We'll do that. I've been the one running this family for the last year and a half while you were out licking your wounds. You handed over the reins. You don't get to come take them back because you don't like how I do things. I'm the head of the O'Malley family now."

"Watch your tone, boy."

Aiden kept his *tone* contained and calm even though all he wanted to do was throw something. "If you'd stopped to talk to me instead of coming in here behind my back—which just proves that you know coming back here like this was bullshit—you would know that I have no intention of letting Keira marry Romanov. It's a stalling tactic while I get the rest of the game into play."

Seamus sat back. "I'm listening."

Aiden couldn't help feeling like he was delivering a closing speech and his father would act as judge, jury, and executioner if he fucked it up. "Taking out Dmitri Romanov would split New York wide open and create a power vacuum. We have no control of who steps into the hole Romanov would leave."

His father made a noncommittal noise, so he kept going. "But if I take his power before we remove him, it lessens the impact of his absence—and allows for *us* to gain a stronger foothold in his territory."

"And how, exactly, is this ploy about marrying off your sister part of the plan?"

Seamus was taking an awfully high horse considering that three years ago, *he* had tried to force Carrigan into marrying the same damn man.

"Romanov came to *me* for help, which indicates that he's in a precarious place at the moment. He wants Keira. He has for some time now, if I'm not guessing wrong. While he's distracted with her, he's not going to be looking for a knife in the back from one of his allies."

"You're underestimating him."

"I can't afford to." Romanov wasn't stupid. He'd expect some kind of betrayal, but he needed Aiden's help badly enough to risk it. What was more, the fact that he was willing to negotiate about Keira meant that he *really* wanted her. His actions at the party last night had only driven that home.

His baby sister was nothing but bait. They might be temporary allies with the Russian, but one wrong move would put it all in jeopardy. Romanov said he'd give her a choice, but that was shit-all of a guarantee that he wouldn't cart her off to New York the first chance he got.

Not going to happen.

Seamus shook his head. "It's too much risk for too little payoff."

"Bullshit. Romanov is going to take us out. He's got the ability to do it, and we both know it. The only reason he hasn't is because we keep Olivia and her daughter safe— and because he wants Keira." When it came right down to it, *that* was the tipping point to the man offering the alliance in the first place. He had to know Aiden would fight him every step of the way if he tried to force his hand.

More flies with honey and all that bullshit.

"You're right. He could have taken us out—and he damn well fucking *will* if he finds out you're planning on going back on your word and crossing him." Seamus shoved to his feet. "I don't care if you've been running things for a day or a year—you're out. It's over."

Nothing his father said made any sense. He shook his head. "So, what? You're going to renounce the engagement and have him come after us for blood? You just said that he could take us all out."

"There's only one option—thanks to you. You will honor

the alliance and do whatever the Russian says. Your sister has to marry Romanov. No schemes. No knives in the back." Seamus strode for the door. "You made your bed. Now Keira has to sleep in it."

* * *

Charlie had just finished getting ready when a knock at the bedroom door drew her out. She opened it to find Keira there, the very picture of nervous energy. "Hey."

"You want to get out of here for a little bit?" She shot a look down the hall like she was afraid someone would catch them and drag them back to their rooms.

Charlie followed her gaze. "Looking for someone?"

"My parents came back into Boston last night unexpectedly." She made a face. "The very last thing I need is to be cornered by either of them."

Aiden's parents were back? Was that why she'd woken up alone?

Reaching out for him when she was half-awake only to find his side of the bed cold was such a silly thing to worry about right now, but it had stung all the same. She stepped back and allowed Keira to put a door between them and anyone who might come by. Aiden's parents would think she was a gold digger the same way the rest of his family did, but they might actually try to *do* something about it.

He'll handle it. He's handled everything else up to this point.

It didn't comfort her as much as she would have liked. "When's the last time you saw them?"

"Over a year ago."

She let go of her own worries and focused on Keira. She

was obviously concerned about facing her parents if she'd sought Charlie out.

A year was a long time not to see someone—especially family. Charlie took in the woman's body, skinny in a way that seemed to indicate not eating, rather than exercising. And the circles under her eyes and the way her cheeks were hollowed out. From what she'd heard of Seamus O'Malley, he cared less about his daughter's mental and physical health than he did about his value as an investment.

It was tempting to think that Keira's mother would be different, if only because she was alive and well and able to *be* a mother to her kids. Charlie's tendency was to give mothers almost godlike power because she didn't have one of her own. She knew that. It was nice to think that every mother who managed to live to see their children grown was a good mother, but it wasn't reality.

The woman hadn't stepped in when Keira's siblings were in need, so there was no reason to think she'd do so now.

"Keira—"

"I know, okay? I know I look like shit, and I don't need everyone and their dog telling me that I look like shit. My mom will lecture me for hours, and my father will just look right through me. I don't have it in me to deal with either."

Charlie knew all about doing whatever it took to survive. Hadn't she been in a similar place a few years ago? Her downward spiral would have lasted a lot longer if Jacques—a bartender she barely knew at the time, not her fucking dad, who should have done it—hadn't stepped in and basically slapped some sense into her. *I wonder how Jacques is doing . . .* She put the thought away and refocused on the woman in front of her.

Keira needed an escape. She needed to feel in control—maybe for the first time in years. Charlie didn't pretend to know the woman inside and out, but she knew what made *her* feel better when she was clawing her way back from the edge.

"Give me two minutes." She went to the dresser. "I just need to grab my gun."

"*Gun?*" Keira walked deeper into the room, curled her lip at the rumpled sheets, and walked to the window to open it. "Holy shit, it smells like fucking in here. God, you two are like teenagers."

"Yeah, well...magic pussy."

She snorted. "I'm never going to live that one down, am I?"

"It's a classic. Give me a second to make a few calls." Charlie was conscious of Keira's attention on her as she figured out which Krav Maga gym was closest, and allowed drop-ins. Then she pulled her gun from her suitcase and strapped on her ankle holster. A few seconds later and the weapon was barely a bulge against her jeans. "Let's go."

"What does a poker dealer need to carry a nine-millimeter for?"

"Good eye." She shot Keira an appraising look. It was tempting to brush off the question, but it also wasn't fair. "I was attacked a few years ago. I was helpless, even with all the training I'd had, and I've promised myself I'll never feel like that again. The gun is just a tool—not some magical protection—but it might make the difference between being the one on the ground and being the one standing over my attacker."

Keira considered her for a long moment. "It's entirely possible that my snap judgment of you was a shitty call. You have a past, don't you?"

"We all do."

"Isn't that the fucking truth?" She followed Charlie out into the hallway. "Not that way. Come on."

They took the back set of stairs down to the kitchen and ducked out a door leading to a walkway to the street. A few minutes later, Charlie caught sight of a man shadowing them half a block back. He was a big dude with shoulders that would do a linebacker proud, and he moved like a fighter—light on his feet despite his size. *Dangerous.* "That man is following us."

Keira craned her neck to look, and sighed. "It's okay. That's Mark."

She seemed to remember Aiden mentioning a Mark at one point. "Does Mark often trail you when you leave the house?"

"Him or another one of Liam's people. Mark is Liam's cousin, so he gets the fun task of being my babysitter more often than most." Keira shrugged. "I'm an O'Malley. There are people who'd snatch me up to use against my family." Something passed over her face, gone too quickly to identify. "Goes with the territory."

"I hadn't thought of that." She had, but it was one thing to know that Aiden routinely sent one of his men to watch Keira and totally another to have the spooky experience of being shadowed by a stranger. Of course, Mark wasn't a stranger to Keira, but the fact remained.

No wonder the woman does whatever it takes to escape sometimes. I would, too.

Her phone rang, and she knew who it was even before she looked at the caller ID. "Good morning, Aiden."

"Where the hell are you going?"

She shot another look at their tail. "That was fast."

"Mark reports to me, so imagine my surprise when I find out that my fiancée and my sister just staged a jailbreak and are walking down the goddamn street without a protection detail."

So much for any lasting feel-good sensation from their night before. Charlie rolled her eyes. "One, we already discussed how much I despise having to check in with you before doing anything. Two, you know as well as I do that I'm more than capable of taking care of myself and Keira."

"There are other factors in play."

So we're just going to ignore logic when it doesn't suit our argument? Nice, Aiden. His icy bullying tactics might work with his family, but she wasn't about to play that game. "It's got to be something of a shock waking up to realize your parents are back in town."

He cursed and then changed tactics. "Just get your ass back here, Charlie. There's trouble."

It was like she could actually see his thought process: *Commanding didn't work. Let's try warning about danger.* Sooner or later, he'd realize that she preferred him to just be fucking honest with her instead of trying that high-and-mighty O'Malley lord crap. "You mean politics."

"They're the same thing."

That answered that. She shook her head. "No, Aiden. Your man can follow us—at a discreet distance—if that will make you feel better, but we both needed out of the house, so we're getting out of the house."

"Charlie—"

"See you tonight." She hung up, frowning when she caught Keira looking at her strangely. "What?"

"No one talks to my brother like that." She shook her head. "Hold that thought. I mean no one talks to him like that and gets away with it, without him putting them under house arrest or some other macho bullshit."

One didn't become the head of a mob family without a certain level of don't-cross-me. If anyone in the family could talk back to Aiden and get away with it, he'd have anarchy on his hands before long, and anarchy was dangerous for everyone.

But, for better or worse, Charlie was outside the hierarchy—and he'd put her there. If he'd wanted a meek little fake fiancée, then he should have called someone else. She wouldn't know meek if it bit her in the ass, and having him try to order her around only made her dig in her heels.

Charlie shrugged. "I'm sleeping with him, and I have his ring on my finger. It gives me the ability to talk to him however I damn well please when we aren't in front of an audience. And, no, before you ask, you don't count as an audience. You're family."

"You know, Charlie, I think I like you, magic pussy and all."

She snorted. "Give it a rest."

"I will. Promise." Keira looked around, her furious attitude melting away in favor of curiosity. "So, where are we going?"

"Keira, my dear, we're going to teach you how to fight."

CHAPTER THIRTEEN

Giving Keira a crash course in Krav Maga ended up being exactly what they both needed. The girl knew the basics in self-defense, but watching the comprehension dawn on her face as she went after the punching bag was a revelation in and of itself. She craved control in a life where she had little—Charlie got that. She felt exactly the same way sometimes.

They grabbed a quick bite to eat and headed back to the O'Malley house, Keira peppering her with questions along the way. The woman was practically bouncing on her toes as they rounded the corner of their block. "What about takedowns, like those guys who were sparring?" Her excitement made her look younger than she was, her hazel eyes dancing with interest.

"You learn those once you hit a certain level. You have to master kicks and hits before you go on to the more complicated stuff—or start sparring." She hesitated. "If you want to pursue this, I think the owner would love to see you back there again. A lot of women check it out and then move on to other stuff, but Krav Maga really is one of the best out there for the lives *we* live." *We.* She missed a step.

Since when did she put herself in a category—*any* category—with someone who was a freaking O'Malley?

But it was hard not to see the similarities between her and Keira. They were both trapped by circumstances—though Charlie's were circumstances of her own making. She could have left New York and gone anywhere. No, she couldn't have been a cop again, but she could have had a normal life.

Instead, she'd chosen to stay and live with the knowledge that she'd never really be the daughter her father wanted, that she would never regain the reputation as a cop that she'd always craved, that she wasn't guaranteed to see justice *at all.*

So, yeah, she and Keira weren't as different as she'd originally thought.

Maybe that means Aiden and I aren't, either…

"Pretty sure Aiden would have a stroke if I asked him to go that gym a couple times a week. Think of all the terrible things that could happen to me."

"I'll talk to him." She wasn't sure what kind of pull she had at this point, but Charlie was prepared to go toe to toe over this. Keira had lit up in that gym, and at this point in her life, she needed *any* life preserver that would keep her from drowning.

She laughed. "Good luck. I'd almost pay to have a ringside seat for *that* conversation, but there's the chance it'd devolve into angry sex and the last thing I need is therapy for that, too." She came to an abrupt halt. "Shit."

Charlie turned to see what had leached the color from her face and stopped short. The man standing on the top step of the O'Malley home could have been a doppelgänger for Aiden, give or take a few decades. The only real difference aside from eye color was that he had more lines around his eyes and mouth and silver dusting his temples.

The eyes were different, too, she noticed as she and Keira came to a stop at the bottom of the steps. It was more than just the color—brown, compared to green. This man's eyes were cold. Aiden's expression could go icy, but it was a mask he wore. When he wasn't paying attention, his eyes conveyed worlds of knowledge.

Charlie didn't get the impression that *this* man bothered with a mask.

This would be one Seamus O'Malley.

If her dad could see her right now, he would be shitting bricks. Charlie straightened her spine and kept her shoulders back, doing her best to ignore the way the man looked at her—as if she was a cheap whore or shit on the bottom of his shoe. He took her in and dismissed her in the space of a heartbeat, turning his attention to his daughter. "Keira."

"Father." A tremor worked its way through the woman, so slight Charlie wouldn't have noticed it if she hadn't been so close. "What are you doing back?"

"I've come to fix the mess your brother created."

Well, hell. That could mean a number of things, and none of them boded well for Aiden's plans to bring Romanov down. Or for the woman next to her, currently shrinking back to the miserable mess she was before their outing. Keira wrapped her arms around herself. "That's fucking wonderful."

"Language."

"Yes, language. God forbid someone talk about what a *fucking* mess our family is." Just like that, she dropped her arms and lifted her chin, glaring at Seamus. "You should go back to Connecticut, Father. No one wants you here, and Aiden is doing a better job of running this family than you ever did." She marched up the stairs and shouldered past him.

It was all well and good that she'd stood up for herself, but without his daughter in the picture, all his attention turned back to Charlie. She shuddered and tried to hide the reaction, but his smirk let her know he'd seen it. "This is what my son lost his damn mind for?" He shook his head. "Pathetic."

"You don't know the half of it." She had no reason to defend herself to this man—nothing she could say would change the opinion he'd formed before he ever met her.

That didn't stop her from wanting to punch him in his smirking face. *That's your anger talking. Calm down.* She took a breath, and then another. This was Aiden's father. That weird note she'd heard in his voice this morning made more sense now. Maybe she should have listened, but she was right that Keira needed to get out for a while. She was *definitely* going to talk to Aiden about getting her set up with regular Krav Maga classes. If the woman got out of the oppressive atmosphere of this house more often, she wouldn't be shrinking into a mere fraction of the person she could be.

That she *should* be.

It was possible Aiden was dealing with some of the same shit. She'd never really considered it before. *I need to consider it now.* She strode up the stairs, putting a little swing in her walk—first, because she was furious, and second, because if Seamus O'Malley thought she was a gold-digging whore, at least she should play the part. *There is no shame in the situation, no matter what he thinks.*

She patted him on the shoulder as she walked past. "Don't be jealous of your son. It's not a becoming look for you."

Charlie made it three steps into the house before his hand closed around her upper arm and spun her around. "Just because my son likes the way you fuck doesn't mean you can talk to *me* however you please, little girl." He shook her, the rage on his face something to behold.

She'd faced down men like him before, and she wasn't about to let this piece of shit manhandle her, Aiden's father or not.

Charlie brought her free hand up to use his pressure points to force him to let go of her, and then she shoved him back. "And just because I'm fucking your son, doesn't mean you get to touch me like I'm one of your yes-men."

He took a menacing step toward her, and she had half a second to wonder if she was going to have to go for her gun, when Aiden's voice cut through the foyer. "What the fuck is going on?"

Seamus straightened and adjusted his jacket. In the space of a heartbeat, icy disdain replaced the rage that had shaken Charlie to her core. "A simple conversation."

How quickly he recovered and smoothed out his expression was more terrifying than everything that had come before. *I was wrong about him not wearing masks. He's even better at it than his son is.*

Aiden stalked down the stairs, his gaze never wavering from her. "Are you all right?"

"I'm fine." She very pointedly didn't look at Seamus as

she said it. Knowing she could likely take him didn't do a damn thing to comfort her, because any confrontation between them wasn't just a one-on-one sort of thing. There were layers and implications, and even if she was willing to shoot someone in self-defense—or *not* self-defense—this was still Aiden's dad.

Did I seriously just consider the consequences of shooting Seamus O'Malley?

She was in so far over her head, it wasn't remotely funny, and it wasn't even about the sex or her heart anymore. It was about her life.

Aiden stopped in front of her and searched her face. Then he touched her arm in the exact place that his father had grabbed her. Charlie flinched before she could catch herself, which caused his green eyes to harden. He spoke without looking away from her. "If you touch my fiancée again, I will kill you myself. Is that clear?"

"If you think—"

"This is not up for debate. You might have resumed control of the O'Malleys—for the moment—but that doesn't give you the right to do what you just did. Apologize, Seamus."

"You're crossing the line, boy. Again." Seamus strode away without another word, leaving them staring at each other.

Instantly, Aiden's eyes thawed. There was still more than a little anger, but he let her see the worry, too. He spoke low enough that she had to strain to hear him. "Are you really okay?"

"Yes."

He huffed out a breath. "No, you're not. I don't even know why I asked."

"Aiden, I'm fine." She reached out and touched his arm, which seemed the only sign he needed to pull her against him. It felt good to have him wrap her up like that. Better than good. Comforting.

But she couldn't let his worry stand.

Charlie's mouth against his shirt muffled her words. "He startled me. That's all." She didn't mention that she'd had half a thought to go for her gun. She hadn't, and that was that. No reason to even bring it up.

The thought still settled in her stomach like a stone, threatening to drag her down. Up until this point, she'd been in the right. The one with the justifiable fury. The innocent who'd been victimized by Dmitri Romanov.

The moment she'd considered shooting Seamus O'Malley in his own home was the moment she'd slipped over a line she wasn't sure she could uncross.

The line that separated the good guys from the bad.

* * *

Dmitri hung up the phone and considered the new information at his disposal. Of all the scenarios he'd played out upon forcing Aiden O'Malley's hand, Seamus O'Malley coming back to Boston and reaching out personally to assure him that his intention to marry Keira O'Malley would be honored...it had ranked toward the bottom. It hadn't even taken the man a full day to make his play—he'd arrived earlier this morning and it was barely eight p.m.

The move reeked of weakness and desperation, which irked him. The O'Malleys had proven to be worthy enemies over the last three years, and he had a certain respect for them as a result. Aiden hadn't agreed to a single thing until

Dmitri had given as good as he got in their deal, and now his father was practically pissing himself as he offered Dmitri his throat.

Something broke in the old man, something he can't get back.

It was useful information, but he wasn't prepared to do anything about it currently. Whatever Seamus O'Malley thought, Dmitri and Aiden had a temporary alliance. The O'Malleys would help him with his Eldridge problem, but the true reasoning behind his request for assistance had nothing to do with an enemy.

He wanted Keira.

More, he'd already decided that he'd have her. There was no other option, no other acceptable outcome. He'd put his ring on her finger, and she would be exchanging vows with him at the earliest manageable date.

There wasn't a damn thing Seamus or Aiden or the rest of the O'Malleys could do to stop it.

He took out a second phone, one he'd secured for a single purpose, and dialed. It rang several times, before a breathless Keira answered. "You know, it's funny, but I distinctly remember only owning *one* phone. And yet I hear a ringing and there's this little sucker in my underwear drawer. Creepy, Dmitri. Really creepy."

Underwear drawer? He drummed his fingers on the desk. He was going to have to have a...talk...with Vance about the appropriate places for him to go digging through—namely, *not* Dmitri's intended's panty drawer. "Apologies on the placement."

"But not on the fact that you had one of your goons sneak into my room." She tsked. "Typical."

It struck him that he'd never heard Keira quite so lively.

Every time they'd encountered each other, she'd been under heavy doses of drugs or alcohol. She sounded downright sober. "How did you like Krav Maga?"

"Stalker much?" Keira sighed, but the sound was almost happy. "I'm only telling you this so you know I can beat your ass if you think about trying some messed-up shit with me, but it was amazing. Hitting made me feel..."

"Powerful. In control." He understood, even if he didn't have a love affair with violence the way some men did. Violence, in its many forms, was a tool. A weapon was a weapon, no matter the flavor, and all weapons were to be utilized.

"Yes."

And if there was one thing his Keira craved, it was power and control. He'd gotten that right, even if she didn't want to admit it before now. "I suppose now I know where to take you for special occasions."

"Careful there, Dmitri. You're starting to sound more man than monster. I might get the wrong idea."

"Make no mistake. I'm the monster. Forgetting that would be detrimental."

"Because you'll beat me?"

He went still, icy rage freezing out the amusement their conversation had spawned. "Does your father beat you?" Aiden didn't. He would have known if her brother—*any* of her brothers—hurt her.

But Seamus O'Malley had disappeared into the country before Dmitri set his sights on Keira. If he had mistreated her, it wouldn't necessarily have come to light. There'd been no hospital records, but that didn't mean a damn thing when someone was wealthy enough to have a personal doctor on call.

"And if he did?" The happiness was gone from her voice, too, leaving the apathy he recognized. "What would you do? Would you ride in on a white stallion and cut him down?" She laughed. "Please. You're all monsters. Hell, I'm a monster, too. You don't get to play the savior when you're no better than he is."

She hadn't admitted one way or another, but Dmitri sure as fuck was going to find out if Seamus O'Malley had hurt his youngest daughter.

For now, he focused on the woman on the other end of the line. "You don't need a savior, Keira. You're more than capable of saving yourself."

Again, that broken laugh. "And you're just telling me what you think I want to hear. Admirable effort, though you missed it by a mile. You're supposed to say that of course you'll save me from my wretched life, and that you definitely aren't the man my family makes you out to be, and naturally I'll be the coddled and protected wife who you'll fall madly in love with."

He stared at the painting on the wall across from his desk. It was a winter landscape, calm even as it was brutal. In that world, like in his, only the strong survived.

Only the monsters.

The picture *she* painted was even further from reality than the one on his wall. There were no white knights or saviors in their world, and he was just as bad as the members of her family. Worse, in many ways.

Love? There was no room in his life for love. Love was for the weak, the idealists, the people who became casualties because they opened themselves up for a shot to the heart.

Keira sighed. "That's what I thought. We both know

what this is—and what it isn't. So do me a favor and don't talk to me like I'm an idiot."

Somewhere along the way, he'd lost control of this conversation, and he hadn't even been aware of it until now. Dmitri resumed drumming his fingers on the desk. "Do you like your ring, Keira?"

A hesitation. "You know that I do."

"I can shower you in gifts that make that look like an embarrassing trinket. You might not have your freedom, but you'll want for nothing as my wife." He should just leave it there. If she had foolish romantic notions, that wasn't his burden to bear. He'd never offered her love, never offered her anything but exactly what he intended.

But it felt too much like a lie to let things stand. "I can offer you anything money can buy. I can't—won't—offer you love. Sex, yes, as much as you can handle and more, but this isn't a love match, Keira. It never will be."

Her exhale, so world-weary and exhausted, made him shift, driven by an urge to do...something. He didn't know. He still hadn't figured it out when she said, "I know, Dmitri. It's cute that you feel the need to point that out, but I'm not a teenager with stars in my eyes. I know what you are—and what this is. And, trust me, I'll never expect love from you. Now, if you're done with this entertaining little whatever-the-fuck-it-is, I'm tired and I'm going to bed."

"Good night, Keira." He hung up, still feeling off-kilter and not sure why. He hadn't lied to her. Dishonesty was one line he didn't cross unless he absolutely had to, and he would never do it with her. If he lied to her and tried to force her to his will, she would be more his enemy than wife. And that was unacceptable.

That's it. That's why it bothers me. I hurt her, even if it was the truth, and now she's going to lash out and there will be consequences.

He put the phone in the top drawer of his desk and shut it, willing himself to focus on the next step. Tensions remained high with Alethea Eldridge, and he had to soothe her pride to ensure that she didn't suspect anything. Irksome, but easy enough to do.

First, though...

He picked up the desk phone and pressed 1. Mikhail answered on the first ring. "*Da?*"

"Send Vance to my office. I have something I need to discuss with him." Namely that his pawing through Keira's unmentionables was a punishable offense.

And he had every intention of collecting.

CHAPTER FOURTEEN

Aiden hunted down Cillian the first chance he got. He found his brother in the library, reading to Hadley. The picture they painted, their heads bowed as his brother read a nonsense children's book, was almost enough to make Aiden turn around and walk out, leaving the discussion for a later time.

Unfortunately, that wasn't an option.

Still, he waited until Cillian had finished the book to say, "We need to talk."

"I know." Cillian set Hadley on her feet. "Take this book to your mama. You know it's her favorite."

Hadley grinned and pressed a quick kiss to his cheek before leaving the room, pausing only to give Aiden a brief wave. "She's a good kid."

"Yes, she is. She's also not why you're here." Cillian stood and stretched. "This is about our parents."

"You called them."

Cillian laughed in his face. "Oh, for fuck's sake. Why the hell would I pull a stunt like that? Did I want to talk to you about whatever plan you've cooked up? Hell yes. Would I endanger all of us because I'm pissed that you aren't letting me in? No. If you think otherwise, you're a goddamn idiot."

When his brother put it like that, it was hard to argue with him. Aiden dropped into the other chair and ran a hand over his face. He'd had such a clear sequence of events when his whole plan had been put into motion, but it seemed like every time he turned around, more threads were getting tangled. "Romanov is a threat that needed to be addressed, but if we come at him from the front, he'll annihilate us."

"I'm not arguing against that. What I *am* arguing against is using Keira as bait—because that's what you're doing, isn't it?"

He didn't know if it was a blessing or a curse that Cillian was so goddamn smart. "Romanov came to me for help."

That got his brother's attention. "What?"

"Two weeks ago. He's having problems with the Eldridges, and he needed someone to help him with a bait and switch to keep them occupied while he gets things in place to remove them entirely."

Cillian whistled. "That's quite the coup—and it would leave Romanov in control of most of New York."

"Yes." Something that would keep anyone with half a brain up at night. "But it's happening whether we like it or not. I agreed to work with him because it means I'll have some say in the fallout—and there *will* be fallout."

Cillian hesitated. "I despise Dmitri. I don't like his history with Olivia, and a year of not being a total shithead doesn't make up for twenty-four years of leaving her to the wolves."

"He's a known factor, and he has a history of keeping his word once he gives it." And therein lay the problem. He wanted Romanov out of the picture—permanently. But he was reasonable enough to acknowledge that killing the man outright wasn't going to do them any favors. He'd spent so long planning in silence, the only person who knew the full story was Liam.

Maybe it was time to change that.

"The Eldridges are just a distraction."

Cillian's eyes went wide. "That's one hell of a distraction."

"Yeah." Alethea took the term *sadistic* to unparalleled lengths, and her heir was even worse. He couldn't fault Romanov for wanting to remove them from the equation as quickly as possible—that was exactly how he'd felt about Brendan Halloran before the man was murdered. "I'm not convinced Romanov couldn't remove the threat without our help, but the fact remains that he asked for help."

"What did you get in return?"

"Keira gets a choice." It was hard to say it aloud. He felt fucking weak for even allowing it on the bargaining table to begin with. Aiden very carefully didn't look at his little brother. "I don't think for a second that he'll honor that—he's put too much time and too many resources into securing her. She's his last-ditch effort to save face and prove that crossing him is a mistake."

"So what's the endgame?" Cillian's tone gave nothing away.

"He breaks his word, which will be enough to prove to both Sheridans and Hallorans that he's a mad dog who needs to be put down. Between the three of us, the war will be quick and brutal, and over before anyone realizes it's started. It's a risk, but a calculated one."

And if he could aim John Finch at the bastard, he could potentially get the FBI agent away from Boston and off Teague's back. If he was lucky, maybe Finch would get caught in the crossfire.

Except that thought didn't bring the same satisfaction it once had.

Finch was Charlie's father, which meant his death would hurt her, and Aiden didn't relish that.

"That sounds great in theory."

He shifted to face Cillian. He could tell his brother knew what he was thinking. "Our father is going to get in the way."

"Without a doubt. He's already started trying to undermine you."

Aiden knew that. But there was only so much Seamus could do. As soon as Aiden realized that his father might be back—and that he didn't necessarily *want* him back—he'd taken steps to ensure the men's loyalty. It wasn't foolproof by any means, but it would make it harder for his father to win them over.

That didn't mean Seamus would play along. If he had his way, Keira would actually marry Romanov. The thought of his sister, already so lost, trapped in a marriage with that monster...

"I'll take care of it." He wouldn't make the same mistake with Keira that he had with Carrigan. He would protect her, even if it meant defying his father and putting both himself and Charlie in danger in the process. He pushed to his feet. "I've got to go."

"What are you going to do?"

"What's necessary." He let calm settle onto his face—a mask was better than nothing. "I'll protect the family—even if that means protecting the family from Seamus."

* * *

Charlie hadn't had a chance to talk to Aiden about Keira taking Krav Maga. She hadn't actually talked to him at *all*, despite sitting six inches from him for the last five hours as they traveled from Boston to New York. The silence had been uncomfortable at first, but when she realized Aiden was thinking hard about what the night would bring and probably strategizing the best way to go about it, she left him alone.

The driver slowed and pulled the car to a stop. They'd arrived.

She leaned over Aiden and peered out the window. "It's a warehouse." And a seedy one at that. When she was still a cop, she'd spent time in some of NYC's worst neighborhoods, and the location of this place was the worst of the worst. Cops barely patrolled this area unless they had a specific reason to be there, because the badge put a target right between their eyes, and the neighborhood mostly took care of its own. They didn't want or need the law interfering. "This is such a bad idea."

If she'd known Aiden would take them to murder central, she wouldn't have chosen a short strapless dress that hugged every curve and left little to the imagination. It was also a red bright enough to stop traffic, and she'd felt pretty damn great about the choice. Until now. "You said we were meeting the Eldridges."

"We are."

She pointed at the building. "We're going to walk in there and get killed."

"It would be bad business for Alethea to murder us, in a warehouse or otherwise." Aiden climbed out of the car and held out a hand to help her from the backseat. If she didn't already know that things were tense, she would have now, by the fact that he didn't comment on her dress or do more than brush a quick kiss over her mouth before they left. He was preoccupied, which was all well and good... if they weren't about to meet two of the scariest women Charlie had ever come across.

"Aiden." She stopped him with a hand on his arm, catching her breath when he turned to face her. He looked downright lickable in his black suit, the sheer lack of color in his clothing somehow bringing out the green of his eyes, even in this light. Charlie wanted to tell him that it would be okay, that whatever it was that was bothering him—father or enemies or otherwise—she'd be at his side to face it. But if she said any of that, he'd laugh in her face, and rightly so. She wasn't his girlfriend, and there might be a ring on her finger but she wasn't walking down the aisle to him. This wasn't real.

So she didn't say any of it. She just adjusted his already perfectly buttoned-up shirt. "I'll tell you a secret."

"Oh?"

Conscious of Liam and the other man just a few feet away and the possibility of cameras and audio equipment monitoring their every move, she inched closer. Her heels—just as red as her dress—put her at almost the same height as Aiden, so it was child's play to lean in and whisper in his ear. "I'm not wearing anything under this dress." *That* would distract him.

Sure enough, his hands came to rest on her ass, palming her as he confirmed what she'd just said. Aiden growled a little. "When I said make a statement, that wasn't what I meant."

"Wasn't it?" Even though her adrenaline was pumping in anticipation of walking through that warehouse door, she smiled. "Doesn't it make you feel just an eensie bit better knowing that you'll be having me in the backseat of that town car after this hellhole of a meeting is over?"

His hands spasmed on her ass. "Christ, bright eyes, you really know how to change a man's outlook."

Apparently, she didn't need sweet and comforting words to get his head in the game and chase that hopeless look off his face. She just needed to remind him of what they did best. "Let's go get them."

He took a step back, claiming her hand as he did, and they turned to face the warehouse. "Try not to bait Mae this time."

"She likes it when I bait her." She squeezed his hand. "If she thinks that we're so in love that you'll actually marry me, she might cut my throat herself. It amuses her to consider me a dalliance and to consider you something of a sure thing for *her*."

Charlie loathed the thought of Aiden with that monster of a woman. It didn't matter that it wasn't something he wanted or planned for—she'd put a ton of money on *Mae* planning on making it happen.

He shot her a look and then cursed. "Fuck, Charlie, I didn't even think about that when I asked you to do this."

"That's because even with three sisters, apparently you don't know how the female mind works." Especially in a sociopath like Mae. Or a psychopath. Charlie had always had some difficulty telling those two apart. "She's set her sights on you, Aiden. She could care less that you're claiming to be desperately in love with someone else, engaged or not."

"Fuck." He slowed to a stop.

"What?" She looked around, but nothing popped out as overtly dangerous, aside from the murder warehouse. "What's wrong?"

"*You* didn't bargain on the Eldridge heir gunning for your blood when you agreed to this. *I* didn't bargain on it. I can't ask you to go through with it."

She blinked. *Of all the responses I imagined, that wasn't on the list.* "Aiden, I'm more than capable of taking care of myself."

"In a fair fight, sure. But she won't come at you fair. Mae will knife you in the back."

She knew that. She also knew that the end justified the means—and the risks ventured along the way. Charlie turned to face him again. Sexual distraction wouldn't work this time. She had to lay it out straight and hope that he'd be rational enough to realize she was right. "Your dad showing up has you all messed up in the head. Stop. Think. If you walk in there without me, either they're going to assume I'm too weak to hold my own and they're going to come gunning for me, or they're going to know that you have no intention of marrying me. We don't have time for you to worry about me."

Though a small selfish part of her warmed at his wanting to keep her safe, the rest of her was doing her best not to be insulted. Didn't he know that the worst for her had already come to pass? It was possible that Mae could kill her, but she had no intention of letting the woman get the opportunity.

"Charlie…"

She could tell he was still wavering, some streak of honor trying to take hold, so she went for the sucker punch. "If we don't do this, Keira marries Romanov."

Aiden took one breath, and another, and then nodded and straightened. "If you change your mind—"

"I won't."

"All the same. If you change your mind, all you have to do is say the word and we're out of there. I'll figure out another way that doesn't make you the target of one of the scariest women I've ever met."

That delicate warmth in her chest spread. He'd do it, too. It might set him back and put his own sister in danger, but he'd get her out if she felt like she was in over her head. Charlie almost laughed. She'd been in over her head the second she agreed to do this.

Truth be told, she hadn't seen the surface for years, not since she'd lost everything.

And *that* focused her.

Justice. Revenge. Two sides of the same coin. That's what this was about. She couldn't afford to lose sight of that.

So she held her head high as they walked through the nondescript door and into the warehouse. It looked like she imagined thousands of other warehouses looked—pallets stacked high and wrapped up until it was impossible to tell what they held. Charlie took it all in, noting the wide aisles that didn't offer much in the way of cover, and the tiny windows overhead that were impossible to climb to. If this was a trap, she didn't think they'd get out alive, Liam and his man at their backs or no.

A woman melted out of the shadows. She was so plain that Charlie had to look at her a second time to make her appearance register. Mousey brown hair, a pleasant-looking face, a normal build. It was only on that second look that she saw the careful makeup designed to downplay her features, and that the roots of her hair were a rich brunette, and that her clothes had likely been picked for their poor fit. This woman could walk into any room and be ignored and overlooked, and the people there wouldn't even realize they were doing it.

Dangerous.

The woman motioned. "This way, please." Even her voice was pitched to be forgettable.

She led them deeper into the warehouse, finally stopping in front of a door. "Inside, please."

So unfailingly polite. Aiden opened the door, and Charlie slipped through, blinking in the low lights. She took in the familiar hexagon table wrapped in green felt, and the dealer—another woman—who was as low-key as the woman who had led them here. Poker.

Footsteps had her turning to face the Eldridge women as they strode into the room from a different door. Alethea had dressed in a sharp pantsuit that highlighted her petite form. Mae wore a dress easily as short as Charlie's and, quite frankly, she rocked it. She looked like one of the women in a WWE show, all glamorous strength and murderous intent— and it worked for her. Charlie could admit that, even when she wanted to be in any other room but this one.

Mae smiled, the expression sending chills down Charlie's spine. The woman motioned to the poker table. "We wanted you to feel right at home."

Somehow, Charlie doubted that very much. But she pasted on a smile anyway and slid into the nearest chair. "That's so thoughtful of you. Are we playing Texas Hold 'Em or Five-Card Draw?"

CHAPTER FIFTEEN

Aiden barely breathed as Charlie faced down Mae for what felt like the millionth time that night. Even though he knew she was playing up the persona of an empty-headed idiot, it was still disconcerting to watch her giggle and joke her way to winning. She effectively took out both him and Alethea in the first hour, manipulating them expertly despite the dramatics—or *because* of the dramatics. She bluffed so well, he still wasn't sure when she actually *was* bluffing. Even though he knew better, he'd underestimated her.

It made him wonder how else he was underestimating her.

But as soon as it was down to her and Mae, Charlie started losing. For the life of him, he couldn't figure out if it was on purpose or not. They still hadn't gotten around to talking business. It would come, though. Alethea hadn't invited them out here for a simple poker game, no matter what her daughter thought of Charlie. The woman was too smart to waste an opportunity as important as getting Aiden on her side, but she was too arrogant *not* to try to play him in the process.

So he focused on Charlie and the game dwindling to a close between her and Mae. He hadn't trusted her before in how she handled the situation with the Eldridge heir. He trusted her now.

"All in." Charlie pushed all her chips to the center of the table with a flirty wink at him. "Dinner's going to be on me tonight, baby."

She loves this. The risk, the role-playing, the outwitting of dangerous enemies.

He made a noncommittal sound. Alethea leaned over from where she sat next to him and murmured, "Trouble in paradise?"

"You're awfully concerned with my love life." He didn't look away from the game, where Mae was considering Charlie like a cat toying with a mouse before devouring it.

She laughed softly. "This is about business and you know it—you also know that your love life *is* business. Since you're going to play coy on the subject, let's put the rest of it on the table. You want us to work with you against Dmitri Romanov."

Finally. Trust the woman to leave it until the last possible moment to broach the real reason they were there. When he looked at her, he found she was wearing the same expression as her daughter.

Normally, Aiden knew which way he wanted to play a person, depending on a number of factors. His sisters got the older brother who was kind of an asshole but still loved the shit out of them. The people under his command got Seamus 2.0, because that's what they responded to best. Charlie got... Well, she was currently beside the point.

Alethea spoke and acted bluntly, but she was capable of subtlety—if she wasn't, Romanov wouldn't consider her such a large threat. So Aiden went the most direct route. "It's in your best interest."

"No, it's in *your* best interest. My best interests lie elsewhere currently."

He reminded himself that he'd expected he'd have to persuade her—if only on sheer principle. He walked the knife edge of danger, and it wasn't only his life on the line. If Alethea turned against him, he wasn't walking out of this warehouse alive. It was a risk, and it seemed a whole lot larger with Charlie at his side. One mistake and they were both going to pay.

He couldn't let fear rule him now any more than he'd let it when facing down his father. Fear was how a man got himself killed. He gave her a lazy smile. "Oh? Is that why Romanov is going to marry my little sister?"

Her blue eyes flashed. "That was a low blow, and rude to boot. You know very well that he turned down my darling daughter."

Yes, Aiden did know—because Romanov had told him. He got the impression that Romanov would have been happy letting them run their territory if they hadn't threatened him, but they'd forced his hand with that proposal. It would have been smart to say yes and merge resources. It's what the O'Malleys and Sheridans had done. Fuck, it was what the O'Malleys and Hallorans had done to a lesser extent. Those alliances made them all stronger.

Then again, having met Mae, he didn't blame the Russian one bit. That woman had black widow written all over her.

"His loss." He sat back, feigning disinterest. "Did he tell you why?"

"Does it matter?" Alethea frowned. "What do you know?"

It was time to dangle the bait and see if she'd bite. Aiden's gaze drifted back to Charlie. "I have it on good authority that your shipment to Romanov in two weeks will be your last."

"It's not." She narrowed her eyes. "He wouldn't dare."

"You know better."

Dmitri Romanov had no shortage of balls. He wouldn't have accumulated so much power if he was afraid to take risks. Taking on the Eldridges was a risk, even with the O'Malleys at his side. He was a smart man. He had to know that turning down a marriage with Mae would be enough to spark a response. So why had he done it?

Surely not because of Keira...

Alethea drummed her fingers on the table. "I'm listening."

"Consider it a token of my goodwill to pass this information along."

"Mm-hmm." She snorted. "It wouldn't have anything to do with you wanting him dead, would it? Easier to put a bullet between those gorgeous eyes of his than to orchestrate all this."

If it was that easy, he would have done it already. But he'd been telling the truth when he talked to Cillian—Dmitri Romanov might be a threat, but at least he was a known quantity. Romanov was also gunning for the O'Malleys—for Keira—and Aiden couldn't allow that to stand. He was still repairing his relationships with his other sisters after putting the good of the family before their individual needs. He'd give his baby sister a choice about her future. "I can't do it alone." Aiden kept his voice low, as if it pained him to admit it.

"Now the truth is out. Though, my dear boy, if you can't do it on your own, how do you imagine you can help me?" She shot him a look from the corner of her eye. "I'm going to put that Russian bastard in the ground the way I have with every other enemy that's crossed me. I don't need you."

The two guards in the room moved closer at the threat in her voice. Liam looked like he wanted to do the same, but Aiden waved him off. He kept one eye on Charlie and Mae as the last card was placed on the table. "We're stronger together than we are apart." It made him feel dirty to offer her an alliance—dirty in a way that nothing he'd done in his life up to this point had managed to. It didn't matter that it was a ruse. He was effectively getting into bed with *both* Romanov and the Eldridges.

I'd do this and worse to keep my family and my people safe.

"Hmm. Well, I guess time will tell, won't it?"

He didn't particularly like where she was headed with this, but he couldn't say that he was surprised. Aiden sighed as if he wasn't coiled and ready to spring into motion the second one of her people moved wrong. "Alethea, all of Boston will take it poorly if you harm me, and *I* will take it poorly if you harm my fiancée. Let's not waste our time with idle threats."

"Who said it was idle?"

"Damn it!"

They both turned to find Mae raking in the chips, a small smile on her face, while Charlie slouched in her seat. She offered Aiden a sheepish smile. "Dinner's on you, baby." She pressed a hand to her stomach and made a face. "Speaking of . . . any chance your business is done? I'm starving."

"Just wrapping up." He stood and adjusted his jacket.

Now was the time when Alethea would spring her trap—if there was one. Showing fear was out of the question, so he kept his gaze on Charlie as he crossed to her. *I will get us out of here alive. I promise.* He spoke over his shoulder. "You have the information. What you do with it is up to you."

Alethea let him get almost to the door before she spoke. "You don't fool me, Aiden O'Malley."

He turned, touching Charlie's back to signal her to keep close. It took more work than normal to keep his expression easy and open. "I'm not trying to fool you."

"Bullshit." She smiled a slow smile that made his skin crawl. "We'll take that help that you're so generously offering, and we'll put Romanov in the ground."

He knew the other shoe was going to drop, and she didn't disappoint.

"For a price."

He sighed. "By all rights, you should be kissing my ass for bringing you this information. You had no idea Romanov was going to double-cross you, and he would likely have succeeded in murdering both you and Mae if left to his own devices. I'm not playing this game with you. Use the information or don't. But I'm not going to bend over backwards when you've already told me quite explicitly how little you need me."

"Did I hurt your delicate feelings? How sad for you." She shook her head. "Wait for my call, Aiden. We'll talk more then."

I'm saving Keira. He had to focus on that and let the rest fall where it may. Dmitri Romanov had done their family wrong several times over. They might be allies for the time being, but that didn't mean he was going to cave to the man's every whim.

Especially when it came to his baby sister.

He wouldn't let it happen. He refused to.

He gave Alethea a tight nod. "I look forward to it." Then he turned around and ushered Charlie through the warehouse and out into the night.

* * *

Charlie hadn't taken a full breath since she'd thrown away that last pot to distract Mae from what Alethea and Aiden were talking about. She'd never had any intention of winning, though she'd had trip aces in her hand. Mae might have reached across the table and tried to cut her throat, and that would have ruined everyone's night.

She hadn't breathed at all when Alethea ever-so-carefully threatened Aiden.

That woman and her daughter were rabid dogs. She'd known that, but she'd comforted herself with the end justifying the means: Romanov had to go down, just like he deserved to. It had made sense in her head, though it had taken some mental gymnastics to get there.

Now?

Now she wanted nothing more than to grab Aiden's hand and take him away from it all. She *liked* him. He wasn't like these other mob bosses, who seemed to relish doing evil things and hurting people. He did what he had to do in order to keep his family safe.

And keep them in power. Can't forget that.

She took his hand as they settled into the backseat of the sedan, the contact grounding her even though it was a lie. She couldn't afford to have romantic feelings for Aiden. Her vision was already clouded because of her need for vengeance against Dmitri Romanov. Throw in something as foolish as love and she'd lose her way completely.

"Are you okay?"

She nodded, too twisted up inside to speak. What if something had happened to him? Through it all, he'd never dropped the mask he'd used to manipulate Alethea—the friendly and vengeful mob boss.

Did he know that we had maybe a fifty-fifty chance of walking out of that warehouse alive?

She squeezed his hand tighter. "You can't do that again."

"What?" Aiden turned to face her fully, his green eyes concerned.

"Meet Alethea like that—on her terms, surrounded by her people, in a place where you can't get out unless she *lets* you out. Not again, Aiden. Not like that."

His brows slanted down, and then his expression cleared. "You're worried about me? Bright eyes, you don't have to be."

Either he was lying to make her feel better or he'd missed the cold calculation in Alethea's eyes when she'd watched them walk out. If he didn't dance to the tune she set, she would have no problem killing him. She wouldn't lose a wink of sleep at night over it.

Charlie gripped his hand tighter. "Promise me."

"You know I can't. I'll do whatever it takes to see this through, and if that means getting into another situation like the one we just left, I won't hesitate."

She wanted to shake the stubbornness right out of him. "Even if it means you don't walk out alive?"

He started to give her a pat answer. She saw the second he registered that she was actually scared for *him*—not herself. The mask slipped, and something like wonder dawned.

Aiden pulled her into his lap and framed her face with his hands. "The end justifies the means. You know that."

She'd thought the same thing earlier. Now she wasn't so sure.

But he wasn't going to listen to her tonight. Either he hadn't seen the danger or he was determined to downplay it. If she kept pressing, it might mean a fight, and that was the last thing Charlie wanted. She'd never been more aware of time flowing, a river that she couldn't fight. Aiden wasn't hers. She couldn't protect him. She didn't even have a real right to demand he take more precautions. She was just a woman whose aims had lined up with his.

"Charlie—"

She kissed him. There wasn't anything left to say that they couldn't communicate with their bodies. She shifted to straddle him, the move making her dress ride up to indecent heights. All Aiden's careful control was gone in an instant, replaced by a frenzy that matched her own. He slid his hands up her thighs to her hips, pushing the dress even higher, and grabbed her ass, grinding her against him.

All her fear and anger turned to desire, creating an inferno bound to incinerate them both. She couldn't care less. Charlie reached between them and undid his slacks to pull out his cock. She palmed him. "Condom?"

He opened his mouth and then considered. "Fuck, I don't have any."

Damn. Disappointment soured in her stomach, but she shoved it away. "Then I guess we'll have to get creative. I need you inside me. I don't care how." She pushed away his hands and slid down the seat to kneel between his thighs.

Or she tried to.

He caught her halfway through the move and shook his head. "No, bright eyes."

"What?" Surely he wasn't rejecting a blow job? That had to break some kind of international law. It just wasn't done. "You're starting to give me a complex."

Aiden lifted her back to his lap, this time facing away from him. The passing lights showed her reflection in the glass separating them from the front seat. Her blue eyes were wild, her hair tangled from his fingers, her dress in danger of slipping off her breasts. Behind her, Aiden was barely a shadow. He moved her hair to one side and kissed her neck. "You come first, bright eyes. Second, too, if I have any say in it."

She licked her lips. "One of these days, I'm going to tie you down and give you all the blow jobs I've been craving."

"One of these days . . ." He bracketed her throat with one hand, keeping her head tilted to the side, and coasted the other hand up her inner thigh, spreading her legs further. "One of these days, I'll let you."

She nodded. "Good answer." The move increased the pressure of his hand against her neck, and she squirmed, turned on far more than she should be.

His wandering hand reached the junction between her thighs, and he parted her, idly stroking. "I think I like that you're worried about me." His finger circled her clit and away. "I like it a lot."

"Mmm." What was she supposed to say to that? She'd already had to face the fact that she didn't have the right words because she didn't have the *right*.

His finger pushed into her slowly. "I won't be without a condom again, bright eyes. Feeling you so hot and wet around my finger makes me crave the same around my cock." He pumped as idly as he'd touched her to begin with. "A woman like you could make a man forget himself."

It was hard to think, with his hard body behind her, his erection pressing against her ass, and his hand moving between her legs. She tried despite that. "Only for a while."

"No, bright eyes. Not just for a while." He dragged his mouth down the line of her shoulder. "When I'm inside you, all I can think of is you. When I'm near you, all I can think of is getting inside you again. If you gave me half a chance, I'd be buried to the hilt right now, condom be damned. That's *crazy*."

She rocked against his hand, letting her head fall back to rest on his shoulder. He let go of her throat. The only warning she got was his thumb brushing her sternum and then he pushed down her dress, baring her breasts completely. Aiden cursed. "Next time you forget such a vital part of your wardrobe, the moment I find out, I'm going to fuck you. I might give you the option of dragging you to the nearest bathroom...if you're lucky."

He lightly pinched first one nipple and then the other. Charlie couldn't hold back a moan. She bit her lip, but the faint pain was nothing against the pleasure of his stroking her. She fought to keep her hips still, to do anything except grind against his hand like an animal in heat, but it was a lost cause. With his hands on her body and his mouth tracing those delicious patterns over her shoulder to her neck and back again, she was in danger of combusting on the spot. "*Aiden.*"

"I like the way you say my name when you're on the edge." He pushed a second—and then a third—finger into her. "Come for me, bright eyes. I want to feel you."

He'd already learned her body in their short time

together. Even if she'd wanted to hold off, there was no denying Aiden. He stroked her G-spot while the heel of his hand pressed hard on her clit, her small movements providing just enough friction to drive her out of her damn mind. For one eternal moment, she was poised on the edge.

And then he set his teeth against her neck and shoved her into oblivion.

CHAPTER SIXTEEN

Aiden led the way up to the hotel room, ignoring Charlie's questioning look. It was crazy to stop before they got back to Boston. There were a thousand different tasks in need of doing.

But she was right—they'd almost died back there. He'd seen it in Alethea's eyes. He'd hoped that Charlie had missed it, but he'd underestimated her yet again.

Fooling around in the backseat had just whetted his appetite. He needed her, naked and in a bed, her skin against his the only feeling that would calm the racing of his heart. The only stop he'd made on the way was to run into a convenience store and grab a box of condoms, because he would *not* deprive them again.

"Aiden, don't you think this is a bad idea?"

"Yes." He used the key to open the hotel door and then held it for her.

She sighed and walked into the room, amusement

creeping into her blue eyes as she watched him throw the dead bolt and then search the room. Charlie propped her hands on her hips. "Are you expecting a murderer to be lying in wait?"

"We're not in Boston. Even if we were, I'd still check." Because she was there with him, and he'd done a shitty job of keeping her safe up to this point. It didn't matter that he hadn't promised her safety—that he'd initially planned to use her as ruthlessly as any tool.

Things had changed.

Satisfied that they were safe enough for the time being, he unbuttoned his shirt. "Strip."

"Aiden..." She pressed her lips together and paused. "You need this."

"I need you." It was the truth. It wasn't the sex that he craved to settle him. It was Charlie.

She shimmied out of her dress. He might live to be one hundred, but he'd never see a sight more breathtaking than Charlie standing before him in nothing but heels. Her makeup was a little smudged from their time in the car, but it only added to the appeal. She wasn't some Photoshopped model. She was real.

Aiden finished undressing as she watched, never taking his gaze from her. "I misjudged Alethea."

"I know." She stepped forward and placed her hand on the center of his chest. Using just that touch, she guided him back to sit on the edge of the bed. "You thought you could manipulate her."

He *had* manipulated her, but it had been a close call. "Do you know what they do to—"

"Aiden, stop." She knelt between his knees and ran her hands up his thighs. "Beating yourself up isn't going to do a single damn thing but ruin this blow job. You made a mistake. We got out alive. We're here. We're alive. We're safe."

That was the problem. He'd made a mistake. He'd gone in overconfident and—

His thoughts slammed to a halt as Charlie leaned over and took his cock into her mouth. She sucked him until he hit the back of her throat, then started the slow slide back up. As if she savored his taste.

She wrapped her hand around the base of his cock and licked around his head. Aiden cursed long and hard. "Come here."

"Nope." She used her free hand to cradle his balls. "There might not be some handy ropes lying around, but I'm collecting—with interest."

He started to reach for her but ended up fisting the comforter of the bed and letting her work. This is what he'd wanted when he booked the hotel room instead of driving back to the O'Malley house. Charlie. Him. They had nowhere to be for the next few hours, and they wouldn't be interrupted. There was no rush.

For her part, she seemed content to take her time—and drive him out of his goddamn mind in the process. As Aiden watched her suck him off, her bright red lips wrapped around his cock were almost enough to make him come from the sight alone. "Bright eyes, I need you."

"You have me." She rose and grabbed one of the condoms from where he'd tossed them on the bed. "Tonight. Right now. You have me. We got out, Aiden. We're okay." She rolled the condom onto him and then braced her hands on his shoulders. "How do you need me?"

The offer was just proof that she saw him better than most people. She recognized that he needed to reassert the control Alethea had threatened. Aiden pulled her down onto his lap and kissed her. He'd intended it to be a silent thank-you, but the notion didn't last past their first contact. Charlie opened for him immediately, her tongue seeking his.

He lost himself in the feel and taste of her. Each second that passed settled the rattled feeling in his chest, until his frustration and fear over how shit had gone so south melted away.

And then there was only Charlie.

He drew back enough to say, "I should be asking how *you* need *me*."

"Are you?"

He grinned. "No. I want you on your hands and knees on the bed."

She climbed off him to obey. He stood, and his mouth went dry at the sight she offered. With her knees parted and the arch in her spine, he could actually see how wet she was. "You liked sucking my cock." He shifted onto the bed, easing up behind her.

"So much so that I'm going to do it again at the earliest available opportunity."

He chuckled. "I can't argue with that."

"Really? Because I thought I was going to have to follow through on my threat to tie you down to just get you to let me do it." She hissed out a breath as he palmed her pussy. "You're very cagey."

"Are you into bondage, bright eyes?" He slipped one finger into her and, satisfied that she was more than ready, he brought his cock to her entrance. Aiden gripped her hips and worked into her with short, controlled thrusts, until he was sheathed to the hilt.

Charlie moaned. "I'm a control freak."

"I noticed." He'd also noticed that she enjoyed their games as much as he did. He pressed his hand against the small of her back and slid it up her spine, guiding her down until the top half of her body was flush against the bed. The position left her ass in the air and allowed him deeper yet.

Satisfied she would stay there, he pulled almost all the way out and then thrust deep. Charlie cried out. "Harder, Aiden!"

This time, he obeyed. Aiden followed her muffled commands, fucking her just the way she needed. She thrust back to meet every stroke. He wanted to maintain this feeling of perfection all night long, but Charlie felt too good. "Touch yourself," he demanded.

She snaked one hand beneath herself, and her pussy clamped tight around him in response. He kept up the angle that had her writhing on the bed, holding tight onto his control and keeping his own orgasm at bay. She didn't make him wait long. Charlie cried out his name over and over again, her shrieks barely muffled by the comforter.

It was too much. Aiden couldn't hold out any longer. He tightened his grip on her hips and drove into her, chasing the pleasure her body offered him. He came with a curse, and it was like every muscle in his body dissipated.

He collapsed half on top of her. "Fuck, Charlie."

"You just did."

Aiden laughed hoarsely and gave her ass a light smack. "Mouthy."

"Every damn day." She rolled to face him and tucked in against his chest. When apparently that wasn't close enough, she draped one long leg over his hip and hugged him. "I needed that."

"Me too." He held her close. The soft cadence of her

breathing washed over him, erasing the last of his lingering unease. Tonight had been a closer call than he wanted to admit, which was bad enough.

Putting Charlie in that position despite her questioning the wisdom of it was inexcusable. "I'm sorry I didn't listen to you."

"You had it under control."

Not nearly as under control as he would have liked. He kissed the top of her head. "Next time your gut says it's a bad situation, we're out. No questions asked."

She tensed. "That's stupid."

What the hell? He couldn't see her face to gauge where her head was at, but her response didn't make a damn bit of sense. "There's nothing stupid about it. You knew it was a bad call. I didn't listen to you, and we almost got into a conflict we might not have walked out of."

"That was just common sense. You can't trust my gut. *I* can't trust my gut."

Ah. Aiden forced his body to relax and waited for the tension to bleed out of his tone. "You couldn't have known the other cops would turn on you."

She jerked back from him. "I do *not* want to talk about it."

"Charlie." He let her go, because the alternative was to wrestle her to a standstill, but it made his chest ache to watch the distance between them open up. "You have to face it at some point. You couldn't have known."

"One, I don't need the therapy session. Two, stop trying to distract yourself from your mistake by focusing on me. Three, fuck off." She scrubbed a hand over her face. "Shit. Fuck. Goddamn it. Now *I'm* sorry. That was out of line. But the point stands—my past is off-limits. Respect it or this ends now."

Her obvious pain made him want to press her, but there was shit he didn't want ripped open. And she was right—he'd latched on to her past to avoid thinking too hard about his present.

Aiden held out a hand. "Come back to me."

"Not until you agree."

He sighed. "I won't talk about it tonight."

"That's a shitty-ass promise." But she still crawled back into his arms. He barely had time to relax when she spoke again. "Keira is going to start taking Krav Maga lessons."

"I'll arrange to have an instructor brought to the house." His little sister knew how to shoot—he and Teague had made sure all their sisters did, even if Carrigan and Keira took to it better than Sloan. They had men whose whole job was to keep them safe, but it was always possible that the time would come when they'd have to defend themselves.

He'd never considered some kind of martial arts. Aiden knew how to fight, but there was nothing formal about it. He was a goddamn brawler.

"Wrong. You'll arrange to have Mark—or whoever—escort her to her classes several times a week."

As much as he didn't like the idea of his sister traipsing out into Boston with any regularity, Charlie's tone said that she'd go to the mat for this. He wanted to know why. "You took her there today."

"Yes, I did." She hesitated, and he found himself holding his breath to see what she'd say next. She rewarded his patience by shifting away enough to meet his gaze. Her expression was as frank as he'd ever seen, stripped of the artifice she'd been wearing like a second skin since agreeing to pose as his fiancée. "I'm prefacing this by saying that it's not an invitation to delve into my past—it's just to give you some context. Understand?"

"Yes." He agreed too readily, but Aiden was hungry for more of her. He knew what he'd read, but reports failed to do Charlie justice. He wanted to know every part of her mind the same way he was beginning to know her body.

She gave him a suspicious look but finally said, "I had plenty of training—as you can imagine—but after my attack...I'd never felt so helpless as I did in those first few months while I was recovering. I was helpless and terrified that someone would decide to finish the job, and I spent too much time hiding away."

The actions sounded familiar, even if the cause wasn't the same. She could have been describing Keira. "I'm with you so far." He deliberately didn't think about what he'd like to do to the men who'd hurt Charlie badly enough to instill that fear in the first place.

"Eventually, I started training again out of spite. I hated that I'd been weak, and wanted to do anything to combat the chance of that happening again. It was about control, which I'm sure you can appreciate." She traced the vein that ran along his forearm. "Keira feels helpless and scared, even if she would rather cut you than admit it. The partying is just an escape, but she's always going to wake up and find herself sober and have to start the whole process over again. Krav Maga isn't going to magically fix everything that is wrong in her life, but it will give her an outlet that she desperately needs."

She snuggled into him again. "You should have seen her going after that punching bag. She needs this. I know it's dangerous to have a schedule that requires her to leave the house, but that's what your security people are for. They can figure it out. Dmitri Romanov"—she choked a little on his name—"doesn't seem to want to hurt her at this point, so the danger is as low as it's ever likely to be."

Aiden fought down his knee-jerk reaction to reject the idea out of hand. The truth was that Keira needed help, and though he'd never have imagined that she'd find a champion in Charlie, their relationship was developing into something resembling friendship. He stroked his hand over Charlie's hair. "You feel strongly about this."

"You have no idea how crazy it drives me to see you and your siblings acting like idiots around each other. I get it—you're big bad mafia people who have a boatload of issues—but you're letting your relationships with them be poisoned for no goddamn reason. It's a fucking tragedy."

He tried to see it from her point of view. Charlie had no siblings. Her mother was gone. Her father had essentially disowned her, though they remained in regular contact, so Finch had to love her—as much as the man was capable of loving anyone. But that didn't mean he was a good father to her. By all accounts, he was just as shitty a dad as he was a person in general.

It made sense that Charlie had come in, taken one look at Aiden and his siblings, and wanted to fix things. "Some things can't be fixed."

"And some things aren't as broken as you might think. How can you tell the difference?"

She had him there. Aiden rolled her onto her back and propped himself up on his forearms. "Would it make you happy if I tried to mend things?"

"My happiness is irrelevant. I'm temporary." She rolled her eyes. "But yes, it would make me happy if you'd at least try. You can send me thank-you flowers when you realize I was right all along."

Fuck, he liked this woman. Somehow she'd managed to survive all the terrible shit life had thrown her way. Aiden kissed her, slow and searching. When he finally lifted his head, they were both breathing hard. "I'll talk to Liam about setting up a detail for Keira so she can start training."

Charlie's blue eyes danced. "And?"

He nipped her bottom lip. "And I'll call Carrigan and see about setting a meeting up. Happy?"

"It's a start."

Carrigan was the easier of the two fences to mend. Which was saying something, because she still hadn't forgiven him for siding with their father when she chose James Halloran. Aiden had tried to force her hand, which had created a fracture between them that he didn't know how to broach.

Truth be told, he hadn't even tried.

He slid off Charlie and stood. "Get dressed. I don't know about *you*, but I want to catch a couple hours of sleep in my own bed tonight." Her laughter chased him into the bathroom, where he disposed of the condom.

Who would have thought that when he sought out Charlie Finch, she'd end up being the kind of woman he'd never realized he might actually need?

Theirs wasn't a love story for the ages. Their differences ran soul-deep despite the fact that they were melding together just fine for the moment. But she'd never stop being a cop.

And Aiden had no choice but to stay on his path.

CHAPTER SEVENTEEN

Aiden waited until Charlie's breathing evened to climb out of his bed. He pulled on a pair of pants and stopped at the door. He was tempted to look back and see her there tangled among his sheets, her face relaxed in the way that only sleep seemed to be able to manage. He didn't. What he had to do to put the next stage of this shit show into motion required him to harden his heart against hurting her, despite what they'd shared in that hotel room mere hours ago.

There was no choice.

He just hadn't expected the guilt to be quite so strong.

At this hour, the house was quiet and felt empty. Maybe it was his conversation with Charlie, but it struck him that most of his siblings were gone, moved out and on, and that if he didn't succeed, Keira would follow the same path and it would only be him and Cillian left of the O'Malley clan. At least Cillian and Olivia were bound to fill the halls with children, though he didn't think she'd be on board for seven kids, the way his mother had been.

And what about him?

Getting married was in the future—he couldn't avoid it indefinitely—and after everything that their family had gone through, he'd have to make a politically advantageous marriage to solidify their power base. Alliances could make or break them, and it was his turn to take a hit for the greater good.

His mind turned to Charlie, despite his best intentions. He was enjoying the hell out of their time together, and she'd more than proven she could play the game along with the best of them. She'd correctly read the situation with Mae—better than he had—and adjusted accordingly. She'd offered him comfort and surrender. She cared about his siblings, and his relationship with them.

But he wasn't keeping her. He couldn't.

Aiden padded into his office and shut and locked the door behind him. It already bore marks of his father being back—papers that had been neatly organized, now scattered across the glossy desk, the bottle of expensive liquor now severely depleted, the very air more stagnant and cloying. The latter was his imagination, but he caught a whiff of the cologne Seamus favored and gritted his teeth.

The man might as well have pissed on the carpet to mark his territory.

At least the burner phones were exactly where he'd left them—in the bottom drawer. He pulled one out at random and considered it. If they successfully removed Alethea and Mae from the New York equation, the new influx of territory would keep Romanov busy for years. He'd have to work his way through the Eldridge operations and ensure that only those loyal to him remained, a time-consuming task. Romanov might very well leave the O'Malleys alone for good and focus on issues closer to home.

But he couldn't guarantee it.

The Russian was a slippery bastard. He could do the logical thing and worry about New York, but he was just as likely to assume that Aiden had lowered his guard, and then attack the O'Malleys instead. They were only temporary allies, and with Romanov's eye on Keira, that alliance wouldn't last past Alethea's fall.

Aiden refused to allow that to happen—which meant it was time to bring in the next wave of his plan—whether it would hurt Charlie or not.

He dialed the number he'd memorized as soon as Liam had tracked down the information. Despite it being well after two in the morning, the line rang only a handful of times before a gruff voice answered. "John Finch."

"Hello, Agent Finch."

Silence for a beat, and then two. "Who is this?"

"I'm surprised you don't know. You've got my brother dancing to any tune you set, so I would assume that you'd have the rest of us down by now." Aiden fought to keep his tone cool and disinterested, fought his anger at this man for fucking with his family, and his anger at his brother Teague for getting caught up in such a desperate situation.

"Aiden O'Malley. Do I want to know how you got this number?"

It struck him that Finch might think Charlie had handed it over. The guilt circling Aiden's throat like a vise tightened. His control wavered. "I have my ways."

"I'm sure you do." There was rustling on the other end as Finch settled in. "What is it I can do for you?"

He didn't miss the fact that the man hadn't addressed his comment about Teague. He didn't expect Finch to. It was one thing for Aiden to suspect it—it was entirely another for him to know for sure. He could have told the fed that it was a lost cause. He had more than enough information to incriminate his brother. That wasn't why he was calling.

At least, it wasn't the sole reason he was calling.

"It's more about what I can do for *you*." He didn't wait for Finch to comment. It didn't really matter what the agent thought of this. The only thing that mattered was him acting how Aiden needed him to. "There's going to be a show-down of sorts between the Eldridges and the Romanovs on October twelfth." He rattled off the specific location. "It might look like a deal gone wrong, but I think you'll find it's much more intriguing. I suspect you'll want to be there."

"Hmm." He didn't sound the least bit impressed. "And what do you expect in return for this tidbit of information?"

"I expect you to back the fuck away from my brother." It came out harsher than he meant it to.

Finch sighed. "Look, kid, even if your brother was an informant, that deal would be between him and the fed who works with him. You making a deal has nothing to do with that."

That was about what he'd anticipated, but frustration still reigned supreme. Aiden drummed his fingers on the desk, staring at the closed door. Part of him had hoped it wouldn't come to this. He'd known better. "Your daughter is very beautiful."

"Leave her alone." All tiredness was gone from the man's voice. "She's been through enough, and whatever problem you think we have is between us."

He'd fully intended to throw their physical relationship

in Finch's face, but Aiden couldn't do it. He'd had every intention of seducing her to hurt her father, but that motivation had changed the first time she touched him. He wanted her for the sake of *her*, not because he wanted revenge.

But he still wanted revenge.

"Did you know we attended a poker game with Alethea and Mae Eldridge tonight?"

This time, the silence stretched on for almost a full minute. "You're going to get her killed."

Over my dead body. But he didn't have to let Finch know how invested he was in Charlie's safety. If the man wasn't worried about his daughter, he wasn't going to be motivated to do what Aiden wanted. "She's assured me she can handle herself."

"You know as well as I do that she's in over her head. My girl is capable, but she's a small fish in an ocean of sharks. Send her home, Aiden."

"I don't think I will." He knew damn well that he'd have to let her go at some point. But not yet. "I strongly urge you to be on that dock on the twelfth. Have a good rest of your night, Agent Finch." He hung up and systematically dismantled the phone. He doubted that Finch's phone was tapped, so there should be no recording of that conversation, but he still wasn't going to leave that burner phone for a second use. Finch knew how to get a hold of him if he was so inclined.

The office door opened, and a sleepy-looking Cillian strode in. He was dressed much the same way Aiden was— a pair of pants that had obviously been hastily thrown on and nothing else. "What's going on?"

"Nothing that can't wait until morning." He glanced at the clock on the wall. It *was* morning, albeit early enough that everyone should be asleep.

"Wrong." Cillian dropped into his customary chair across from Aiden. "I've been patient while you danced around this, and while you plotted and schemed and left me in the dark. Now you're going to tell me everything, and you're going to do it now."

He'd had every intention of looping Cillian in at some point, but he raised his eyebrows at the underlying threat in his brother's words. "Or?"

"Or nothing, you asshole. You're my brother, and while I might not fully support every move you make, I can still appreciate the direction you're taking this family." He took a deep breath, and when he spoke again, his tone was more subdued. "But if you're doing something that's going to bring Romanov down on us, I'm getting Olivia and Hadley out of town until the smoke clears. So you *will* tell me. You owe me that much."

Aiden could argue that Cillian wasn't in charge so he was on a need-to-know basis, but that was something their father would do. Seamus O'Malley believed that he owed no one anything and that everyone else was responsible for jumping through hoops to keep him happy.

Once, he'd thought that emulating his father was the best way to go about things.

These days, he knew better.

The strength of the O'Malleys—of Boston as a whole—was in their family connections. Aiden was good, but he wasn't the end-all, be-all. Pretending he was a god and everyone else was under his control was a good way to end up like Seamus had—with his entire family ready to chew off their own arms to get away from him.

Charlie was right. It was time to start to mend the relationships he had with his siblings—and to ensure his with Cillian didn't get broken in the first place.

Aiden stood and grabbed the bourbon bottle that his father had already helped himself to. He set two tumblers on the desk and poured a healthy dose into both. Then he sat down and told his brother everything.

* * *

Charlie woke up alone in what was becoming a nasty pattern. She wasn't used to sleeping so soundly that someone could get up and move around the room without her realizing it. Even with everything going on around them, she'd been sleeping better in the last week than she had in the two years previous. It didn't make a lick of sense, except maybe to chalk it up to being sexed into submission.

She stretched and smiled at how sore she was.

Last night had felt like a turning point. She didn't know what they were turning toward, but in that hotel room, they hadn't felt like a criminal and a former cop. They were just a man and a woman who had narrowly escaped harm and needed to feel alive.

She touched the ring on her finger. It no longer felt so foreign. Now, she was almost used to it...which was something she didn't want to think about too hard. Better to keep busy and moving than to give in to the temptation to lie here and replay their time together.

That was the problem, though—keeping busy. She never thought she'd miss her crappy job working the poker table at Jacques's, but between running the poker games and spending time at the gym, the hours had passed quickly. She didn't have that here.

It didn't feel right spending Aiden's money in general,

let alone because she was bored. And while the O'Malley household had its own personal gym, it always seemed to be populated by the steely-eyed men who provided the muscle to the family. Charlie had faced down equally cranky dudes who didn't want to share their space when she was going through police academy, but she didn't think Aiden would appreciate being tattled to about his new fiancée throwing down with his men.

So what the hell was she going to do until the next thing Aiden needed her for?

Charlie showered and got dressed, then pulled on a pair of her favorite jeans and a shirt that she'd owned before Aiden came into her life. The way things were going, she was in danger of forgetting who she was—*what* she was. She might not be a cop anymore—or ever again—but that didn't alter where she'd come from.

Fancy clothes and money couldn't change that.

Going with Keira to the gym had been good for both of them. She pulled her hair to the side and braided it loosely. Keira didn't know yet that Aiden had given her training a thumbs-up, but it would do them both a world of good to get out of the house—especially since Seamus O'Malley was back. Charlie knew she'd have to face him down eventually, but she wasn't looking forward to it.

She found Keira exactly where she expected to—holed up in her room, though at least the customary cloud of smoke wasn't present. Keira looked her up and down from mascara-smudged eyes. "You look way too spunky this morning. I'm going back to bed."

"No, you aren't." Charlie dropped into the same chair she'd taken the last time she was in the room. "I'm bored."

"That sounds like a personal problem."

She poked the pile of laundry with her toe. "I think you're bored, too. You had fun yesterday."

Keira yawned. "What's your point?"

"My point is that we should get out of here for the day again. There's got to be something we could do." She hadn't spent much time in Boston, despite living relatively close, but the touristy thing didn't appeal—and she doubted that would be enough to tempt Keira out of the room. "Don't you have something you need to do that you haven't been doing because of all this?" Charlie waved her hand.

"It's too early to party. My coke dealer never answers his phone before three." Keira saw the look on her face and burst out laughing. "Fuck, Charlie, I'm kidding. That bastard stopped calling me back months ago. I'm pretty sure Aiden threatened his life if he didn't eighty-six me."

She chose not to comment on that. "Well?"

"Oh, *fine*." Keira dug her phone out from beneath a pile of pillows and thumbed through it. "You're not going to like this." Before Charlie could ask what she meant, she had the phone to her ear. "Carrigan?... Yeah, I know, it's been way too long. What are you doing for lunch?... Perfect." Her hazel eyes lit on Charlie. "Oh, and I'm bringing our brother's gold-digging fiancée with me... No, don't be a bitch. I like her."

Charlie pressed her lips together, wondering if she'd just made a mistake. It was one thing to run around the city with Keira, pretending they were just friends who happened to like the same things—like punching a bag until their arms felt like limp noodles. Going to lunch with Carrigan was something else altogether. That woman was formidable, and it was readily apparent that she had no problem getting her hands dirty. She hadn't done anything to confirm that, but Charlie couldn't shake the feeling.

Then again, I told Aiden it was time to start reaching out to his family. Maybe it's time I learned what that really entails.

Liam didn't look happy when they told him where they were going, but he assigned them a security detail, saying he would call ahead to the Hallorans and ensure that things were covered on their end as well.

It wasn't until they were in the backseat of yet another town car that Keira slouched in her seat and expelled a long breath. "God. It's always a gamble if they're going to let me out of the house. With my father back, I thought someone might throw a bitchfit—especially since we're going to see Carrigan, and she's supposed to be dead to the family."

It took a few seconds for the pieces to click into place. Carrigan was with James Halloran. It didn't seem to bother Aiden all that much. After all, he'd invited her to the dinner he'd put together, but if their father didn't agree with his stance . . . that would complicate things.

"Dead to the family?"

"Ridiculous, isn't it? I mean, we all have mixed feelings about the whole Halloran thing, but James isn't that bad, and he obviously worships the ground Carrigan walks on." Something like longing flickered over Keira's face. "Could be worse."

"Could definitely be worse." She sent a quick text to Aiden, wincing when she realized she should have done it before she left. Going to see Carrigan.

Her phone vibrated almost instantly. I know.

Of course he knew. Liam would have told him before they drove out of the building. Problem?

No. Be careful.

She started to set her phone aside, but it buzzed again. Have dinner with me tonight. Just us, no plotting.

I'd love that. A smile pulled at the edges of Charlie's mouth despite her best intentions.

"Oh *God*. You two are disgusting."

She looked up in time to see Keira roll her eyes. "Really? Because I'm pretty sure you were giving Dmitri Romanov all sorts of come-fuck-me looks. And now you're wearing his rock on your finger." The memory killed any feel-good she'd gotten from Aiden's plans for the night. "He's dangerous, Keira. I don't think you understand how much."

Keira gave her a look that had no place on a twenty-one-year-old's face. "Everyone in our world is dangerous. If you haven't figured that out yet, you should get out while you still can. My brother might like to pretend that he's holier-than-thou, but he's just as ruthless as Dmitri. And I'd be really surprised if he didn't have as much blood on his hands—if not more."

"You don't..." Surely she wasn't hearing this right. "You sound like you have feelings for him." She very carefully didn't think about the claims Keira had aimed at Aiden.

All emotion disappeared from the woman's face. "Don't be silly, Charlie. Only an idiot would fall for Dmitri Romanov."

* * *

Keira regretted setting up the lunch with Carrigan and Charlie the second they sat down at the table. It was early enough that the restaurant wasn't very busy, which was a blessing in disguise, because her sister turned to Charlie and immediately said, "Keira is right. You must be a gold-digging whore to get into bed with this family."

Charlie took a sip of her water. "Let's get this out of the way. I'm marrying your brother. You can throw a bitchfit, but the wedding is going to happen. You might as well come to terms with it now, or you won't be invited."

Keira knew she should probably step in, but Charlie seemed more than capable of holding her own. She was an interesting woman, and despite herself, Keira kind of hoped that Aiden didn't fuck it up.

Her phone vibrated in the pocket of the jacket she'd tossed over her tank top before they left the house. She slipped it out and blinked. When had she thrown Dmitri's burner phone into this jacket? "Excuse me."

Neither her sister nor Charlie paid much attention as she rose from the table and walked to the back of the restaurant, where the bathrooms were. She answered as soon as she turned the corner. "Are you sneaking into my room again and moving this damn phone around?"

He didn't miss a beat. "If I were in your room, it wouldn't be because I sneaked in there, but because you let me in. And I certainly wouldn't be prioritizing moving a phone around."

He seemed to do that a lot—appear to answer a question without actually answering it. She tapped her toe against the trim on the bottom of the wall. "Well, knock that shit off. It's creepy."

"It's probable that you drank too much and misplaced the phone."

She glared, tapping harder. He had a point. When she'd gotten drunk last night, she seemed to remember wanting

the phone on her in case he decided to call again. *Stupid.*
"What do you want? I'm busy."

"Out to lunch with your treacherous sister."

He *would* think that. Carrigan breaking her word to him
was the catalyst that had turned Dmitri Romanov into the
bogeyman that the O'Malleys feared. Keira froze, feeling
sick to her stomach. Of course. This had all started with
Carrigan. *Of course* Dmitri wanted Carrigan. He always
had. "Don't call me again."

"Keira." He spoke sharply enough that she knew she'd
surprised him.

If she was smart, she'd hang up and throw the damn
phone in the nearest trash can, but she'd already proven that
she was too stupid to live when it came to Dmitri Romanov.
"If you want Carrigan, that's your problem. I'm not interested in being sloppy seconds, or a younger, meaner version
of the woman you really want." It hurt far more than it had
the right to for her to say those words.

And, goddamn him, he laughed. "Is that what you
think?"

"You're answering a question with a question. Again. I
hate that."

"You didn't ask a question. But let's pretend for a moment that you did. Do I want Carrigan? No. I never did. She
would have been a suitable wife, but I had no strong feelings for her one way or another."

"Then why force my family to its knees?"

She could almost hear the smile in his voice. "You know
why."

She licked her lips. "Yeah, I know why."

Because Carrigan breaking her word and running off with
James Halloran had weakened him. If he couldn't hold on to

a woman who'd agreed to be his wife, then he might not be able to hold his people in place. Having Olivia flee Romanov hands, defying their father's dying wishes, and ending up in O'Malley hands had only further weakened him.

"Are you wearing my ring, Keira?"

Her gaze dropped to the massive rock on her finger. Even knowing she should have taken it off, she couldn't make herself do it. She loved it, just like he seemed to have known she would. "Yes."

"I never gave a ring to your sister. I never touched her as I've already touched you." He took a breath, but it didn't do anything to decrease the intensity in his voice. "You have driven me to distraction from the moment we met. I would move mountains to ensure that you end up as my wife, in my bed. You would do well to remember that."

He could be lying...

She shivered, not sure if he was threatening her or making a promise that she might look forward to, just a little. Or both. "Why are you telling me this?"

"Because I want there to be no misunderstanding between us. I don't want your sister—either of your sisters. I want you."

I want you.

She leaned against the wall, her knees suddenly feeling a little out of whack. "Why are you calling, Dmitri?"

"You're in danger."

"What?" She shot off the wall, spinning around. The hallway was just as empty as it'd been the last time she looked. "Next time, Romanov, lead with *that.*"

He called so I'd leave the table and get out of the line of fire. She ran back the way she'd come. "If you—"

"I'm not responsible."

No, but he'd known there was a threat and he'd removed her from the situation, rather than warning Carrigan and Charlie. "Damn it, Dmitri, if something happens to my sister or Charlie, I will hunt you down and cut your fucking balls off. Take *that* into account next time you try this bullshit." She hung up and sprinted back toward the dining room.

CHAPTER EIGHTEEN

Get down!"

At Keira's yell, Charlie's instincts kicked to the fore-front, and her body took over before her mind could catch up. She grabbed Carrigan and hauled her to the ground. They hit with a bone-jarring thud. She expected the other woman to screech and shove her off, but Carrigan pressed herself even closer to the floor and kept her head down. *She's done this before.*

Charlie lifted her head to look around, finding Keira crouching under a table near the back of the room. She was paler than usual, but her eyes were bright and her expression determined. They stared at each other, and she couldn't help feeling a bit ridiculous. "Keira, what's—"

The rest of her sentence died in the boom of gunshots and the cascade of glass showering the seats they'd just been sitting in. Something hit the top of the table hard enough to knock it over, but she was already moving, shoving Carrigan in front of her and army-crawling across the floor to a more secure spot. *Where are Liam's men?*

More shots rang out, and then the screech of tires. Charlie counted to ten, then twenty. At thirty, Carrigan twisted to face her, shaking glass out of her long, dark hair. "Well, shit, gold digger. I guess we have to be friends now, since you just saved my life."

She hadn't, though. If Keira hadn't yelled, she wouldn't have known there was danger until it was too late. Charlie pushed herself up to a crouching position, wincing at the cuts covering her forearms and knees. Most of them were small—though it was hard to tell with all the blood—but there was probably still some glass embedded. *This is going to suck.*

"You okay, Keira?"

"Yeah." She sounded a little shaky, but the glass hadn't reached her spot.

Charlie's stomach lurched at the bullet holes in the wall above their table, though. If she'd been standing there...

She wasn't. None of us were. Stop worrying about what-if and move.

"Stay down." Charlie didn't think the shooters would come back around, but it wasn't worth the risk.

Carrigan had her phone out. "Get back here now... Yes, I know I said you could grab food. Plans have changed. *Now.*" She hung up and immediately dialed again. "James. I'm fine." Her eyes met Charlie's, and she gave a wry smile at the lie. She was just as cut up, if not more so. "Okay, not totally fine. There was a drive-by." A pause. "Yes, you're right. The O'Malley house is closest. I'll be there. Love you."

Charlie belatedly realized she should probably be making a call of her own. She winced as she grabbed her phone, the move pulling on half a dozen cuts. The phone had barely rung when Aiden picked up. "What's wrong?"

Of course he would know something was wrong. The only reason she would be calling was if plans had changed, and they never changed for positive reasons. *Stop stalling and tell him what happened.* She took a deep breath, but it did nothing to calm her racing heart or remove the shakiness from her voice. "There was a drive-by."

"I'm on my way."

"What? No. Aiden, you can't. I'm okay. We're all okay."

She didn't know if she was telling the truth about the O'Malley men who'd been stationed out front. It sounded like Carrigan had let her security detail go get food, since it didn't seem necessary to double up. She swallowed hard and knew without a shadow of a doubt that they hadn't made it if they'd been in the last place she'd seen them— right outside the window. "I..."

You can do this. You've faced down worse than this.

It was a long time ago, though.

She did her best to draw on her training about how to operate in an emergency. What had Carrigan said? "We're coming back. We can get to the house faster than any other place—and it'll be faster than it would be to wait for you and then turn around and go back."

"I'm coming with a group of my men to meet you halfway. Can you reach the car?"

She started to say yes but stopped. Normal drive-by shootings—it was so sad that such a thing existed—were over as soon as the car drove away from the scene. But she couldn't be sure there was anything normal about this situation. "I think so."

"Then get your ass in the car, bright eyes."

She hung up and looked around the room. "Aiden's sending men to meet us." They had to get out of here. The restaurant staff hadn't ventured out, and she wasn't in the mood to hunt them down. "Keira, come on."

The younger woman stood on shaky legs, her eyes too wide. "I'm going to kill that motherfucker."

Charlie didn't ask what she meant, just turned to Carrigan. "Can you walk?"

"Yes." She shoved to her feet, teetering a little in her heels. She made a face at the blood running down her legs. "I guess that's one way to ruin a pair of shoes."

"My least favorite way." Charlie's jeans had saved her legs from the worst of it, but Carrigan's bare legs..."Do you have a doctor on staff?"

"Keira can call Doc Jones as soon as we get to the car." She sighed. "You're a New Yorker, right? I guess that means I'm driving." She pulled a gun out of her tiny purse, checked to make sure it was loaded, and nodded. "Let's go."

They still had to get out of the restaurant. It made sense to leave the back way, into the alley, but Charlie had to know if there was some kind of body count.

If we hadn't left today... No. She couldn't afford to think like that. The men knew what they were potentially signing up for when they took jobs as enforcers for the O'Malleys.

That knowledge didn't make her feel the least bit better.

Carrigan's phone rang before she took a step. She frowned. "Yeah?" Whoever it was didn't have good news. Her gaze cut to Charlie. "We'll go out the back and meet you at the O'Malley house. Take care of it."

Even though Charlie was certain she didn't want to know, she had to ask. "What?"

"The two men working your security detail didn't make

it. I'm sorry." She glanced at the front door. "We have to leave now."

"But—" She cut herself off. "You're right." There was more than her guilt to think about right now. Carrigan could clearly carry herself just fine in a crisis, but Keira's adrenaline was obviously running rampant. She had to get the girl to safety.

She pulled her own gun from her ankle holster. *Should have pulled it before now.* Apparently, her instincts weren't as great as she'd thought. She took up the rear position in their little group.

The back entrance let out through the kitchen. A chef and two servers were huddled near the walk-in freezer. Carrigan ignored them, but Charlie stopped. "Stay here until the police arrive. You're safe." They didn't look like they believed her, but she couldn't do much about that. She'd tried.

Carrigan's town car was two blocks over, and they made it there with no trouble—though everyone they passed gave them a wide berth.

Not a single person asked if they needed help.

Anger rose, pounding in time with Charlie's heart. Three women, two covered in blood and limping, and...nothing. She jumped when Keira took her hand. "Deep breaths, Charlie."

She didn't want to take deep breaths. She wanted to rail and scream at how fucked up the universe was. The longer she was on this earth, the harder time she had convincing herself that people defaulted to good. They didn't. They defaulted to selfish.

Every. Single. Fucking. Time.

"I'm fine."

"I know."

Carrigan pulled a key out of her purse. "It pays to be paranoid and carry and extra key. Let's get the hell out of here."

Charlie took one last look down the street in the direction of the restaurant and then climbed into the car. "You took the words right out of my mouth."

* * *

Aiden barely waited for his SUV to pull to a stop next to the town car before he jumped out of the passenger seat and rushed around the front of the car. It didn't matter that they were at a red light in the middle of the street. All that mattered was the fear he'd heard in Charlie's voice when she'd called him to tell him what happened.

A drive-by.

All he could think when he heard was, *Not again*. He yanked open the back door and stopped short at the sight of Charlie covered in blood. She blinked. "Get in the car before people start honking."

He slid onto the seat next to her and slammed the door shut. "Doc Jones will meet us at the house." Carrigan and Keira were in the front, clearly visible, since the tinted glass was retracted. Carrigan seemed to be doing okay, since she was driving, though she was covered in as much blood as Charlie was. Keira alone looked unscathed.

He gently took Charlie's hand, his chest tight as he turned it to see the cuts littering her arms. "Did you see who it was?"

"It was Romanov," Carrigan said. "It had to be."

"No, it wasn't." Keira turned fully around to look at

him. "I know you hate him, but it wasn't him. If he hadn't warned me, we'd all be dead."

He'd circle back to how Romanov had managed to warn her once they were safe and patched up. Right now, he had bigger priorities. "He could have set it up so you would think that."

"No, really?" She rolled her eyes. "But if he was behind it, he would have called it off the second he knew I was back in that room."

They were *definitely* going to have a conversation once things settled down.

"You're delusional." Carrigan turned onto their block.

Was she, though? A drive-by on a public street was hardly Romanov's style. It was too...blunt. He had no reason to strike. By all appearances, Aiden was setting him up to get exactly what he wanted. Taking a shot at Carrigan would sever any alliance—and it would ensure that all three of Boston's families turned their fury directly at him. To say nothing of Keira's reaction.

It's something the Eldridges would do.

Alethea and Mae had let him and Charlie walk out of the warehouse alive, but that didn't mean that they were going to play right into his and Romanov's hands.

This whole thing had started when Romanov turned down a marriage alliance with Mae in favor of Keira. Put Charlie in the same room—another woman Mae couldn't stand—and it was practically waving a red flag in front of a bull.

He'd assumed that because they were in Boston and surrounded by O'Malley and Halloran men that Charlie and his sisters would be safe. He'd obviously been wrong. It was something he'd have to deal with. Later.

Right now, all he could see was the blood on Charlie's pale skin. Even though they were obviously all surface wounds, he couldn't help connecting the sight with the night Devlin was killed. She could have *died*. If things had played out differently, she would have—the same way his youngest brother did on that night three years ago, shot down like a dog in the street.

A shudder worked its way through him, and he tried to fight it off. Now wasn't the time for his control to waver. There was *never* time for his control to waver. He realized his hand was shaking and went to let go of hers, but she tightened her grip. Charlie shifted closer, lowering her voice. "I'm okay, Aiden. We're all okay."

Twice now, she'd dodged being hurt severely. Who was to say she'd be so lucky if this happened again?

"I'll find who did this and I'll put them in the ground."

Carrigan snorted. "You're going to have to arm-wrestle James for the right." She parked, and the man in question appeared as if by magic at the side of the car. He yanked open the driver's door and stopped short. Carrigan held up a hand and then seemed to realize that all the blood made it look worse. "I'm okay. I promise."

"Lovely, we need to have a conversation about what okay means. This?" He pointed at her. "Not okay."

She climbed out of the car, glaring at him in the same way she used to glare at Aiden when she was a kid and would skin her knee, almost daring him to make an issue of it. "If you try to carry me, I'm not going to take it well."

Aiden half expected James to override his sister's protests, but he just cast a critical eye over her. "You collapse, I'm carrying you."

"Deal." She turned back to the car. "Hey . . . Charlie."

Charlie smiled, as if sharing some joke Aiden wasn't party to. "Yeah?"

"We're having a fundraiser tomorrow night. I'll make sure you and Aiden are on the list." Then they were gone. Carrigan might be an O'Malley still, but she was now a Halloran first. James would have his own doctor on staff to get her checked out.

By the time they all made it inside, Doc Jones had arrived. She'd intimidated the shit out of Aiden as a child—she was tall and broad and had flame red hair streaked with gray—and his impression of her hadn't changed much as he got older. He paid her very well to be available when they needed her, but there wasn't enough money in the world to ensure that she had a good attitude while she did it.

She propped her hands on her hips and looked them over. "Well, hell. I've never seen a more motley crew, and in my line of work, that's saying something."

"Doc Jones." He touched Charlie's back, urging her forward, the warmth of her body through her clothes reassuring him as he shadowed her, sure that she was going to drop at any moment.

The good doctor, naturally, called him on it. "Let the girl breathe. Back off or you'll wait outside."

Aiden instantly took a step back. As hard as it was to put distance between them, being forced out of the room while she worked on Charlie would be even worse. He watched like a hawk as Doc Jones examined her arms and huffed. "Did a number on yourself, didn't you?"

"I have a deep desire not to be shot."

She chuckled. "Don't we all? You're miles ahead of this idiot's siblings." She jerked a thumb at Aiden. "Though *he*, at least, hasn't called me up because of a bullet wound yet."

"He'd better not."

Doc Jones went to work, cleaning the worst of the blood off and then carefully prodding the wounds in search of glass. Aiden gritted his teeth every time Charlie winced. She put a brave face on it, but then she would. She was too tough for her own good.

He wanted her to be able to let down her guard around him. It was such a foolish desire—to be her safe harbor— that he didn't know how to deal with it. He wasn't safe for Charlie. He'd *never* be safe for her. Asking her to be vulnerable around him because he craved the ability to take care of her was selfish in the extreme.

Knowing that didn't do a single damn thing to detract from the desire.

Watching her tough it out when she was obviously in pain, scared, and pissed off broke his fucking heart. It took every ounce of control he had to sit still and offer silent support, when all he wanted to do was shove Doc Jones away and carry Charlie up to his room.

By the time Doc Jones was finished, Aiden was shaking nearly as much as Charlie. The doctor adjusted the bandages on her arms. "It could have been a lot worse."

"I know."

"I'm giving you pain meds. You had better damn well take them." She continued before Charlie had a chance to answer. "No one likes a heroic idiot. Take the pills and slow down enough to give your body a chance to start healing. You don't have a cock, so whipping it out to prove yours is the biggest is going to waste everyone's time."

Aiden stepped up and plucked the pill bottle from the doctor's hand. "I'll make sure she takes it."

Doc Jones managed to look down her nose at him

despite the fact that she was sitting. "I should give you some damn Xanax, because, God knows, you aren't going to sleep tonight. But I know better."

He managed a small smile. "Yes, you do." The closest Aiden got to pills was ibuprofen, and even then he had to be seriously hurting to take it. He knew damn well it was his control-freak nature, but that didn't mean he was about to change.

"Should shoot you with a damn horse tranq." Doc Jones shook her head and stood, her gaze narrowing on Keira, who was sitting meekly on the couch. "And you. Don't get me started on you. That shit you put in your body is going to kill you, girl."

"Not if a stray bullet gets me first."

Aiden turned to tell Keira not to joke like that, but Doc Jones boomed out a laugh. "At least you've got your sense of humor." She packed up her stuff and headed for the door, pausing next to Keira. "Eat something, girl. Suicide, whether it's fast or slow, is the coward's choice. Find something to live for." Then she was gone, the door shutting softly behind her.

Keira barely waited for her heavy footsteps to disappear down the hallway before she jumped up. "I need a hit like nobody's business." Then she was gone as well, though her exit was much quieter.

Alone at last, Aiden finally moved to crouch in front of Charlie. She didn't say anything as he took her hands and extended her arms, turning them this way and that, examining Doc Jones's bandage job. It was impeccable, as always. "How are you doing?"

"Terrible." She sighed. "It's been a while since I was in the middle of a crisis like that. I forgot how hard the adrenaline spike is afterwards."

There were half a dozen things he needed to be doing right now, starting with having Liam smooth things over with the Boston PD, but he didn't give a damn. She was hurting and shaky, and he wanted to be the one to hold her until it passed. "Let's get up to our room. I have one call to make and then I can help you get settled in." His men deserved that much.

Aiden would figure out if the Eldridges were responsible, and if they were, he'd make them pay. That was his job. He took no joy in it. This shit never ended. Even as he took steps to secure their future safety, some other threat would come along and pull the rug out from beneath his feet.

There were several smaller organizations who weren't too keen on the hold the O'Malleys had over central Boston, but this drive-by was a bold move. Colm Sheridan's massacre of the MacNamara family was the stuff of nightmares, and no one was willing to push either the O'Malleys or the Hallorans hard enough to risk an outcome on that level.

No, the Eldridges were the only ones crazy enough to attack this boldly.

He put that all on the back burner, to think about after he got Charlie relaxed enough to sleep. He stood, letting go of one of her hands but maintaining his grip on the other. "Are you hungry?"

"No."

He'd still call and have some food brought up—something that would go easy on an upset stomach and would keep overnight. She might not be hungry now, but in an hour that could change. If she managed to sleep, she'd definitely wake up hungry.

She must have seen something on his face, because she gave a wry smile. "You're something of a mother hen."

"I'm worried about you. Let me fuss."

They made it back to his room without running into anyone, a small miracle, and he locked the door for good measure. "Sit. I'll grab you some clothes."

It was a token of how shaken up she was that she actually did what he told her instead of insisting she was capable of doing it herself. He headed for the bathroom to grab a washcloth to finish cleaning off the blood, then paused in the doorway. Charlie looked so small sitting on the end of his bed, her head bowed and her shoulders shaking, just a little.

He didn't know how to do this. Aiden was the sword and shield that stood between his family and the rest of the world. He wasn't a nurturer. It was so much easier to fight than it was to comfort.

For Charlie, he'd learn. "I'll take care of you, bright eyes. I promise."

CHAPTER NINETEEN

Charlie knew better than to dwell on what-if. What-if didn't matter. What could have happened was irrelevant. What *did* happen was all that mattered. At least in theory.

The truth was that she kept replaying the drive-by and counting down the seconds from when Keira ran into the room until the bullets pierced the glass in the same spot they'd been sitting. Thirty, maybe thirty-five. Not even a full minute's difference between life and death.

You're okay. You're all okay. That's all that matters.

It didn't seem like it. She should have known there was danger. Hadn't she just told Aiden that very thing last night? And then she just waltzed out to lunch and picked a table near a window, as if that danger was all in her head. Stupid. Very, very stupid.

"Charlie." Aiden sat next to her on the bed, a washcloth in his hands. He tipped her chin up and slowly ran it over her face. "Talk to me."

Words bubbled up, pressing against the back of her lips, despite the fact that she wasn't usually a sharer. Apparently, two years out of commission was all it took for that hard-won training to disappear like it'd never existed. "It was close. Too close. If Keira hadn't come back when she did..." She shuddered. "I'm sorry. I'm not usually such a basket case."

He didn't speak until he'd finished with her face and moved on to her shoulders. "Lift your arms." He carefully maneuvered her T-shirt off and threw it in the trash can next to the dresser. "It's okay to be shaken up. *I'm* shaken up. When I saw you in that car, covered in blood"—his hand hitched and then resumed its path along her collarbone— "that scared the shit out of me."

Strangely enough, his admission of fear calmed her. She covered his hand with hers, fighting not to flinch at the pain that shot through her arm. "I'm okay. I've said it, and I'll keep saying it until we both believe it."

Aiden's green eyes still showed concern as he cupped her face with one hand. "You're alive. You're safe now." He kissed her lightly. "I'll keep you safe."

When this man said it, she actually believed him. It was dangerous in a way she wasn't prepared to combat. Charlie needed to be sharp and at the top of her game, and she couldn't do that while standing in Aiden's shadow as he took on the role of protector for her the same way he'd done for everyone else around him—whether they wanted it or not. That wasn't what she'd signed up for, and that wasn't what he needed her to do.

But maybe it would be okay to allow...just for tonight.

He let his hand drop and stood. "You're going to want long sleeves so you don't pull at the bandages."

"Okay." She was more than capable of dressing herself, but if she was going to let him take care of her for tonight, that meant she had to relax enough that she wouldn't fight him every step of the way.

It seemed to make him feel better to fuss—and it *did* make her feel safe, as he'd promised—so she sat there while he found a loose shirt and a pair of sweats—both his—from his dresser. It brought her back to when they'd had sex while she was wearing his shirt and how hot that had made them both. Despite everything that had just happened, her body responded, her thighs clenching and her nipples pebbling.

Aiden turned around and stopped short, his gaze narrowing on her face and then sweeping over her, lingering on her breasts—her nipples easily visible through the lace of her bra—and her thighs pressed together. "Bright eyes..."

"I know." She stood and crossed to him. "It would make me feel really safe if you'd touch me." Charlie went up on her tiptoes and kissed him.

"You're hurt."

"I didn't even need stitches." It had been a close thing, though. She had butterfly bandages on a few of the cuts, but even if they were actual stitches, that wouldn't be enough to keep her from wanting him. "I need you."

She didn't know if there was a single threat under the sun that could keep her from wanting Aiden.

"I don't want to hurt you."

You will, no matter what you do. She didn't say it, just like she didn't say so many things when they were together. All it would do would be to fast-track her heartache. Better to enjoy the time they had to the fullest, and worry about the future when it punched her in the face. "Then be gentle if it will make you feel better."

He inched one eyebrow up. "If it will make *me* feel better? You're being rather accommodating."

Despite everything, she smiled. "Considering I'm about to take advantage of you, yes, I am. Now strip."

"That's my line."

"Then say it." She sat up, careful to keep her expression pain-free, and reached behind her back to undo her bra. It hit the floor, closely followed by her panties. "Oops. Too late."

The worry disappeared from his face, leaving heat in its wake. "Damn it, bright eyes, you're making it hard to do right by you."

That was the thing. She didn't *want* him to do right by her. Her definition of what that entailed and his differed greatly, and she wasn't about to give him reason to cut her free any sooner than absolutely necessary. "Then just do me."

Aiden barked out a laugh. "Do you? For Christ's sake, Charlie, where do you come up with this shit?"

He was trying to get the control to talk her out of it. She could see it on his face. Aiden wanted to take care of her, and as attractive as she found the prospect, if she let him steamroll her right now, she knew he'd try to keep her out of things in the future in order to keep her safe. Like hell was she going to let him.

Charlie gave him a sweet smile. "That's okay. You don't have to do me."

"Now that we've got that—"

"I'll just do myself." She climbed further onto the bed, knowing damn well that he was watching every move she made, and that his eyes were glued to her ass. She rolled onto her back and ran her hands over her breasts. "Mmm."

A muscle in his jaw jumped. "You're playing with fire."'

In more ways than one. "No, I'm playing with myself." She slipped a hand between her thighs and stroked her clit. She wasn't quite primed yet, but it wouldn't take long with his stare heating her skin. She watched him through half-closed eyes. *He looks like he wants to fuck me into submission.* He had his arms crossed tightly, as if clinging to the last shreds of his control. *We'll have to do something about that.* If he was willing to let himself off the leash now, when she was at her weakest, then he'd be more willing to trust her to do what needed to be done when the time came.

She just needed to push him over the edge and into a free fall.

She spread her legs wider and circled a finger around her opening. It felt good, so she did it again, letting loose a breathless little moan.

The only warning she got was the slightest dip in the mattress, and then Aiden was on top of her. "Goddamn it, bright eyes." He kissed her, thrusting his tongue into her mouth. She tangled her tongue with his, but he didn't give her a chance to sink into the sensation. Aiden pushed himself up onto his hands, his green eyes thunderous. "Arms above your head."

She considered arguing, but she was getting what she wanted. Charlie reached up to grab the headboard with a laugh. "Okay."

He didn't look amused. "I refuse to fucking hurt you, so you will keep your damn hands there until we're through. Understand?"

"I understand."

"Good." He reached between her legs, picking up where she left off. There was no teasing tonight, no playing with her until she begged for him. Aiden had her barreling toward an orgasm with the speed of a freight train, driven by something she didn't have a name for. She came between one breath and the next, her back bowing, a small helpless sound escaping her mouth.

He shifted enough to dig through the nightstand for a condom. As he rolled it on, he looked like a man possessed. Maybe he was as desperate to escape what-if as she was. She hadn't died. She was okay. She was safe. But they both needed the physical connection of sex to prove it.

He speared her with his fingers once, twice, a third time. And then his cock was pushing into her, filling her completely. She wrapped her legs around his waist, holding him in the only way he'd allow right now, while he thrust into her and wedged one arm beneath her hips to force them closer yet. He slid the other arm up her spine to cup the back of her neck. "Don't ever do anything like that again."

She kissed him because she understood what he meant— she'd felt the same thing less than twenty-four hours ago. He met her with tongue and teeth, driving into her even as he plundered her mouth. Like he couldn't get enough. Like maybe he'd never get enough.

Charlie already knew that Aiden O'Malley had ruined her, but the moment he came, with her name on his lips, she could have cried. She blinked back the threat of tears, determined not to show how affected she was. No matter what he said, no matter how good it was between them, they had an expiration date. She held him, shaking now from her own orgasm, and murmured, "I'm okay. It's okay." Over and over again.

Finally, Aiden lifted his head and pressed a devastatingly sweet kiss on her lips. He didn't say anything, but there was nothing more to say. They were alive. They'd made it another day. They would continue to move forward with their plan, because they had no other options.

Charlie's heart gave a painful lurch. The end was in sight. It might not be today, or tomorrow, or even next week, but the writing was on the wall.

She and Aiden wouldn't last the month.

For better or worse, it would be over by then.

* * *

Aiden stared down at the two dead men. Ben and Donovan. Both had worked for the family for years, and they'd deserved better than to be gunned down in the street. He was ashamed that he didn't know more about them than their names. He didn't know if they'd left families behind. Partners. Children. Fucking pets.

Liam stepped up to stand at his shoulder. As always, he knew what Aiden was thinking. "They were both single. They both were loyal, and you treated them both with respect. This isn't the way that I would have chosen for their lives to end, but it's not as bad as it could be."

That didn't make him feel better. He didn't think it made Liam feel better, either. Aiden stepped back from the bodies and rubbed a hand over his face. "What the fuck are we doing?"

"This is the price sometimes."

But what was the gain? Power? They had a shit-ton. Money? More than he could spend in a lifetime. All they did was breed enemies and get people they cared about killed. Maybe it was the last couple years taking their toll, but he wasn't sure if he saw the point anymore.

He couldn't do anything about that. He couldn't even

fucking *say* that. There was no one else, and the problem that Romanov presented—taking him out would open the door for someone even bigger and badder—also applied to the O'Malleys. If they suddenly were to step back and go legit, it was all but guaranteed that the next power player to move into their position would be even more a monster than Aiden felt like.

It was equally likely that whoever that player was would come after them, if only to ensure that they wouldn't try to get back into the game.

No, there were no other options but to continue forward, bearing the price and doing whatever it took to guarantee that they stayed in power—stayed as safe as anyone could be in this life.

He turned away from the dead men. "This doesn't read like Romanov." As much as he'd like to lay the whole damn problem at the Russian's feet, it didn't line up.

"No, it doesn't." Liam fell into step next to him as they walked up the stairs to the garage. "How sure are you of the Eldridges?"

"Not sure enough." He scrubbed a hand over his face. "Fuck, this is my fault, isn't it?" He should have just left well enough alone, or gone after Romanov himself instead of putting together a plan that involved far too many wild cards. He couldn't control Alethea. *That* was abundantly clear.

"You didn't order a hit on your woman and sisters." Liam shook his head. "Don't go taking this on, too. You know damn well that we can't predict every move every enemy will make."

He did know that. It didn't make it any easier to bear. "I should have known she'd go after the women." That was what bothered him the most about the situation. There was a time when even the most twisted of enemies would hesitate to strike out against the women and children of a family, but it appeared they were long past it. If he was being honest, they'd been past it for a very long time now.

But Alethea *was* a woman. She wouldn't have that same code.

Aiden stepped forward to grab the door and open it. "I would have predicted that she'd at least have waited until she took out Romanov to start looking to remove the other competition."

A mistake they'd both made. Maybe if he'd consulted with Carrigan, she would have had better insight on the way Alethea's mind worked. But he hadn't.

Something else I needed to change... and now have an opportunity to do so because of Charlie.

"The question is how you're going to respond."

He followed Liam out into the night. They climbed a second set of stairs to the porch situated at the back of the house. Most of the family ignored it, preferring to either be inside or completely out of the house, but he and Liam had spent quite a few evenings out here, sharing a beer and just sitting in silence.

Silence wasn't an option tonight. They needed a plan for moving forward. "What's my father been up to today?" He hadn't seen much of Seamus, which wasn't comforting in the least. The man was up to something, and hell if he could figure out what it was.

Everyone in his fucking family seemed to be up to something these days.

"He's been in meetings with the gunrunners. I don't know where he's planning on sending the shipment he's currently negotiating."

"Find out." He needed to cut that shit off at the knees. Aiden hadn't really expected his father to back off just because they'd exchanged words, but it appeared Seamus was more than happy to use his current distraction to undermine him. He couldn't allow it to happen, no matter what else was going on.

They were only as strong as their foundation, and infighting would weaken the family at a time when they needed their strength the most.

"We need proof that it was the Eldridges. Once we have that, I'll make my move." He just needed to figure out what his move was going to be. He stood before an impossible choice. If he didn't strike back after an attack like that, it would be a weakness his enemies would want to exploit. If he did, he ran the risk of screwing up his plans.

His original plan to set the Eldridges on Romanov and Romanov on the Eldridges was all well and good, but he couldn't allow Romanov to fight his battles.

Or James Halloran, for that matter.

Fuck.

He pulled out his phone, cursing himself for not thinking of it sooner, and dialed James. He had the man's number out of sheer necessity, though he hadn't had cause to use it up to this point. It rang until he was sure it would click over to voicemail, and then a surly voice answered. "What do you want?"

There was no reason to mince words. James wouldn't take it well if he tried to manipulate him. His only option was blunt honesty. "That attack was against Charlie and Keira, not Carrigan. I want you to stay out of it."

"Too fucking bad. She has three sets of stitches and she's cut all to hell. If your woman hadn't reacted when she did,

Carrigan would be dead. So don't try to start a pissing contest with me, Aiden. You know who's responsible? You had better fucking tell me, or *you* will be next on my list."

He closed his eyes, praying for patience. "I'm glad my sister is okay. But her being there changes nothing."

"What would you do in my position?"

He wanted to lie, to tell whatever convenient truth he could come up with to get James to stay out of it. He couldn't. "I'd do exactly what I'm planning on doing and make an example of this piece of shit so that no one comes gunning for my fiancée or my sisters again."

"Exactly." James hesitated and then grudgingly said, "I'm willing to hold off and work together since our purposes line up. That's as far as you can push it. Don't fucking cut me out of this."

Fuck. He considered his options. There really weren't any. James would move forward on his own if he didn't agree to these terms, and they'd likely be stumbling over each other in their effort to get to the Eldridges—or whoever was responsible—which would weaken them both. "Fine. Don't move until I contact you."

"Your sister wants you at that fundraiser tomorrow night. Don't fuck this up, Aiden. You keep saying that you're not your old man—now's the time to prove it."

He'd totally forgotten Carrigan's comment about the fundraiser. It couldn't be worse timing. He opened his mouth to say exactly that, but the image of Charlie's face imprinted itself on the back of his eyelids. *A chance to fix things.* "We'll be there."

"Good." James hung up.

"That went well."

Liam snorted. "It sounds like it. Can you blame him?"

"No, but the situation just gets more twisted the further into it we are. The last thing we need is more complications." The words were barely out of his mouth when his phone started ringing. He stared at it. "Check the porch for bugs. Now."

As Liam moved to obey, he answered. "It's awful late for a chat, Dmitri."

"And yet you're awake."

He stood and stalked around the perimeter of the porch. "Our next meeting isn't for several days. Why are you calling?"

"You know why."

Yeah, he did. "If you had a warning about the attack, you should have warned me instead of Keira."

"That unnecessary step would have wasted time the women didn't have."

He couldn't argue that point, no matter how much he wanted to. It was entirely too easy to lay every single sin he could think of at Romanov's feet, but the unfortunate truth was that the man had moved to protect Keira in the most efficient way possible. "There had to be a better way." A way that didn't include Charlie and Carrigan getting cut all to hell as bullets whizzed over their heads.

"How shall we deal with the responsible party?"

Should have seen that coming from a mile away. It struck him for the first time that there were fiancées from the O'Malleys, the Hallorans, *and* Romanov in that restaurant. If Dmitri hadn't sounded warning, that would have been a blow that every single one of them would have had a hell of a time coming back from—if there was any coming back from it at all. Aiden's chest tightened painfully again at the thought of Charlie sharing the same fate as

Devlin. "Prove it's the Eldridges—with evidence—and I'll take care of it."

"Unfortunately for both of us—and James Halloran, I imagine—I'm not handing over that information unless you give your word that we will cooperate in bringing down our mutual enemy."

"No. Our alliance doesn't cover this, and you damn well know it."

Dmitri sighed, as if Aiden had disappointed him. "That is the wrong answer."

Frustration had his control cracking and his mouth getting away from him. "What the fuck do you even care? Keira is merely a means to an end. I'm sure you have other women lined up if that falls through." A man in Dmitri's position—*Aiden's* position—had his pick of political hopefuls who wanted to marry off their daughters to accrue more power for their families. No one was quite on the O'Malleys' level, but there were other players in New York who would fall all over themselves to step in if Dmitri so much as crooked a finger at them.

"Your lack of understanding doesn't change the fact—if you want the information, you will loop me into whatever retribution you have planned."

He could find the information on his own given enough time, but it presented the same problem he'd run into with James. Aiden stepped to the side as Liam came back to the porch with a handheld device that he promptly ran over every piece of furniture they had out there, before turning it to the deck itself. He cursed and lifted a chair to yank something off the bottom. *I knew the timing of his call was too convenient.*

Aiden watched with satisfaction as Liam crushed the

surveillance device under his heel. "Do not bug my house again."

"I make no promises. How can I expect to know when you're planning things if you refuse to call me and inform me when *my* fiancée is involved as well? What is your answer?"

There was no choice, as much as he hated to admit it. "Fine. You're in."

"Delightful. We'll meet in neutral territory. I trust you'll ensure that James Halloran minds his manners." Dmitri ended the call.

Aiden leaned against the railing and glared out into the night, wondering where the fuck he'd gone wrong. He was supposed to be orchestrating the downfall of Romanov to ensure that he didn't end up actually marrying Keira, and yet here he was, working with him *again* to bring down a common enemy.

The world had gone topsy-turvy when he wasn't looking. He felt like he was moving through a foreign land without a map or compass. It didn't matter. He wouldn't let it.

All that mattered was the bottom line.

CHAPTER TWENTY

Charlie picked at her breakfast, not feeling much like eating. She took a bite of the eggs out of principle. With all the chaos going on, she needed her strength. Waking up alone—*again*—had put her in a foul mood. Add to that the fact that Keira wasn't in her room and Liam wasn't lurking at the bottom of the stairs like she was used to and she felt completely out of place.

The two men who worked in the kitchen took pity on her and threw together a late breakfast, even though it was obvious that they were on the way out the door. Now she sat alone, wishing she'd just gone back to sleep instead of coming downstairs.

Footsteps had her perking up, and for half a second, she thought the man who walked through the door was Aiden. But then his features registered. *Seamus*. She braced herself, but the contempt that appeared in his dark eyes still hit her hard enough that he might as well have reached across the kitchen island and slapped her.

Seamus O'Malley crossed his arms over his chest and looked her up and down—or at what he could see of her upper half. "At least my son has good taste, even if thinking with his dick has put our family in jeopardy."

Even though she knew that was the part she played and a necessary one at that, irritation bloomed. "I happen to like his dick quite a bit. And you've already made your opinion known. Now you're just being mean."

He cocked his head to the side. "What I can't figure out is how you got Liam on board. He's usually the more level-headed of the two, and he won't hear a word spoken against you. Are you fucking him as well?"

Charlie carefully set aside her fork, because if she didn't stop holding it right now, she'd throw it at him. She pushed back her stool and stood. He was the same height as Aiden, so he towered over her, even with the table between them. Every instinct she had screamed not to show Seamus her back. She lifted her chin, refusing to let him intimidate her. "If I *was* fucking him, it wouldn't be any of your business."

"Wrong, girl. Anything and everything that happens in this house—with my children or my men—is my business."

She widened her eyes and pressed a hand to her chest. "Your men? Oh my God, I'm sorry. I didn't know Liam's dick had your name tattooed across it."

She expected him to come at her. Most straight men with anger issues couldn't stand even the slightest homoerotic accusation leveled at them.

Seamus surprised her, though. He raised his eyebrows in an expression that almost perfectly mirrored the one Aiden had given her just hours before. The similarity made her skin crawl. He shook his head. "You aren't doing yourself, or my son, any favors by continuing this charade. You can't make it in this life—your temper is going to get you both into hot water, and it's *Aiden* who will have to get you out again." He reached into his jacket. "How much?"

"Excuse me?" She was still trying to process the lightning-fast change in his demeanor, and it took his pulling out a pen for her to understand what he meant. "You can't pay me off."

"I think we both know that's not true." He opened his checkbook. "A hundred thousand should be enough, don't you think?" Seamus glanced at her. "Don't look like I just kicked your puppy, girl. You might love fucking my son, but you don't love him. Anyone with eyes can see that. Take the money and get something better than a bullet for your troubles."

She swallowed past a suddenly dry throat. This conversation was like barreling down a winding road in the middle of the night with no headlights. "Are you threatening me?"

"I don't have to. Someone else already has your number, don't they? Neither of my daughters have been attacked in over a year, and you come along and, within days, there's a drive-by. Coincidence? I think we both know it's not."

"We both seem to know a whole lot, according to you."

He frowned. "I don't understand why you're being difficult. Do you need more money?" He appeared to do some quick math in his head. "I can offer you a million, but not a penny more."

Charlie stared. "You... You're offering me a *million* dollars to break up with your son. That's insane."

"Insanity would be not taking it." He straightened, replaced the checkbook, and adjusted his jacket. "I can see that you need some time to mull it over. The offer stands." He turned around and walked out of the kitchen, leaving her to stare after him and wonder what kind of rabbit hole she'd fallen down.

People didn't *do* that. They didn't offer to pay money to break up a couple they didn't approve of. That was so crazy, she didn't know how to put it into words.

Even worse was the tiny traitorous voice inside her whispering that this thing with Aiden wasn't for real, so there shouldn't be anything wrong if she decided to take the money and run.

Except there would be everything wrong with it.

She hadn't agreed to this because of money. She did it because she wanted justice done. Or vengeance. Or both. At this point, she'd settle for Dmitri Romanov being taken out of the equation in any way.

The problem was that things had ceased to be that simple almost immediately. She liked Aiden. She admired his strength in the face of impossible odds. She liked his sense of humor, which she'd only gotten glimpses of before last night. She liked how he made her feel...safe...even though she'd never been in more danger than in the last week and a half.

Charlie couldn't remember the last time she'd felt safe.

The fact that she'd been shot at should negate that feeling. Not to mention Aiden's many masks. He actively manipulated the people around him by using their expectations of him against them. As much as she wanted to believe that he dropped the mask around her, Charlie couldn't be 100 percent sure of it. He told her to trust her instincts, but her instincts hadn't told her that men she'd considered brothers were dirty cops. They hadn't told her that her father would turn against her.

They hadn't told her that she'd go and fall for Aiden O'Malley, a man who should be the enemy.

But he was so much more than the coldly calculating crime lord that she'd first met. He had a bone-deep honor that might not fit with society's standard, but it functioned in the world he moved within. He loved his siblings, despite occasionally making decisions that hurt them—his bottom line to always keep them protected. It was for that love and responsibility that he'd stepped into his father's place as head of the family.

Who would have thought that Aiden would have more loyalty than both Charlie's father and her brothers-in-arms?

She didn't want to let him go. Not yet.

The mindless work of rinsing off her dishes in the sink did nothing to settle the feeling inside her, like one step wrong would send her hurtling off a cliff. She felt guilty for even considering taking the money. She was supposed to be the righteous one, and she was just as fallible as anyone else when push came to shove.

It wasn't a comfortable thought.

She turned around and went still. "How much did you hear?"

"It's a good deal." Aiden stood in the exact same spot that his father had just a few minutes earlier, though the icy feeling his father managed to project was nowhere to be found. He looked calm—too calm. "A million dollars to end a relationship that wasn't real to begin with."

Hearing her treacherous thoughts come out of his mouth hurt. A lot. Charlie started to wrap her arms around herself but stopped the motion halfway through. This wasn't who she was—this weak woman who went with the flow and didn't dare stand against the current. It used to be that she saw what she wanted, and God help anyone who tried to stand between her and her goal. Everything she'd staked her

life on—that Justice saw in black and white, and the good
guys always won—had proved to be false, and reality had
almost broken her. She survived, but she'd lost part of herself in the process.

I want to be that woman again.

I want Aiden.

She walked slowly to him, studying his face like her
very life depended on it. *Too calm.* No expression showed,
though he looked like he was holding his breath while waiting for her response. *He doesn't want this to end any more
than I do.* She wanted to believe that was the truth and not
just another mask, but she was terrified she was wrong.

"It's a good deal." She stopped in front of him, close
enough that it would be the simplest thing in the world
to slip her arms around his neck and press against him.
"Though I'm inclined to tell your father to fuck right off.
Unless you want me to take it."

He stepped into her, pulling her against him. "Fuck no, I
don't want you to take that deal. I want you to stay." Aiden
gently touched her bandaged arms. "Though you'd be safer
accepting that money and getting the hell out of Boston—
and New York."

"Maybe." But maybe not. There were a lot of things to
fear from the world if someone looked closely enough, and
she'd spent most of her adult life doing exactly that. The
crime statistics in most major cities were enough to keep a
person up at night.

She laid her head on Aiden's shoulder and inhaled the
clean woodsy scent of him. She had no business feeling safe
in his arms, but that didn't stop the sensation from curling
around her again. "We'll figure it out."

"Charlie . . ." He kissed the top of her head. "You're right.

I've already set some things in motion to figure out who the responsible party is. It'll be taken care of."

It'll be taken care of. Those words could only mean one thing.

Aiden wasn't going to hunt down the evidence and call the cops. He was going to deal with it outside the law. *The same way we're dealing with Dmitri Romanov.* She took a shuddering breath. Crime statistics aside, she was lying to herself if she said that things were the same here as they were in the rest of the country. Boston might have law enforcement and lawyers and judges, but none of those people played a part in dealing with enemies on O'Malley territory.

She shivered. Right now was her opportunity to suggest he try something new—like actually calling the cops—but when she opened her mouth, that wasn't what came out. "Okay."

"Trust me, bright eyes." He tipped up her chin and kissed her. "I'll keep you safe."

God help her, but she actually believed him.

* * *

Aiden found his father sitting with his mother in the library. He stopped in the door, struck by the fact that they looked *old*. Rationally, he knew they were almost sixty, but there had always been something ageless about both of them. *The events of the last few years would be enough to age anyone.* Even Aiden had new lines around his eyes that had never been there before.

His mother looked up and smiled. "Aiden." She stood, and he crossed the room to give her a hug.

"Mother." It was probably better that they were both here

for this, because he didn't doubt that his mother was capable of pulling the same shit Seamus had earlier. "Father."

Seamus hadn't stood, and he didn't do more than nod now. "I trust you're not going to do something stupid."

"Stupid like offering my fiancée a million dollars to break off the engagement?"

Aileen turned to Seamus. "A million dollars? Are you insane?"

"She made a tough bargain."

Aiden's control snapped at its leash, but he fought back the anger as best he could. Punching his father in the face might feel satisfying in the moment, but ultimately it would cause more problems than it solved. So he sat down on the couch across from his parents with a perfectly contained demeanor. "You haven't been in Boston for over a year—either of you. I don't fault you the need to get away, but the fact remains that I've been running the O'Malley enterprises in the meantime. Though you seem to be under the impression that I'm going to ruin everything, the world hasn't ended in your absence. Coming back here to resume control is out of the question. Meeting with gunrunners behind my back is out of the question. You're putting our men in a hard situation, and this push and pull for leadership is going to get our people killed."

Seamus lifted a single eyebrow. "Which is why you should step aside immediately."

Aiden gritted his teeth. "Which is why you will go back to your early retirement in Connecticut."

"Son, you know damn well that's not going to happen." His father leaned back and crossed his ankles. "You mishandled the Romanov situation. We've dealt with that Russian bastard time and time again, and nothing we've done has made the slightest impact on him. It's time to face the fact that he's a bigger fish than we are."

The sheer lack of trust in Aiden made him see red. He'd successfully managed Romanov for well over a year, holding him off until things were in place to move. He hadn't done that by being a fucking coward. "Sacrificing Keira is not the answer."

His mother touched Seamus's leg and leaned toward Aiden. "Have you asked your sister what she wants?"

He didn't have to. Aiden already knew what Keira would say. He'd seen her face the night Romanov sent his delightful little note with the ultimatum in it. A year wouldn't have changed how his sister felt about the entire thing. "She'll marry him just to end it." That was why he'd fought so hard to allow her the ability to choose—*truly* choose—without the threat of potential war hanging over her head.

"That's her choice."

He stared at his mother. "You've got to be joking. Her *choice*? You didn't give Carrigan a choice when you were going to shove her out the door and down the aisle to that monster. You would have done the same fucking thing to Sloan if she didn't disappear."

"If Carrigan had done her duty, none of this would be happening." Seamus pushed Aileen's hand away. "Don't shush me, woman. You know I'm right. Keira's a good girl, and she's going to do what her older sisters failed to."

Aiden shook his head. "Keira is an *addict*. She sees Romanov as just another form of killing herself, the same way she's been killing herself since Devlin died."

"*Aiden.*"

"It's the goddamn truth." He'd already talked to Liam before this meeting and figured out who on the staff would be a problem if it came to forcing his father out. There were surprisingly few of them. Most of his men had made the transition with him the week Seamus left. To have his father randomly show up and try to assume control was making everyone edgy. They might back Aiden if push came to shove, but he wanted to avoid putting them in that situation if at all possible.

Aiden stood and buttoned his suit jacket. "You will abide by my wishes in this, or you will be removed from the house. For now, we'll move forward with planning the wedding, but it's ultimately *my* decision with how that proceeds. Do you understand?"

Seamus's face turned a mottled red that couldn't be good for his blood pressure. "Crossing me is a mistake."

Almost definitely. But the alternative—letting his father ruin the plans that had been over a year in the making— wasn't much of an alternative at all. So he didn't let his turmoil show on his face. "Do. You. Understand?"

"Oh, I understand all right."

"And, Father? Stay the fuck away from Charlie. I'm marrying her, and if you corner her again, I'll consider you an enemy and move forward appropriately." He turned away and strode out of the room, leaving his father sputtering behind him.

It brought Aiden no satisfaction, but if he didn't do something about his father trying to drive off Charlie now, he was afraid that she'd disappear and they'd find her body in the river. That was the normal escalation of things—a sly payoff, something to scare her into doing what he wanted, and then an untimely death.

I can't lose her.

He barely allowed himself to articulate the thought. He was already going to lose her, if not because of their arrangement expiring, then because he seemed to be getting in deeper with Romanov by the minute. *Or maybe I'll lose her when she figures out that I'm using her to blackmail her father.* He was in a tangled web of his own making, and he hadn't anticipated it getting so complicated so fast.

It would be easier if he didn't care about her—if it was just sex.

He could barely be in the same room with her without wanting to drag her off somewhere private and slake their mutual desire. He admired her strength. She'd been to hell and back, and it hadn't broken her. And there was the fact that she slid almost seamlessly into his life here. She didn't blink at facing down Romanov or the Eldridges, or even his father. Her courage scared the shit out of him. But knowing she could take care of herself only heightened his attraction.

And there was the fact that she pushed him to mend fences with his siblings. Keira actually looked like something resembling healthy since Charlie had moved into the house. Carrigan had invited them to an event, which was an olive branch if he ever saw one. Give Charlie another week and she'd have him sitting down to dinner with Teague and doing his damnedest to forgive his middle brother.

He . . . *cared* about her.

He wanted to wrap her up and send her away to somewhere safe until this was all over. Fuck, he wanted to keep her safe *forever*. To stand between her and the world so she never had to be hurt again.

It wasn't possible, even if she'd let him. He needed her here, and so he'd ride this out to the bitter end and see where all the pieces fell.

He just hoped like hell that they'd both still be standing at the end of it.

CHAPTER TWENTY-ONE

Charlie did her best not to clutch Aiden's arm as they walked up the steps to the hotel where Carrigan and James were holding their fundraiser. The last twenty-four hours had been a whirlwind of activity, and though Charlie had fully expected not to see Aiden for most of it, he checked in with her several times throughout the day.

He covered her hand with his. "We don't have to do this if you don't feel up to it."

"I'm fine." She felt like she'd been hit by a car, and her arms ached fiercely, but it was the truth. Plus, she got the feeling that he was just as off-center about the night as she was. Allied or not, his relationship with Carrigan was problematic at best. They obviously loved each other, and just as obviously had been close once, but Aiden had been genuinely surprised by the invitation to tonight's charity dinner.

She'd have to be way more banged up to be the reason he skipped it.

Charlie squeezed his arm. "Everything will be fine."

"I know." He held the door open for her, and they checked their coats. Aiden stopped and grinned. "Bright eyes, you've outdone yourself."

"This old thing?" Charlie smoothed her hands down the deep purple dress she'd chosen for tonight. Really, it was the only option, since it had long sleeves, which would cover her arm bandages. But she loved it all the same. The high neckline cut across her collarbone and created sharp points off her shoulders, and the back dipped all the way down to the base of her spine.

He circled her, his green eyes intense. "If we make it through the night without my dragging you to a room upstairs, it will be a goddamn miracle."

She licked her lips. Under his gaze, her body flashed hot, as if he'd reached out and touched her. "How much time do we have?"

"There you are!"

Aiden's expression shuttered. "Not enough, apparently." He moved to her side and pressed his hand to the small of her bare back as they turned to face Carrigan.

She looked absolutely stunning. She wore a black dress with long sleeves, though hers left her shoulders bare. It hugged every curve and was just shy of being too short for respectable company, even with her black tights. Paired with her wild dark hair and berry lipstick and she was a showstopper.

Carrigan came in and gave Charlie's cheek an air-kiss. She raised her eyebrows. "Look at us, practically twins."

"Carrigan."

She ignored the warning in Aiden's tone and carefully looped her arm through Charlie's. "Since we're friends now,

I think it's best we pretend all of that nasty business with my calling you a gold-digging whore never happened."

"How charitable."

She laughed. "Yes, well, James had some strong words about the whole situation, as I'm sure you can imagine."

"Aiden and I had the same...talk." She glanced over her shoulder to find him a few steps back. He didn't look particularly happy to be there, but even as she watched, his expression smoothed out and a practiced smile took the place of irritation. If Charlie hadn't been paying such close attention, she would have missed the transition entirely.

Carrigan led the way to a circular table near the front of the room. "This is a plated dinner, so you don't have to deal with any of the silent auction nonsense that we sometimes do."

When Aiden mentioned that his sister was married to James Halloran, Charlie had pictured a life...well, a life more like she imagined Dmitri or Aiden had. Out of the spotlight and in the shadows.

Apparently, she couldn't have been more wrong.

There were people in this room who populated both the local and national news cycles, and even a handful of major celebrities. She turned to Carrigan with renewed interest. "What is the money from this dinner going to?"

"Aiden didn't tell you?" Some of the sharpness bled out of the way she held herself, and her smile turned downright soft. "This money goes to fund housing, education, and various needs of women and children who were victims of sex trafficking. If they don't have a home to go back to, or don't *want* to go back, we do our best to give them the tools they need to support themselves and have what passes for a well-adjusted life."

Charlie considered her. "You do other things to combat sex trafficking, don't you?" *Illegal* things.

"I could tell you, but...you know." Carrigan raised a finger to her lips, her green eyes amused. "Don't get it into your head that we're superheroes or any of that bullshit. I just hate the fuckers who deal in the flesh trade, and I'll do whatever it takes to see their businesses ground to dust."

Sex trafficking was one of the biggest world trades, and modern times hadn't slowed down the numbers any. It was also one of the most frustrating elements of working for law enforcement—as soon as they arrested one sex-trafficking cell, two more popped up, and the original cell often ended up maneuvering out of the charges. It was a lesson in insanity and frustration, made worse by the fact that innocent women and children were suffering as a result.

Charlie stopped next to the chair with her name on it. "Do you think we could talk frankly about it at some point?" She wanted to know what, exactly, Carrigan and James were doing, and what kind of difference they might be making without the red tape of the law holding them back. The possibilities sent a thrill of excitement through her.

"Sure. I've got some free time next week if you want to talk the down and dirty planning of it. I can't show you everything, of course, but I can speak in broad strokes."

"I'd like that."

. "Carrigan."

Charlie jumped, having been so focused on Carrigan that she temporarily forgot Aiden was behind them. She slid out of the woman's grasp and moved to his side, offering him silent support. The siblings faced off, and the light disappeared from Carrigan's eyes. She gave him a mocking smile. "Aiden."

"Don't do that." He stepped closer and kept his voice low enough that the people milling around wouldn't be able to hear without actively trying to eavesdrop.

Charlie had every intention of giving them their privacy, but Aiden's hand against her back kept her in place. The tension in his fingers wasn't apparent in the rest of his body, which just went to show how locked down he had himself.

He pressed his lips together and then sighed. "I'm sorry."

"You'll have to be more specific."

"I'm sorry that I made the call I did about Romanov. It was fucked, and I was wrong."

From the shock on Carrigan's face, this was the first time Aiden had said any of this. She recovered quickly, though. "You know, it's funny."

"What's that?"

"I really did you a favor by telling you and Seamus to fuck off. The balance of power in Boston is stable for the first time in a few generations."

"I know."

She did a double take. "What?"

"Did you know Seamus ordered me to drag your ass back to the house about a week after he changed his mind about letting you go?" Aiden shook his head. "I told him no. I might not like that big blond bastard of yours, but the fact remains that you two have changed the Hallorans—and our relationship with them. Devlin would have been proud."

The "blond bastard" in question appeared behind Carrigan as if by magic. He wrapped an arm around her waist, which was when Charlie realized Carrigan was shaking. *Damn it, I should have noticed before.* Though it wasn't as if Carrigan would have allowed her to offer comfort.

James shot them a look that wasn't entirely friendly. "I think you should leave."

"No, it's okay." Carrigan leaned back against him. "It's just family business—mending fences and all that. Can't fix things without reopening a wound or two."

"Bullshit."

She lightly smacked his arm. "You're being overprotective, and I think my injuries must have gone to my head, because I'm actually enjoying it." She turned her attention back to Aiden and Charlie. "Enjoy dinner. And...Aiden." She hesitated. "I hear what you're saying. I'm not going to pretend either of us can wave a magic wand and fix shit, but I'm willing to try if you are."

Charlie didn't think he breathed for a full ten seconds. "I'd like that."

"Good." She nodded. "And if you're really serious about mending fences, this is your chance to do it right."

She followed Carrigan's gaze and found Teague and Callista moving through the crowd toward them. *Things are about to get interesting.*

* * *

It felt like a fucking ambush. Aiden had come here tonight intending to start to set things right with Carrigan. No one had said a goddamn thing about Teague being here. When Callie latched on to Charlie and switched seats so that he was next to his brother and the women were occupied, he knew it for a fact. "You planned this shit."

Teague set down the beer he'd carried over. "You've been dodging my calls."

"I've been busy." He hadn't been ready to pull the figurative trigger when it came to dealing with his brother's betrayal. But it had to be done, and thanks to his slip a year ago, Teague knew that *Aiden* knew. They'd been circling each other ever since.

"That's bullshit, and you know it." Teague's body language was relaxed and his face open, so anyone watching them would have no idea the intensity of their conversation.

When had his little brother learned to lie so well?

Aiden cast a glance around. Most people were starting to move to their seats, but the rest of their table was empty for the time being. There was no avoiding this confrontation any longer, even though the last place he wanted to deal with it was here in the middle of such a public place.

Maybe it's for the best. I'm not as likely to punch him in the fucking face.

At least in theory.

"You want to do this here."

Teague nodded. "I never pegged you for a coward, Aiden. Let's get this out and done with so we can move on."

As if it was as easy as that. He laughed, because it was the only acceptable reaction that wouldn't draw undue attention. "You betrayed the family. You informed to the fucking feds." He kept his tone even, because he hadn't given Charlie the details of his falling-out with Teague. She had no idea her father was his brother's contact with the FBI. She *wouldn't* know if Aiden had anything to say about it.

"Yeah. I did."

He stared. He'd half expected Teague to deny it. "That's all you have to say for yourself."

"What the fuck do you want me to say? You know what it was like living in that house under his thumb. You know what our life entails. I didn't see any other way out."

"That's no excuse." He'd felt exactly that trapped more often than not, but he never would have hurt the ones he loved in order to be free.

"I know." Teague scrubbed a hand over his face. "I can't go back and change things. And I *wouldn't*, because that fed is the reason I'm still alive today."

"That's no excuse for feeding him intel that could hurt us."

His smiled grimly. "And yet the O'Malleys still stand and the only person in prison is Victor Halloran." He held up a hand. "There's nothing I can say to fix this. I know it. You know it. I don't expect you to trust me again—but you were never going to, because I'm married to a Sheridan now."

Aiden nodded to concede the truth. Teague's loyalties lay with his wife and their new family. It should be that way. But that didn't erase the sting of the betrayal of his own family...

Aiden sighed, suddenly exhausted. They could keep beating this dead horse until the day they died. That's what Victor Halloran, Colm Sheridan, and their father had done for decades, until no one could pinpoint exactly what it was that had created the conflict in the first place. The only outcome of that path was a whole lot of heartache and, eventually, someone they cared about getting killed. That was how their world worked.

"You know," Teague said suddenly, "we found out this week that Callie's having a boy."

Aiden blinked. "I hadn't heard."

"We aren't exactly announcing it." Teague sat back. "We're going to name him Devlin. I'd like you to be his godfather."

His chest tightened and he couldn't draw a full breath. "Teague—"

"We tried it our father's way. We can sit here and throw stones at each other and keep making the same goddamn mistakes for the next fifty years…Or maybe we can try a different direction."

Ultimately, the future was in Aiden's hands. He could keep pushing this. Teague wouldn't roll over and play dead—not with Callie and Moira and little Devlin on the way—and there was no way everyone would walk unscathed from that confrontation.

Or he could let it go.

Carrigan had given voice to something he'd been mulling over for months. Boston was *stable* for the first time in several generations. Even things with Romanov were at a mild simmer—and could possibly stay that way once they dealt with the Eldridges. Starting shit for the sake of some archaic idea of loyalty to family above all else…

If Seamus had been a different father, their family would have functioned differently. Aiden wasn't prepared to lay the blame fully at his father's feet, but ignoring the part he'd played in the whole thing was idiotic.

He and Teague and Carrigan—and even Sloan—had a chance to heal the wounds of their fathers.

All he had to do was take the olive branch Teague was extending.

He looked over and met Charlie's gaze as she chatted with Callie. He could feel her emotional support even across the distance, and it struck him that if Charlie could still see the good in people after all the terrible shit that had been done directly to her, he was being petty as fuck for even considering letting this peace offering go unmet. He managed what he hoped was a reassuring smile for her and twisted to face Teague again.

The hope in his brother's dark eyes actually hurt to look at.

"I look forward to meeting this godson of mine. Devlin, huh?"

Teague shrugged, though his expression was now full of emotion. Relief. Happiness. Hope. "Devlin was the best of us. It seemed wrong to pick any other name for our son."

"I like it. I think he'd approve." And for the first time in three long years, Aiden actually felt something resembling peace about his younger brother's death. As if a jagged broken piece had slid into place to create something completely new.

This night had been unexpected across the board. He and Teague and Carrigan weren't going to go merrily skipping through a field of daisies—and they might never have the same close relationships that they had before everything went to shit, but...it was a start.

And he had Charlie to thank for it.

On that note, he leaned toward Teague and lowered his voice further. "I'm prepared to put this all behind us, but there's something I need in exchange." Charlie would never forgive him if he had the cops who'd hurt her removed completely, but there was another avenue available. It had the added bonus of tangling up Romanov, but he couldn't pretend that was his motivation as he laid out what he wanted.

When he was through, his brother's gaze skated to Charlie. "Finch's daughter." He shook his head. "And you care about her. You wouldn't be willing to trade in this favor otherwise."

"I care about her." He hesitated, but they were past the point of pride. "I also miss the fuck out of you. This will satisfy both debts." Because he had no illusions about that—if he wanted Charlie to stay, he had to give her a reason beyond outstanding sex. Aiden was who he was, but that didn't mean they couldn't find some kind of compromise.

He just hoped like hell that it wasn't as long a shot as he suspected.

Teague finished his beer. "I would have taken care of it just because you asked."

The possibility of a future working together instead of fighting was enough to make Aiden smile. "Let me know when you have it lined up."

"Will do." Teague set his empty glass down. "I missed the fuck out of you, too. I'm glad we got this figured out."

"Me too." It was one less thing for him to carry around, and strangely enough, trusting his siblings made him feel stronger instead of like he was diluting his power base. Imagine that.

Carrigan stepped onto the stage. She looked perfectly at home as the center of attention, the head of a nonprofit that was doing actual good in the world. His sister was a goddamn inspiration, and it might be worthwhile for Aiden to take a page from her playbook and consider making his corner of the world less shitty for everyone who lived in it. Protecting them was all well and good, but why not take it a step further?

Slow down. Learn to walk before you run.

He had to deal with the threats posed by both Romanov

and the Eldridges before he could do anything else. But maybe, just maybe, he'd find some time to talk to Charlie about what a future would look like if he was more than just a mob boss.

Would it be enough for her to consider staying?

CHAPTER TWENTY-TWO

Dmitri had allowed Aiden and James to agree upon a place to meet, mostly because he was the one holding all the cards. It made no difference if he was in New York or Boston, O'Malley territory or Halloran. They needed him, no matter how much they might hate him, and he would use that to his advantage.

It served a dual purpose, after all.

The anger, which had never quite left him upon receiving news of the attack, spiked. That fool Eldridge woman had no idea what she was unleashing when she went after one of his—after *Keira*. His skin crawled just thinking about her rushing back into that room and danger. He should have known she'd respond like that and approached the whole thing differently, but he hadn't stopped to think and analyze. He'd discovered she was in danger and acted. She could have been killed or seriously injured—because of her connection with him.

Unacceptable.

If Mae Eldridge was going to act like a mad dog, he would put her down like one.

He was too close to finally having Keira. He wasn't going to let some sadistic woman with a chip on her shoulder and a jealous streak a mile wide ruin his plans. He'd already planned on removing the Eldridge family, because their increasingly erratic violence was starting to gain federal attention that no one in New York could afford. It had been strictly business.

No longer.

Now it was personal.

He met Aiden and James at a dingy little bar on the line between their territories, one of those places that seemed to cater to both Hallorans and O'Malleys, depending on the day. Apt.

Dmitri left his man in the car, as previously agreed upon, and strode through the front door. Negotiation was a funny thing. It relied as much on the perception of power as actual power. Slinking through the door as if he was afraid would send a clear message that he was weak and start things off with him at a disadvantage.

It was always better to have enemies and allies alike overestimate his power. Reputation was everything. A man had a strong enough reputation and he'd never have to fight another day in his life. But the slightest scent of weakness, and enemies would come out of the woodwork to nip at his heels. That was what had happened with the Eldridges, and if he didn't deal with them effectively, there would be someone lining up behind them to take a swing at the Romanovs.

Romanovs. I'm the only one left.

James burst into motion the second he caught sight of

Dmitri. He pushed off the bar he'd been leaning on and drew a gun from his shoulder holster in a smooth move. "Give me one good reason why I shouldn't shoot you and put us all out of our misery."

He would pull the trigger if he was smart. Dmitri was a threat that wasn't going away as long as he was alive. Saying as much wasn't in his best interest, though, so he just shrugged. "I have information you need."

"You almost killed both me and Carrigan."

"Carrigan was never in any danger from me." He looked James up and down, comparing what he knew of the man against the woman he'd almost married. "I suppose I understand what she sees in you. You're rather rough around the edges, aren't you?"

James narrowed his blue eyes, his finger hovering on the trigger. "You're a piece of work."

"Guilty as charged." He shouldn't bait Halloran. James had every reason to hate him, and he would have killed the man if his plans had gone as they were supposed to. "Where is your lovely wife? I would have thought she'd be in the middle of this conversation." She hadn't struck him as someone content to sit on the sidelines while her man took care of business.

When James didn't immediately answer, Dmitri laughed. "Did you have to threaten to tie her to a chair? That must have brought back fond memories."

"Stop fucking talking or I'll give you another hole in your head."

Dmitri eyed the tumbler at the bar next to the man. *Likely whiskey.* "Do you have any passable vodka in this place?"

"You do realize I could shoot you right here and there isn't a person in this place who would testify against me."

Apparently, the time for fun and games had passed. Dmitri sighed, already bored. "Yes, you could. Just like I could have had you killed several dozen times over the last two years. I didn't, so let's move along, shall we?"

He felt someone at his back a few seconds before Aiden calmly said, "Put down the gun, James. We need him."

James lowered the gun, but he didn't put it away. He glared over Dmitri's shoulder. "Don't think I've forgotten *your* involvement in this shit storm, O'Malley. You stirred this up, and you put Carrigan in danger because of it. She's willing to forgive that."

James wasn't.

It would have been smarter for Halloran to play this softer. Of the three men in this room, he had the smallest number of resources to bring to the table, since a good portion of his were tied up in the nonprofit Carrigan ran. *Interesting thing, that.*

But then, James Halloran wouldn't know cautious if it smashed him over the back of the head.

Aiden skirted Dmitri, and Dmitri let him do it. When facing down rabid animals, showing fear didn't get a person anywhere but dead—the same rule applied to the Boston Irish. He'd misjudged them during his short time in negotiations over Carrigan with Seamus O'Malley, and Dmitri had been paying the price for that oversight ever since.

He waited for Aiden to take a seat, and then got down to it. "Mae Eldridge is responsible."'

"For fuck's sake, you could have told us that information with a phone call." James downed the glass of amber liquor in front of him.

"I want evidence." Aiden O'Malley didn't so much as blink, but Dmitri hadn't expected him to.

The man was as cold as ice—something he appreciated—except, it seemed, when it came to Charlie Moreaux. There was something about that woman that Dmitri found familiar, but he couldn't place exactly what it was. He had a man working on digging through her history to figure out what she was really doing with Aiden O'Malley, but the drive-by had sidelined that temporarily.

He focused on the two men glaring at him. "Of course." Dmitri pulled out a file that he'd had put together. It wasn't as thick as he would have liked, but it had enough information—and photos—to prove his claim as truth. He strode over to the bar and set the file down, and then retreated to watch their reactions as they flipped through it.

James was furious, as well he should be. Carrigan would have died in that restaurant and Halloran loved her to distraction. A loss like that could kill a man and yet leave his heart beating.

Dmitri had no intention of falling under a woman's spell—not even Keira's. Love was a weakness, no matter what society would have one believe. It offered a bright target for anyone and everyone who had reason to hate him. He wanted Keira, yes, but it was a purely physical thing. If he didn't need an O'Malley to compensate for the blunders with both Carrigan and Olivia, he wouldn't have bothered.

Liar.

He ignored the snide voice inside him with the ease of long practice. Dmitri did his best work by manipulating people around him, and allowing himself to get entangled, emotionally or otherwise, was not in the cards.

Aiden looked over every piece of paper in the file and then closed it. "I assume you have a plan."

"On the contrary—consider myself merely along for the ride."

It was clear neither Aiden nor James liked that idea much, but Aiden shook his head and dropped onto a bar stool several down from Halloran. "If we take out Mae, we might as well declare war on Alethea."

Dmitri considered him. "It will have to be handled carefully. But then, this was always the plan." He smiled. "Why don't you contact that delightful brother-in-law of yours? What was his name? Jude MacNamara?"

Aiden narrowed his eyes. "Jude is out of the game. He's got more important things to focus on."

"How is your little…nephew, was it? You O'Malleys certainly breed like rabbits."

"Watch it, Romanov." Aiden handed him the file. The only indication of anger he gave was a slight clenching of his jaw. "Our alliance only lasts as long as I say it does. Stop dicking around."

"In that case, let's get down to business."

* * *

Charlie looked up from the book she'd picked at random to find Keira humming under her breath, twisting a lock of hair around her finger as she paged through what looked like an art magazine. "Do you draw?"

"Hmm?" Keira flipped another page. "No, I used to paint."

"Used to?" She kept her tone politely interested. Aiden had mentioned that Keira dropped out of art school, but even without that information, Charlie would have put two and two together. There was evidence of art all over Keira's room, though she'd destroyed most of it in one way or another. The fact that she was showing *any* interest in something that had obviously once been very important to her was a big deal.

She flipped another page, still not looking up. "It was a long time ago."

"That's quite the safe, pat little answer."

Finally, Keira looked at her, hazel eyes flashing. "What do you want me to say? If you haven't noticed, my life is pretty shitty these days. You can't paint when you're not inspired. I used to try before I realized it just made me more depressed."

She'd spent enough time around Keira to know she lashed out rather than deal with something painful. It was easier to attack than to try to heal a soul wound. That was probably why she and Charlie got along like a house on fire—they both reacted to pain the same way. "Did you go to Krav Maga today?"

"Yeah." She narrowed her eyes at the change in subject but finally said, "I feel like I got hit by a train, but I have another class tomorrow."

"It might seem counterintuitive, but working those same muscles every other day or so will keep them from tightening up and will help with the soreness."

"That's what the instructor said."

"He's a smart man." She sat back and considered how to approach the art thing—or if she even should. As Aiden kept reminding her—she wasn't here to fix his family. But she'd seen the way he'd relaxed last night at the dinner once he'd had it out with Carrigan and then Teague. It was like some part of him that was always coiled had actually relaxed for once. He had rocky relationships with several of his siblings, but Keira was the one who worried him the most.

She worried Charlie, too.

The Krav Maga helped, but it wasn't a magic pill that would fix everything. Learning a new skill that worked her body as well as her mind was just the first step of the journey—an opportunity, if Keira chose to take it.

That gave her an idea. "Could you teach me?"

"You're a fucking brown belt, Charlie. It will take me years to get to a point where I actually have the ability to take you down, let alone teach you anything."

She laughed. "You'll be there before you know it. But no, I meant will you teach me to paint?"

"Why the hell would you want me to do that?" Despite the incredulity in her voice, there was a spark of interest there. Just like there'd been when Keira had watched the two black belts spar at the gym the first time they'd gone.

That's as good of an opportunity as I'm going to get. Charlie set the book aside and sat up. "Sure. My dad was big on shooting ranges and hand-to-hand grappling, and that sort of thing. But I've never even taken an art class. You liked Krav Maga when I shared it with you. Maybe I'm harboring an artistic streak."

Keira snorted. "Let's stop pretending that you're trying to do anything but manipulate me by bringing this up."

"For fuck's sake, Keira. I'm not trying to manipulate you. Call me crazy, but I thought we were getting to the point where we were something like friends. Friends share shit. If you want me to back off, just say so, but don't pull the pissy teenager act. You want to be taken seriously as an adult? Then be one."

Too harsh, Charlie. What the hell are you doing?

But Keira sat up and really *looked* at her. "No one talks to me like that."

"We covered that already."

"I know." She ran a hand through her hair. "Look, if you haven't noticed, I'm not all that good at the friend bit—probably because I don't actually have friends. There isn't a convenient playbook, and I'm kind of an asshole by default."

Charlie frowned. "You're not an asshole."

"Yes, I am. And that's okay." Keira stood. "We can play with charcoal for a little bit. You can't do too much damage with that."

Charlie laughed, but the sound faded as Aiden walked into the room. She drank in the sight of him, feeling like it'd been days since she saw him last, instead of a few hours. He looked tired, but that seemed to be the norm for him. It made her want to take him away from here and spend a week or three on a beach with white sand and turquoise water.

Keira made a disgusted noise. "You two are so gross." She headed for the door. "It's going to take me some time to hunt down the supplies if mine have gone bad—and they probably have, since I just tossed them into a box instead of storing them correctly. We'll do it tomorrow afternoon."

"Sounds good."

Aiden waited for his sister's footsteps to move away before he sat next to Charlie on the couch and pulled her against his side. "What was that about?"

"Keira's going to display the patience of Job and teach me how to paint." She cuddled into his side, the feel of him settling something deep inside her. "I think she's starting to make peace with the fact that I want to be her friend."

Surely they could stay friends even if she and Aiden weren't together. *Stop thinking about it.*

Just like that, the frown disappeared, replaced by a hope so fragile, it broke her heart a little. "She's painting again?"

Charlie hated to crush his optimism, but she didn't want to lie. "Not exactly. She hasn't done anything of her own, but she also didn't totally tell me to fuck off when I asked her to teach me. So I guess it's not all bad?"

"It's more interest than she's shown in years." He shook his head. "You know, she used to have a full scholarship to RISD before she dropped out. Not that she needed it. The point is that she was good enough for one of the most prestigious art schools on the East Coast. That's probably the saddest part of this whole thing."

"She's got time." Even though she'd spent the last few years spiraling, she had more life than most people Charlie knew. If she had the chance, she'd recover and be one of those people who changed the world. "She'll be okay."

"Not if she marries Dmitri Romanov." The light went out of Aiden's eyes. He cursed and squeezed her shoulders. "Sorry. I didn't track you down to talk about that Russian bastard."

"It's fine." She shifted to straddle him, like it was the most natural thing in the world. It *felt* like the most natural thing in the world. "What do you want to talk about instead?"

Aiden sifted his fingers through her hair. "I ended up enjoying last night."

"I did, too." She'd been unexpectedly taken with Callista Sheridan. The woman was smart and driven, and she obviously had a deep love for her family.

That seemed to be the common thread that ran through all the power players in Boston, with the possible exception of the Hallorans—they valued family above all else. They were also everything she'd been taught to hate by both her father and other cops—career criminals who would never totally leave the life, no matter how many of their businesses they took legit. But even with all they'd been through, they still reached out with forgiveness, instead of cutting the very people out of their lives that they were supposed to protect.

Then there was Carrigan, who spoke so passionately about the work she was doing to combat sex trafficking. And Callista, who had mentioned in passing that she was working with several key people in Boston to fund a program that provided designated drivers to reduce the number of drunk-driving accidents.

These people were doing *good* in way she never could have dreamed. It didn't mean they weren't also bad, but it was a factor Charlie had never considered and didn't know how to process.

"Are you hungry?"

"Actually, yes."

Aiden guided her to her feet and stood. "I have something to show you."

He led the way up the back stairs. He paused in front of a door that led out to a deck that she hadn't had time to explore yet. "Wait here." Charlie didn't have a chance to argue. He ducked down the hallway and reappeared two minutes later with jackets for both of them and shoes for her. "It's not exactly warm outside."

"Thanks." She pulled on the jacket and stepped into the shoes, her heart warming in a way that had nothing to do with the extra layers. It was thoughtful of him…as if he wanted to take care of her.

Her breath caught at the sight of candles flickering on a table laid out with a bottle of wine, two glasses, and a whole spread of Chinese takeout. She let go of his hand and wandered over to peer into the boxes. "How did you know that crispy pork belly was my favorite?" Just like that, the pieces clicked together. She snapped her fingers. "You had Keira feel me out." She'd thought the other woman was asking about her favorite food so they could pick a place to eat the next time they ventured out of the house. "Shady. Very shady."

"I prefer to call it resourceful." He poured them both a glass of wine. "I have it on good authority that this Cab pairs well with Chinese takeout."

"How classy of you." It was like stepping into another realm of existence as she sat down and accepted the glass of wine while he filled two plates. "You know, when you said you wanted a dinner date with just the two of us, I assumed you meant dressing in those fancy clothes you insisted I buy and dragging me out to some restaurant with a menu I can't read, because it's in another language."

He snorted. "Those kinds of dinners serve a purpose. Either you're making a point, or ensuring you're seen by someone specific, or conducting a business meeting. We've been making points and playing parts since we met. I'd like to try something new—having a relaxing conversation where we're not coming down off an adrenaline high for one reason or another. Just me and you—Aiden and Charlie."

"Dropping all the masks? Do you think that's even possible?" She'd seen so many different versions of Aiden in the time they'd been together, she could almost convince herself that she didn't know the real one. Almost. But the truth was that she still felt like she knew Aiden on a soul-deep level. How could she not when his actions spoke louder than any of the words he doled out so carefully?

This was a man who loved his family and was fighting against the legacy his father had left him in order to make something better for all of them. He'd done bad things—of that there was no doubt—but he had more honor than most people she'd met who were supposed to be on the side of good.

I like him.

I might even love him.

She didn't know how she could reconcile their differences. She didn't know if they should even try. Hell, with her luck, Aiden was only enjoying her body and would enjoy seeing her walk out of his life just as much.

"We won't know until we try." Aiden took a drink of his wine. He looked so deliciously rumpled in his jacket, with his tie half-undone—more real somehow. Even as she watched, he let the distant mask drop and focused all of his attention on her.

It was like standing in the face of the sun.

Without anything holding him back, his green eyes spoke volumes. Every brutalized instinct she had clamored that this man wanted her—and wanted her for more than just orgasms.

That he *saw* her.

She couldn't breathe. Couldn't move. Couldn't do more than sit there and stare at him dumbly while she tried to process the onslaught of information he passed on without saying a word.

In the end, Aiden took pity on her and looked away first. He nudged one of the plates to her side of the table. "Eat before it gets cold."

She tried to swallow past her dry throat. "Sure." Charlie took a hasty sip of wine that did nothing to calm the racing of her thoughts.

He waited for her to settle down a little before he spoke again. "What would you have done if you weren't a cop?"

"I'm not a cop." When he just watched her, she sighed and relented. "Okay, fine. I don't know. My dad's a cop, my granddad was a cop. My uncle was a cop before he was shot in the line of duty. There wasn't another path for me." She'd never found that sad before. She'd been so determined to do good in the world and eradicate evil that she'd just charged forward, full throttle, until she'd hit the brick wall that ended her career. It had made sense at the time.

Except she'd spent the last two years adrift and drowning, with no end in sight. Her entire identity had been tied up with being a cop's daughter and then a cop herself and now... "I don't know."

"You're great with Keira."

"Keira just needs someone who's not family and isn't demanding anything of her." At his flinch, she softened her tone. "I'm sorry. That's not fair. Even when you aren't asking her for something, she *feels* like you are. There's no help for it. I'm an outsider, so it's easier for her to be around me, because we don't have the history she does with everyone else in the house."

She didn't tell Aiden that she suspected Keira to be harboring feelings for Dmitri. It wouldn't help the situation or change his plans, and she couldn't afford for him to be conflicted when it came down to the wire.

Ruthless.

Shut up.

"Family is endlessly complicated." He took another drink and then leaned back to stare at the sky. The overcast night didn't offer much of a view, but being outside the walls of the town house still provided a much-needed change of scenery.

"You can say that again." Maybe things would have been different if her mother was still around, but with only Charlie and her dad... Yeah, complicated didn't begin to cover it.

As if divining her thoughts, Aiden leaned forward. "How's your father these days?"

"I wouldn't know. He's not too pleased with me."

"He doesn't like me much."

She choked. "That's the understatement of the year. He wouldn't shed a tear to see your head on a pike."

"Would you?"

She opened her mouth but closed it just as fast. Telling him that she'd be completely devastated if anything happened to him was exposing too much of her already-damaged heart. Aiden might like her, but that wasn't enough. He was still the man he was. She was still the woman she was. They were too different.

If it weren't for Dmitri Romanov ruining her life, she and Aiden would perpetually be on the opposite sides of the law. *We still should be, even if I'm not a cop anymore.* The thought made her uncomfortable, so she poked at her food. "What are we doing, Aiden? I know I blurred the lines a bit when I threw myself at you—"

"Pretty sure I was right there with you."

She kept going, because if she stopped, she might not have the courage to get it all out. "All the same, this has an expiration date. It's always had an expiration date. The sex doesn't change that." *Couldn't* change that.

He finally raised his head and looked at her. "What if we didn't have an expiration date? What if we just . . . did this?"

She went still. "What?" Surely she'd had too much wine and was now hallucinating. "Did *what*?"

"Dated. We could postpone the wedding, of course."

"Postpone the wedding," she repeated through numb lips. "There isn't going to be a wedding."

"Not anytime soon."

She set her wine carefully on the table, shocked when she didn't spill any of it. "Let's pretend we were going to do *this* for real. How do you imagine that would look? I've spent the last two weeks basically twiddling my thumbs. I'm managing to hold it together, because there's the endgame to think of. But that doesn't mean I can do this indefinitely."

"Why do you think I asked you what you'd do if you weren't a cop?" He pinned her in place with those intense green eyes, as if he could see through all her protests to the fear of being hurt that lay beneath.

Or maybe those are my issues talking.

Aiden drummed his fingers on the table. "Of course I'd want you to have a career, and I value your happiness more than I care about using your skills to benefit the family."

She took a hasty sip of wine and then set the glass down just as quickly. "This is insane."

"Is it? I've noticed that the people in my family tend to fall hard and fast, and the feeling doesn't dissipate over time. I had chalked it up to idiocy." He shrugged. "I was wrong. I like you, Charlie. A whole hell of a lot. I admire your strength. You've fought back against things that would have broken another person. You've been here two weeks, and already the dynamic of my family has changed. I can actually envision a future where my siblings and I are friends again, and that wasn't something I would have thought possible without you there to push me."

She blinked. "I...This is crazy."

"Tell me you don't feel anything for me beyond lust and I'll let it go."

CHAPTER TWENTY-THREE

Aiden read the hesitance in the way Charlie held herself and knew he'd pushed too hard. He should have guessed that she'd dig in her heels if he threw the idea of a real marriage at her with no warning, but the notion of losing her had been weighing on him for days. The last forty-eight hours, with the shootout and then the breakthrough at the fundraising dinner, had only cemented it.

He wanted Charlie in his life, and he wanted her there for good.

Obviously, she'd take a bit more convincing before she got on the same page, but he was more than up to the task. If he'd learned anything about her, it was that she didn't respond well to feeling like she was cornered. He'd broached the subject, and now the ball was firmly in her court.

He wanted her to choose *him*. And not because he'd used sex to manipulate her into staying.

Patience. You have time. He sat back and smiled. "We can talk about it later."

She gave him a look like he'd just whipped out a poisonous snake and threatened her with it. "What's your angle?"

They hadn't had time to build more than a superficial layer of trust. It was tempting to try to charm her, but she'd asked for him to be just *him* tonight. So he went with the honest answer. "The subject obviously freaks you out, and forcing you to talk about it isn't going to do anything except ruin our night. I'm willing to be patient while you figure out how you feel about the whole thing. This wasn't part of the plan you agreed to when you first came here." He lifted his glass of wine. "So we won't talk about it until you're ready."

"You're being awfully agreeable right now."

And she was being understandably suspicious. He scrubbed a hand over his face. "What would you do if I tried to force your hand or manipulate you into doing what I want?"

"I'd leave."

Even hearing the words made his chest ache. He set the wineglass down. "Exactly. No games. No masks. No manipulations. Just the truth. I want you. I put myself out there and took the first step. I think you want me, too, but you need time. I get that. So take your time, and we'll talk again after the Eldridge threat is removed."

"Removed. Is that the only solution you have for enemies?" She flinched and held up her hand. "Sorry. I'm lashing out. That's not fair. You just caught me off guard."

"I know." Aiden let himself take her in the same way she had when he'd first walked into the office. Today, she wore a pair of jeans that looked new enough that he figured they were among the items Liam had strong-armed her into buying, with a tank top that clung to her frame in a way that made his mouth water. The jacket covered up the fact that the majority of her bandages were gone, leaving only the butterfly ones on a few of the cuts. She looked like a grunge warrior with her alternative hair and ever-present bright red lipstick.

"Tell me about your day."

She hesitated, but eventually relented. "Carrigan called me to schedule a time to get together next week, and we ended up chatting for a while about the new moves she's making with her nonprofit."

He was glad his oldest sister had already made overtures. "She and James have done a lot of good in the last few years." If he'd pulled his head out of his ass and stood up to their father, she could have been doing the same things under the O'Malley name.

But that was in the past now. Carrigan was happy, which was all that really mattered.

It didn't hurt that her relationship with James Halloran had effectively doused what was left of the brewing conflict between their families.

"Do you..."

"Do I have any charitable shell company set up to do good in the world? Not yet." He wished that he'd taken the time to do something exactly like that so he could show Charlie that a life with him didn't have to be one spent in the darkness. There was that element, of course. He couldn't change that. But it wasn't *just* that element. "I like how Carrigan's run things over there, though."

"Me too. It's not like I thought at all." She gave him a half smile. "None of this is."

"But not all bad."

That earned him a laugh. "No, not all bad." She finally picked up her wineglass again and swirled the dark red liquid around. "Though I have to get out of this house. I'll go crazy if I'm cooped up much longer. The only reason I haven't up to this point is because you keep sexing me into submission, and it's hard to work up the energy to bolt when I'm all blissed-out."

He laughed, just as he suspected she had intended. "It sounds like it's a terrible problem to have."

"It is. Just awful. Keep it up."

"In that case..." He took her hand, urging her up out of her seat and into his lap. "It sounds like I've left you wanting for too long."

"More than twelve hours? Without a doubt." She ran her hands down his chest. "You'd better talk me down so I don't find a convenient window to slip through in my escape attempt."

He liked her like this, relaxed and flirty. He suspected he was getting a glimpse of the woman she'd been before her world came crashing down around her. Aiden hooked a hand into the band of her jeans, his fingers teasing the top of her panties. "If you have that much energy, maybe I should keep you with me in my office. You'd have to wear something, naturally, because I'm not overly fond of the thought of anyone else knowing that you're half a second from coming for me...A dress. Or a skirt." He used his other hand to flick open the top button and pull down the zipper, allowing him to dip inside her panties. "Nothing underneath, though, unless you want to get inventive with garters and thigh-high stockings."

"I'm not really a garter-and-thigh-high-stocking kind of

woman." She hissed out a breath as he created a V with his fingers and slid his hand up and down, stroking her clit between them. "But I might be willing to make an exception."

"You could wear anything and it would do it for me. I'm not picky."

Charlie laughed. "Not picky except when it comes to what I'm wearing *under* my clothes."

"Except for that." He kept his pace slow and controlled, teasing her. He liked the way her lips parted and the intensity of her eyes on him as her breathing picked up. There was no danger in her forgetting who was making her feel like this. They were both here. They were both present in a way he'd never been during sex. He enjoyed the hell out of it because it was Charlie. He wanted what was inside her head as much as he wanted what was between her thighs.

She gripped his shoulders hard enough that her nails pricked him through the fabric. "*Aiden.*"

"Tell me what you need." He already knew, but he wanted to hear the words from her.

She shifted, widening her legs and then whimpering when the move tightened her jeans so he couldn't move as freely. "More. I want all of you."

"Then take all of me." It felt like he was offering a whole lot more than his cock, but he didn't take the words back. Instead, he undid his slacks as she stood and shimmied out of her jeans and panties. Charlie didn't once look behind her at the door leading to the house or seem all that concerned that there were people who could walk in on them at any time. He'd made sure they *wouldn't*, but the fact that she trusted him without asking made his heart give a strange leap.

She straddled him again, but he stopped her with a hand

on her hip. "Condom, bright eyes." He dug around in his jacket until he came up with the one he'd stashed there earlier.

"Carrying some around with you? You're learning."

"It appears I can be taught." He guided his cock to her entrance with one hand, using the other to urge her to sink onto him. As tempting as it was to let her guide this encounter, he knew what she liked—what they both liked. "You're not on top tonight."

"What—*oh*."

He stood and set her in the chair he'd previously occupied, while he knelt on the floor in front of her. Their height difference meant they lined up perfectly like this. He spread her legs wider and draped them over the arms of the chair. A quick adjustment had her ass at the very edge. "Take off your bra. Let me see you." His position blocked the line of sight from the door in the minimal chance someone managed to make it past Liam to the deck, and he wanted to see her breasts bounce with every stroke as he fucked her.

"I wish I was wearing your shirt."

The memory only made his cock harder. He thrust a little. "Later." She slipped her bra off without taking off her shirt completely, then pulled up her tank top to reveal her breasts. The sight was even hotter than if she'd been completely naked. "Stroke your nipples. They're feeling neglected."

"God forbid." She did as he told her, pinching them slightly, the way he did, her hissed exhale music to his ears. To reward her, he started moving, sliding slowly out of her and then back in, just as measured and controlled.

"Now cup them. Yeah, just like that." He managed three more strokes and then he couldn't take the temptation any longer. Aiden pushed her hands away and cupped her breasts himself, flicking his tongue over one nipple and then the other. She went wild beneath him, her hands going to his hips and pulling him closer yet. He surged into her once, twice, a third time. "I know you're on the edge, bright eyes. Let me take you there." He set his teeth against one of her breasts hard enough that she jerked.

"Oh God."

"You like that?"

"Yes." She pulled his head back down to her other breast, and he gave it the same treatment. She was so close, she was quaking around him, but she hadn't reached the point of no return yet.

He hitched her legs higher and wider and was rewarded with a curse. Aiden bore down, fighting off his own orgasm in pursuit of hers. He reached between her legs and circled her clit, and that was all it took to send her over the edge. Charlie came with a sweet cry that had him seeking out her mouth in a devastating kiss. She clung to him, her pussy milking his cock until he couldn't resist any longer. He slammed into her again and again. The sound of flesh meeting flesh filled the night, and then it was too much. Aiden came with a curse and let his head drop to rest against her neck.

She shivered a little and wrapped her legs around his waist, holding him to her. "If that's your argument against underwear, I think I might be convinced."

He chuckled against her skin. "I'll keep that in mind next time I want to persuade you to see things my way."

Then just like that, his desire disappeared. *I didn't tell her.* He hadn't meant to keep his meeting with Romanov and Halloran a secret, but he'd been busy putting things into place and…

No, that was bullshit.

He knew Charlie wouldn't like it that they were working with the enemy, even if it was to bring down the person responsible for almost killing his sisters and her. She was in this game for Romanov, and if she wouldn't even have agreed to date him without that in the picture, he didn't like his chances of explaining the situation without her reacting poorly.

"What? What aren't you telling me?"

He realized he'd gone tense and cursed himself for not watching his reactions. If he told her it was nothing, he'd be lying to her, and that wasn't something he wanted to do. It wasn't something he *could* do if he wanted to earn a place in her life. *Fuck.*

Aiden pressed a kiss to her neck and backed up. He couldn't break the news to her while he was still inside her.

They dressed in silence, and the nervous looks she kept shooting him only made him feel guiltier. There was no fighting it. He'd fucked up, even if he hadn't had a choice in the matter. *I should have talked to her the second the plan changed.* He could pretend that the reason he'd left her out of the loop was because he wasn't used to having to answer to another person, but it was bullshit. "I need you to hear me out before you react. Can you promise me that?"

"What the hell kind of question is that? If you're asking in the first place, you know damn well that I can't promise that."

Yeah, he did. There was no backing out now, though. So he sat down and explained the situation, trying like hell not to notice the way her face fell as the story came out.

I fucked up. I fucked up big time.

* * *

"Let me see if I've got this straight." Charlie was so angry, she could barely get the words out. What he'd just told her..."You contacted me because you wanted Dmitri Romanov. That is the *only* reason I agreed to this." But now, if Keira and Aiden were to be believed, Romanov was partially responsible for saving her life. That was fine. He could play the savior. That didn't erase what he'd done to rip her life apart, piece by piece.

She paced, the deck not nearly large enough to work off her growing rage. "Now you're working with him. Not pretending to be his ally while scheming behind his back, but actually *working with him*."

"Temporarily."

"You can say that all you want, but the more you work with him, the harder it's going to be to finish this."

The look of regret on his face made her stomach drop. "There might be no removing him after this."

"Excuse me?" That was the *only* reason she'd agreed to this, and now he was reneging on the deal?

"The Eldridges are worse than I'd anticipated—and I anticipated them being complete monsters. Romanov is bad. There's no question about that. But he's also a known quantity. If he's gone, it paves the way for another power player like Alethea Eldridge, or worse. I can't allow that."

Rationally, she understood Aiden's logic, but if she'd been operating on rational, she wouldn't have agreed to this charade in the first place. She turned and nearly ran into him. She danced back a step. "Just...give me space for a few minutes." *For longer than a few minutes.*

Good sex didn't negate this withholding of information

any more than Dmitri Romanov being not a total monster to Keira negated all the bad things he'd done.

Was *still* doing.

"You're talking about murder, Aiden." Murdering Mae Eldridge because she was responsible for the drive-by. "I should have never come here. If Mae didn't think I was your fiancée—"

"You aren't the cause of this. If she wanted to kill you and you alone, she wouldn't have done it like that. She knew Keira was there, and so she wanted to kill two birds with one stone, so to speak." Aiden shook his head. "This isn't about me, and it's not about you. It's a political hit aimed at both the O'Malleys and Romanov."

That was just it. Charlie didn't know if she could live in a place—with a man—who got into bed with enemies to take out other enemies. She'd allowed herself to forget, to focus on the good that they were doing and ignore all the rest. To ignore the truth. The law had no place here, and she was mostly convinced that *she* had no place here. "I can't do this."

"Charlie..."

She dodged his reach. "Why do you even need me if you're not going ahead with Romanov?"

He pressed his lips into a thin line. "Romanov is no friend of mine."

That didn't quite answer her question. It struck her that one of the very things she'd admired about Aiden was what made him so dangerous. He'd do what was good for the family, no matter the cost. A couple weeks ago, that had meant removing Romanov. But the second that didn't fit, he switched lanes without so much as a backward glance. She didn't work like that. She couldn't. "I need some air."

"We're standing on the porch."

She shot him a look. "You know what I mean."

"It's not safe."

He kept saying that, which meant he was completely missing the point. She started for the stairs leading down the back of the town house. "Unless you plan to put me under house arrest, I'm leaving." She held up a hand when he moved to follow her. "Space, Aiden. You just dropped a lot of information on me that you've been withholding, and I need some time to process. If you're serious about making a go of this, you have to respect the fact that you can't keep me on a leash." It was a low blow, but she could feel panic boiling up inside her. If she didn't get out of here now, she'd say or do something that they'd both regret. "Please."

He stepped out of her way, and she felt his eyes on her as she descended the staircase. It was too much to ask for him not to send some protection detail to follow her, but as long as she could put some distance between herself and the O'Malley house, she didn't care. Charlie picked up her pace, the comforting feeling of her shoes hitting the sidewalk allowing her to draw her first full breath since Aiden asked her to withhold judgment.

Withhold judgment. How am I supposed to do that?

He'd had more than one chance to tell her that things had changed. When Romanov contacted him initially. Before he went to meet the man who was supposed to be the enemy. Immediately *after* the meeting. He'd decided to keep his plans from her every single time, and then turn around and talk about dating for real. About marriage.

He was out of his goddamn mind if he thought she'd tolerate this kind of crap from a boyfriend, let alone a *husband*.

No matter how much she cared about him.

CHAPTER TWENTY-FOUR

Charlie's phone rang and she jumped, having taken it with her by reflex. She sighed when she recognized the number. *As if my night could get any weirder.* "It's not a good time, Dad." She had nothing to say to him at this point. What *was* there to say? He wouldn't approve of her choices for the last two weeks—he'd made that explicitly clear—and he certainly wouldn't understand how conflicted she felt about Aiden. To him, Aiden and his family were criminals who needed to be in prison. There was no nuance. No give.

Her life would have been much simpler if she could view them the same way. But it was too late for that. Charlie had already spent days on end up close and personal with Aiden and everyone in the house. She knew that he cared about the people around him, no matter how tightly he kept those feelings locked down. She knew that Cillian was a great dad and loved both his wife and stepdaughter to distraction. She knew that Keira had a bright future ahead of her if she could just get out of her own way.

She knew that the O'Malleys had a whole hell of a lot more loyalty than her father did.

"Listen very carefully." He spoke low and intense.

Charlie stopped, straining to hear him. "What?"

"There's a car coming. It will be at your side in fifteen seconds. Get in the backseat. I can get you to safety."

Safety?

Just like that, it clicked into place. "We talked about this. I'm where I want to be." She wasn't sure if that was true anymore, but Aiden O'Malley hadn't kidnapped her and locked her up in his house. She'd agreed to go. If she changed her mind and left, she was reasonably sure that he'd let her leave. He wouldn't be happy, and she doubted it would be the last time she saw him, but he'd let her walk out the door.

"That bastard is using you to get to me."

She turned to look down the street, eyeing the cars that approached. "Dad, Aiden could give two fucks about you." He'd tracked down her real name, and Aiden wasn't the type of man to leave anything to chance, so she had no illusions that he hadn't put two and two together about who her father was. But he hadn't said anything about it, and he hadn't tried to press her for potential information…and she had bigger fish to fry in the form of Dmitri Romanov.

"You really went into that house knowing that he was using you."

Anger rose, black and ugly. "At least he's doing something about his problems instead of just ignoring them and pretending like they never existed. I want justice. Aiden is going to give it to me."

"You are so goddamn naive, Charlotte. Someone within the O'Malley household is an informant. Their identity is classified information, but Aiden O'Malley picked you in order to get back at me for what he perceives as a betrayal."

The fact that he was telling her this now meant that either the information was compromised...or he was so worried about her that he was doing whatever it took to get her to safety.

She wanted to believe it was the latter. She wanted to believe it so badly, she almost got into the car that pulled up next to her, its tinted windows and nondescript coloring marking it as government-issued.

But she knew her father too well. John Finch was all about the bottom line, and the bottom line included every member of organized crime he could get put behind bars. The only reason he'd admit that there was an informant in the first place was because Aiden knew and had taken steps to cut off his contact. "How long has he known?"

"I can't be sure..."

Which was an answer in and of itself. Aiden was a planner. Despite some astronomical differences of opinion, he loved the hell out of his siblings. Someone like Dmitri Romanov wouldn't hesitate to make an informant disappear—permanently. But to do that to a sibling? Aiden would hesitate. He would gather information, and he would plan, and when he moved, it would be to shut down the threat without harming his sibling.

In this case, the threat was Charlie's father.

She swayed on her feet, feeling sick to her stomach. "Did he threaten me?" She couldn't wrap her head around it. He was ruthless, yes, but the man who'd taken her to bed and told her that he wanted a real relationship was not one to coldly use her for his own gain. Except...her own father had allowed her to walk into danger because it served his purposes. He might not have liked it, but he hadn't given her any warning, because he didn't trust her.

Because the bottom line mattered more.

If her dad would do that, why wouldn't Aiden? They'd known each other only a couple weeks, after all. Her instincts told her that he'd never hurt her, but she'd already established that her instincts couldn't be trusted.

Her dad hesitated long enough that she knew he was considering lying to her. "Not directly. But he threw your relationship—if you can call it that—in my face and threatened untoward things if I didn't do what he said."

Untoward things. For her dad, that could mean anything from murdering her to dating her. She sighed, suddenly so tired that she could barely form words. "What did he want from you?"

"That's not important."

Traffic had the car in front of her veering away from the curb and back into the stream of cars in the road. *Good riddance.* "It's important to *me.*"

Her dad cursed, his legendary patience having apparently run dry. "He wanted me to be at a dock in New York at a specified time and date. It's obviously a trap, and I'm not in the business of jumping when mob bosses tell me to jump."

A dock at a specific time and date—likely when he'd orchestrated for Romanov and the Eldridges to be in the midst of a gunfight. Despite everything, she almost smiled. That was really smart of Aiden. If the two enemies didn't kill each other off, the FBI would be there to clean up the mess.

But getting them there in the first place was the problem.

Her father wasn't the type to respond to anonymous tips without a whole bucketful of doubt. He'd be so busy looking for the trap, he might miss the opportunity to see justice done once and for all.

"You should go. His tip is solid."

"You're just saying that because he said it. The only reason you believe him is because you're sleeping with him."

She jerked back and almost ran into a man walking past. The stranger gave her a dirty look and kept walking, but she barely paid him any attention. "Do you really think that little of me?" Sure, she'd gotten carried away with Aiden, but she was also an adult and in possession of most of her common sense. He might try to tell her the sky was pink, but that didn't mean she'd believe him, no questions asked.

That her father thought she was so stupid—so easily swayed—stung more than she wanted to admit. But then, she shouldn't be surprised. It was just more of the same, after all. Bitterness clawed its way up her throat and emerged from her mouth. "When your daughter is a dirty cop, all her decisions are subject to criticism."

"I didn't say that."

"You didn't have to." She'd seen it time and time again, every time he'd looked at her for the last two years. She was so *tired* of it. If John Finch had a family, it was the FBI. Not Charlie. "Good-bye, Dad. Please don't try to send anyone for me again." She hung up before he could say something to make the emotional bleeding worse.

A car pulled up next to her, and the back door opened. She cursed. "Tell my dad..." Charlie trailed off as she registered the gun pointed at her. Distantly, she heard running and yelling, but there was no way whoever was on her protection detail would reach her in time.

Mae smiled, her dark lipstick stark against her pale face. "Get in the car, bitch."

Charlie weighed her odds, but even at this hour, there were other people on the street. She'd get someone killed if she tried to run—Mae didn't seem the type to spare innocent bystanders if she thought she could shoot Charlie in the back. And she was too far away for Charlie to rush her without getting shot at least twice, maybe three times, depending on how fast Mae could pull the trigger.

"This isn't going to get you what you want."

"Maybe what I want is you—dead." Mae motioned with her free hand. "Either get in the car or I'll put two in your chest right here. Your choice."

Rule number one in any hostile scenario was to never get into the car and be transported to a secondary location. Charlie didn't have that option. Mae would definitely be true to her word, and she liked her chances of escaping better if she could lull the other woman into underestimating her.

She lifted her hands slowly. "No need to shoot me. I'm coming with you."

She was almost to the car when Mae's smile widened. "You may be, but I'm not a fan of your men." She grabbed Charlie's arm and hauled her into the backseat as she pulled the trigger. Charlie twisted around and caught a glimpse of Liam lying on the ground, blood leaking from his chest. Then the car shot away from the curb.

Oh my God, what have I done?

* * *

Aiden's heart stopped when he heard the sound of gunshots. *Too close.* He ran down the porch steps, sprinting in the direction Charlie had taken just moments before. He wanted to chalk it up to a car backfiring, but here in the upscale Beacon Hill neighborhood, where he'd lived his entire life, he could count on one hand how many times he'd heard that sound and still have fingers left over. It was too much of a coincidence.

He picked up speed. There weren't many people out this late, but a small group had gathered halfway down the block. *No. Not Charlie.* To have narrowly avoided this exact thing mere days before and then find her bleeding—*dead?*—on the street...If he lost her, it had damn well better be because she walked away on her own strength.

Not because she was dead.

He slid between two men who were shifting nervously, like they knew they should be doing something but had no idea what. Aiden nearly tripped over his own feet as he went to his knees. "No."

Liam had a hand pressed to his chest, but even in the low light, it was easy to see he was covered in blood. "Mae took her."

"Save your strength." Aiden stripped off his own shirt and adjusted Liam's hand so he could press the fabric to the wound. Aiden pointed at one of the nervous men. "Call 911. Now. Tell them we have a gunshot wound and that he's lost a lot of blood." He leaned closer to Liam and lowered his voice. "I'm not losing you, damn it, so if you see a light or some shit, you stay the fuck away."

"Yes, sir."

He watched for coughing up blood, his memory of the night when Devlin died trying to superimpose itself over this one. One of the Halloran bullets had pierced his little brother's lung, and Devlin had drowned in his own blood.

He tried to judge where Liam had been hit—and what vital organs there were in that part of his chest—but he couldn't be sure. Liam's breathing was labored but not wet-sounding, which had to be a good thing. If Aiden could keep him from bleeding out, they might have a chance.

Sirens cut through the night, and Liam grabbed Aiden's wrist with a surprisingly strong grip. "Mae took her. Dark car. Didn't get plates."

"You were a little busy being shot." He'd deal with the ramifications of Charlie being in Mae's tender care as soon as the paramedics loaded Liam into an ambulance. He couldn't leave one of his oldest friends here on the street like a piece of trash. He just couldn't.

An ambulance screeched to a halt next to the curb and dispatched two tired-looking paramedics, a man and a woman. They knelt on either side of Liam and looked at Aiden. "Sir, you need to step back. We can take it from here."

He didn't want to. Some part of him believed that if he let go of his shirt—now soaked with Liam's blood—that it would be the end.

"Sir." The female paramedic gently touched his shoulder. "Please. Every second counts."

That got him moving. He nodded and forced himself to move back a few feet. He watched the paramedics with an eagle eye, but they were above reproach. They took Liam's vitals, muttering to each other in a language that might as well have been Greek for all he understood it.

Within five minutes, they had Liam on a stretcher and loaded into the back of the ambulance. The woman paused long enough to say, "We can't say for sure yet, but barring complications, he should make a full recovery." She hesitated. "Are you going to ride in the ambulance with him?"

"My brother will meet him at the hospital." He'd send Cillian to wait with Liam.

He had to figure out where the fuck Mae took Charlie. Aiden turned and backtracked to the house, shoving through the back door loud enough to send it banging against the wall. Mark, stationed in the kitchen, started to draw his gun, then seemed to register that it was Aiden and not an enemy. His gaze went to the blood on Aiden's hands and the fact that he wasn't wearing a shirt. "Trouble."

"Trouble." He started to rub a hand over his face but stopped when he realized he'd just be making a bigger mess. Aiden strode to the kitchen sink and started scrubbing at his hands. "Charlie was taken, and Liam was shot trying to stop it. He'll be okay, but he's on his way to the hospital."

"Who did it? Romanov?"

"The Eldridges." He never thought he'd long for the days when Romanov was their only enemy—or, hell, when the Hallorans were—but he was getting there fast. Certain rules applied to their world. They weren't always upheld, but sacrificing innocents or near-innocents was almost always avoided. Even Romanov balked at killing women and children. Mae's problem was with *them*, so he or Dmitri should be her target—not Charlie. That was how every other player in this game would operate.

Not the Eldridges.

He'd been a damn fool not to realize that, and he'd put two of his sisters and Charlie in danger as a result. He never should have let Charlie walk away tonight, but it honestly hadn't crossed his mind that she'd be in danger in the middle of O'Malley territory, not two blocks from his home with a protection detail on her heels.

Idiot.

"What do you need?"

He took one breath and then another, but the buzzing of his thoughts didn't abate. When all he could see was Liam on the ground, bleeding out, it had been easier to ignore the screaming in the back of his mind that Charlie was in the hands of a monster. Now, he didn't have the distraction.

He was the leader of this family now, and that meant he had resources. He didn't have to go charging into the night alone. He would call in every single fucking favor owed him to see her safely back. Aiden closed his eyes for a long moment, and when he opened them, he felt more in control. It was a lie, but he'd take what he could get at the moment. "Get Cillian and as many men as we have in the house. Keep it quiet so we don't panic Keira and Olivia and Hadley."

"Got it." Mark disappeared, and Aiden belatedly realized that he should have been more comforting. Mark was Liam's fucking cousin. He'd send him to the hospital and take someone else to lead the attack-and-rescue mission.

First, he had to figure out where Mae had taken Charlie.

He flipped through his phone to find the last person he wanted to call. But pride and old vendettas had no importance when Charlie's life was on the line.

"Da?"

"Romanov."

"What can I do for you at this hour?" He didn't sound like he'd been asleep, but then the man seemed to possess the supernatural ability to stay ten steps ahead of the rest of them. Maybe he knew what had happened already.

Aiden wasn't going to waste time playing games, though. "I need information."

"I'm listening."

Every instinct hammered into him by his father demanded he avoid putting himself in a position of owing favors to an enemy, but he had bigger things to worry about right now. "Mae took Charlie. I need to know where she is."

"That is unfortunate." No emotion in his voice, no concern that Mae was most certainly going to make Charlie suffer before she killed her.

He fought down panic. It wouldn't do anyone any favors. "What do you want for your help?"

"Always the tit for the tat with you." Romanov sighed. "My Keira seems quite fond of your Charlie."

"She's not your Keira." The words were reflex, but he didn't try to take them back. They were the truth as far as he was concerned, and no temporary alliance would change that.

Romanov continued as if he hadn't spoken. "I think that riding to your rescue and saving your fiancée would be the perfect wedding gift."

He gritted his teeth. Working together or not, that didn't mean he was willing to go along with the Russian's intention of marrying his baby sister. Now wasn't the time for that argument, though—not with Charlie's life on the line. "Can you find her?"

"I suggest you start for New York. By the time you're here, I'll have pinpointed her location."

That wasn't a distinct confirmation, but if Romanov was half as interested in Keira as he let on, there was a good chance he'd follow through on helping Aiden find Mae. "How can you know where she'll go? She's barely an hour ahead of me."

"The Eldridges are nasty creatures, but also habitual. Mae has several locations where she likes to bring her victims. She'll have planned this and set up the appropriate onc. I suggest you start driving, because I doubt she'll want to wait upon arrival."

He was already heading for the door. "I'll see you in three hours." It would require some creative driving to cut the time that much, but at least there shouldn't be much traffic at this time of night. He hung up and stopped short when Mark appeared at the bottom of the staircase with one of Aiden's shirts. "You should go to the hospital."

"I already called. The bullet was a through-and-through. It didn't hit anything vital, so he doesn't even need surgery." Mark gave a brief smile. "I imagine he's pretty pissed she got the drop on him."

He would be. *At least he's okay.* He couldn't think about that yet, though, because Charlie was in danger of worse than a gunshot wound. Mae could hurt her in ways that would make Devlin's death look like a blessing. Yet another thing he couldn't dwell on. "If you're coming, let's go. We don't have time to waste."

"I have a contingent of men already waiting in the garage."

"Good." Aiden yanked on the shirt and strode out the door and into the night. Three hours to New York, and they were almost a full hour behind Mae. The woman could do a lot of damage in sixty minutes.

Hold on, bright eyes. Just hold on. I'm coming for you.

CHAPTER TWENTY-FIVE

Charlie woke up in the trunk. She wasn't even sure how she got there to begin with. One second, she was eyeing Mae's gun and considering how best to attack, and the next, she was waking up *here*. She moved, realized her wrists and ankles were zip-tied together, and cursed. Apparently, Mae was taking no chances when it came to her. *Damn it.* She tested the ties, but they weren't in a good spot to try to break them and she didn't have enough range of motion to even attempt it.

Her heart beat harder despite her best effort to remain calm. She'd been in sticky situations before, but she couldn't remember one *this* sticky. As tempting as it was to pretend Aiden or her dad would ride in on a white horse to save her, she couldn't plan on it. She'd just gotten done telling her dad off, and as far as she knew, Aiden was still waiting for her to get over her snit and come back.

She was beginning to understand why Aiden wanted to eliminate Mae altogether.

Shouldn't have been so single-minded. Should have stayed and talked to him—talked it through.

It was too late now to worry about making the crappy decision to walk away from Aiden. She suspected that Mae had been just waiting for the right time to swoop in and take her. If it hadn't been tonight, it would have been the next time she and Keira ventured out, and then there would have been another potential victim in the mess.

Like Liam.

She pressed her lips together against a sob. *I hope he's okay.* So many mistakes, all hers. But she couldn't focus on that. If Liam survived, she was going to do something to make up for being the biggest pain in the ass in the world— just as soon as she got out of this trunk. If *I get out of this trunk.*

As if on cue, the car rolled to a stop. Charlie listened hard, picking out the sounds of the door opening and shutting, and heels on pavement circling around to the trunk. She tensed, ready to spring out as best she could, but when the trunk opened, she once again found herself facing down the wrong end of a gun.

Mae flicked her a glance, not looking particularly impressed. "At least you didn't piss yourself."

"How about you let me out of these restraints and we fight it out like real women?"

"Do you think you're funny?" She cocked her head to the side. "You're not. You know what you also aren't? A dim-witted gold-digging slut. I checked up on you, Charlotte Finch. What's a dirty cop doing with an Irish mob boss?"

A man appeared at Mae's back, his whole bearing translating to "hired muscle." He lifted Charlie out of the trunk as if she were a paper doll and tossed her over his shoulder. She couldn't see Mae as they headed into what appeared to be a warehouse identical to the one they'd met in several days ago.

She didn't know if she should be more terrified by their location or the fact that Mae Eldridge apparently knew her real name. Neither of the implications was good. *Have to figure out a way out of this*. She didn't have a lot of options.

The muscle dropped her into a chair and shoved her shoulders back. She tensed, waiting for him to cut the ties and maybe try to attach new ones. As soon as her hands were free, she'd attack.

But he didn't give her the opportunity.

Mae stepped up, wielding the gun almost casually. "Don't make trouble."

"You know, if my options are to get shot in the brain or to let you tie me to a chair and torture me . . . I think you can guess which option I'm going with."

Mae shook her head. "What makes you think I'm going to shoot you in the brain, Charlotte? All I have to do is shoot you in the kneecaps and you'd have to drag your body out of here. I don't imagine you'd get far enough to call for help before you bled out, even if you miraculously managed to kill both David here and myself."

"I think I'm up to the challenge." It was sheer bravado, though. Charlie knew a helpless situation when she saw one. She'd lived through one before, but that was only because those cops wanted to hurt her badly—not kill her. Mae was most definitely planning to kill her.

That didn't mean Charlie was going to give up. It wasn't her nature, and she couldn't help but think that Aiden would never forgive himself if she died on his watch. *Stupid reason to keep living…* There was so much she wanted to say to him that she wouldn't get to if Mae went through with whatever she was planning.

"David, secure her."

He struck Charlie in the head almost casually, but the blow stunned her long enough that he was able to cut her zip ties and retie her to the chair. She blinked and shook her head, but the pain blossoming from the point of impact wasn't going to go away anytime soon. "Cheater."

"What winner isn't?" Mae finally lowered her gun. "You and I are going to talk, and at the end of it, if I'm satisfied, I'll kill you quickly."

"Painlessly, you mean."

"Did I say that?" She smiled at David as he brought over a low tray filled with tools that made Charlie's stomach try to wrap itself around her spine in fear. Mae selected a scalpel and held it up so that it gleamed in the low light. "Torture is an acquired taste, I'm afraid. My mother started me young, and it turned out that I had a knack for making people divulge their secrets."

Charlie tried to swallow past her dry throat. "Secrets given out during torture are suspect as a general rule."

"Indeed. Which is why I always verify the information before I finish the job." She stepped forward and caressed Charlie's face. "You really are beautiful. Unfortunately, that's going to be past tense." Mae forced Charlie's chin up and ran the scalpel along her cheekbone, leaving a trail of fire in its wake. "Now, Charlotte, let's have a nice little chat. Just us girls."

* * *

Aiden made it to New York in record time. It didn't matter. All he could think of was the wasted hours and how much danger Charlie was in. Before he left Boston, he'd called Carrigan to inform her that shit was going down faster than expected. She sent James to follow them and offer what help he could, but there was no telling whether he'd reach New York in time. After a rapid mental argument with himself, Aiden also called Teague to warn him that this might all be misdirection. Teague had his men up in arms, and all three families were prepared for any kind of attack.

Knowing that his people were as safe as they could be left Aiden to focus on the only thing that mattered—Charlie.

He followed his directions to the Romanov residence. Aiden knew where the man lived, of course—everyone did—but seeing the place in person was something else altogether. The O'Malley town house had been designed to create an impression, but this massive building was in another realm. It was a town house, but Aiden had it on good authority that Dmitri Romanov owned every one on the block. His father had purchased them when he first settled in New York.

He couldn't imagine Olivia, one of the most down-to-earth women he'd come across, growing up in a place like this.

Mark parked the car, and Aiden barely waited for it to stop moving before he had the door open and was striding up the steps for the front door. There was an honest-to-God gargoyle as the door knocker, the little creature's face twisted as if daring someone to use it. Aiden raised his hand, but the door opened before he had a chance to touch it.

Dmitri himself stood on the other side, looking as unruffled as he always did. "Come in."

"Where is she?"

"I'm working on it."

"You said you'd have the site nailed down by the time we got here."

"Yes, well, the Eldridges have a horrible habit of complicating the best-laid plans." He moved deeper into the house, forcing Aiden to follow or be left standing outside. He kept his focus on the man in front of him, but he still got the impression of tall ceilings and a staircase that would look at home in a castle.

Romanov led him into a study, and Aiden stopped just inside the door to take in the room. It was masculine in the extreme, all dark wood and cool colors, with a fireplace that matched the rest of the house completely. There were also shelves and shelves of books, though he didn't move close enough to pick up the individual titles.

"If you're done with your perusal..."

"Tell me." He moved to the desk—very similar to the one in his office—and looked at a map of the docks that Romanov had laid out. There were two spots marked on nearly opposite ends of the docks. "What's this?"

"I have my people surveying the area for Mae and *her* people." He pointed to first one location and then the other. "Mae has been to both in the last hour and she's got a perimeter in place for both. It's impossible to know which location contains your fiancée, and it's likely that as soon as we attack one, there are safeguards in place to kill Charlie before we can get to her."

Aiden fought against the fear trying to take control, but he could only hold it off for so long. There had been too many close calls lately. Fate wasn't kind, and it was only a matter of time before he arrived too late.

Not this time. Not with Charlie.

He couldn't think about what pain she might be facing while they delayed. His grip on the edge of the desk went white-knuckled. "We have to hit both spots at the same time, and we have to do it stealthily."

"Agreed."

A man poked his head into the room and nodded.

"Thank you, Mikhail." Romanov sighed. "James Halloran has arrived."

Sure enough, the big blond strode into the room a few seconds later. There weren't any men with him, but he wouldn't have come alone any more than Aiden. *I would have if Mark wasn't on top of things.* Aiden pushed that thought away. "We have a problem."

They quickly outlined the issue to James, who cursed. "How much open ground is there around the warehouses?"

"Too much." Romanov circled a finger around the southern one. "And Alethea owns the surrounding buildings, effectively removing the ability to get a clear shot."

So snipers were out. They could theoretically work their way through any sentries in the buildings, but it would take time that they didn't have, and if one of the Eldridge guards got out a call for help, it would ruin everything.

Aiden could feel the seconds ticking down. If Mae had visited both warehouses, it meant she was trying to confuse the trail—and she hadn't been at Charlie nonstop for the last hour and a half. He had to hold on to that knowledge, because if he thought too closely about what she was going through—and whose fault it was—he'd drive himself mad.

"Then stealth is out to some extent." Aiden looked up at

Romanov, his fear for Charlie threatening to get the best of him. Was he content to play "Who Has the Biggest Dick?" when her life was on the line? *No fucking way.* "What do you suggest?"

To Dmitri's credit, he didn't gloat. "If they follow the same schedule they have for the last eighteen months, their guards will change shifts at three. If we attack in the midst of that, it will confuse things and give us the chance we need in order to succeed without undue casualties."

Without Charlie being killed.

Aiden looked at his watch, feeling sick. "That's two hours from now."

"Yes, it is." There was no sympathy on the man's face. "Can your woman hold up for that long without breaking?"

She could. He *knew* she could. But that didn't mean he wanted her to have to. Charlie had been to hell and back because of the man in front of him, and now Romanov was telling him that she'd have to do it again. He couldn't blame the Russian this time. The only person who'd put her firmly in the path of danger was Aiden himself.

He stared at the map. "What do you think our odds are if we attack now?"

"Perhaps fifty-fifty. If we wait until the shift change, I would increase that to seventy-five–twenty-five."

He didn't like either of those odds, but he wasn't going to be happy with odds that weren't 100 percent in favor of her getting out of that warehouse safely. "We're not leaving her in there."

"You're risking a significant amount."

"Yes. I am." She was being hurt right this goddamn second. If he'd left her in that little bar two weeks ago, she'd be safe right now. It was his fault she had a target painted on her back, and he wasn't going to leave her to bear the burden of it. "We'll get her out. Now. I'll take my men here." He pointed to the north warehouse. Aiden was pretty damn sure that was the same one where he and Charlie had gone to play poker last week. "Halloran, you will hit this one." He moved his hand to the south building. "Romanov, you will split your men between us."

"We'll talk about your giving me orders another time."

Yeah, just like they'd talk about Romanov's determination to make Keira his wife another time. Aiden looked up and met his gaze directly. "Tonight, we're allies. This isn't the timeline we'd set up, but it will serve the same purpose. Once the Eldridge threat is eliminated, we'll get back to politicking and that other bullshit."

"Indeed." Romanov moved to a cabinet built into the center of the shelves and pulled out a bottle of vodka and three tumblers. "I know you Irish with your unrefined palates enjoy your whiskey, but you'll have to make do with vodka tonight."

"Now isn't the time to be drinking."

"We're about go into battle. It's the perfect time to be drinking."

Aiden took the tumbler without another word and downed the entire thing. It burned his throat, and he welcomed the feeling. Two years ago, the three of them would have happily gunned each other down in the street, and yet here they stood, ready to take on a mutual enemy and trusting one another other not to fuck them over. He looked at Dmitri Romanov and James Halloran and wondered how they'd gotten to this point.

Love, you idiot.

His thoughts once again turned to Charlie. He hadn't told

her he loved her, hadn't wanted to scare her more than she already was. He regretted that now. Didn't he know better? There were no guarantees in life—especially a life like theirs. They had to live and love and do whatever it took to keep moving forward.

He had to believe that she'd walk out of that warehouse. She'd faced down more than her fair share of shit, and Mae might be the worst yet, but Charlie was so damn strong. She'd survive. She had to.

Stay strong, bright eyes. Just stay strong.

CHAPTER TWENTY-SIX

Charlie had thought she was tough. She might not have always admitted that to herself, but it had been a deep core belief she'd needed to keep moving. Being at Mae's mercy threatened to prove her wrong a hundred times over. Time lost meaning as Mae asked her questions over and over again. A cut here. A punch there. More questions.

To which she claimed she didn't know. She denied. She did anything but give Mae the information she wanted.

The woman had taken a call maybe five minutes ago, which was just long enough for the hopelessness of Charlie's situation to sink in. She shifted and winced. She definitely had a broken rib—or three—and her exposed skin was covered in blood from the shallow cuts Mae seemed to enjoy giving her. It was more blood than she should be losing, but overall she wasn't in danger of dying. Yet.

With each minute that passed, she was less and less likely to make it out of this warehouse alive.

The door opened, and she tensed. Mae strode in, a smile on her face. "Now that that little task is off my plate, I can devote the rest of the night to you."

There couldn't be that much of the night left. She'd been snatched off the street around nine, and it had taken several hours to make the drive to New York from Boston, even if Mae had broken all the speed limits. It might feel like she'd been torturing her forever, but it couldn't have been more than an hour or two. She didn't know if that was comforting or if it meant that Mae planned to condense a whole lot of pain into a very short period of time.

Mae disappeared deeper into the warehouse and came back with a giant jug of water and a hand towel. Charlie stared, her entire body shaking. She wasn't afraid of being cut or beaten. She'd experienced both before and lived to tell the tale. Being shot? It would suck, but it was a risk she'd had to come to terms with before she became a cop.

But drowning?

Drowning scared the shit out of her.

When she was twelve, she'd heard some of the older cops joke about waterboarding terrorists, and she'd even gone so far as to ask her dad about it after. John Finch wasn't one to coddle his daughter, so he'd sat her down and explained how it worked. She'd had nightmares for weeks afterward, though she'd managed to stifle her screams so that her dad never knew.

Mae saw where her attention was, and her smile widened. "If it's good enough for the US government, it's good enough for you, don't you think?"

"I'm ready to talk." Anything to keep that water away from her.

"You're just going to lie some more." Mae sighed.

"Though I suppose you can't answer questions if you're hacking up water. Okay, I'll play. Let's have a chat." She grabbed a nearby chair and turned it around so she could straddle it, resting her chin on the back.

The woman looked so...young. Maybe even innocent. She was all smiles and big brown eyes—at least, as long as Charlie didn't pay attention to the knife she'd set close enough to grab with ease. *I'm in a nightmare. I'm going to wake up soon.*

She knew it was a lie. This wasn't some construct of her sleeping brain. This was real.

"How does a cop's daughter end up engaged to Aiden O'Malley?" Mae picked up the knife and ran her finger along the edge.

Charlie debated lying, but she didn't see much point in it now. These questions were a formality. If Mae knew who she really was, then she knew that Charlie never would have ended up with Aiden unless there was an ulterior motive involved. "He wanted my help bringing down Dmitri Romanov."

Mae blinked. "What makes you so special?"

She'd been asking herself that for most of the time they'd been together. As time had gone on, it was clear he hadn't needed *her*. Not really. He could have accomplished his goals without the charade of being engaged. It added a layer that didn't make sense. But she'd been so blinded by her need to make Dmitri pay that she hadn't cared about the inconsistencies as long as the end result remained the same. Then sex came into the picture and further muddied the waters.

Apparently, she'd taken too long to answer, because Mae swiped out with the knife, leaving another blazing trail in its wake, this time across Charlie's thigh. "Hey, I'm asking you a question. If you don't want to talk, we can skip right to the next event."

Waterboarding.

She tried to swallow her fear, but it lodged in her throat. "I don't know why he picked me." There were plenty of women who would have jumped at the chance. Yes, she was qualified because she knew the world he moved in, at least in theory, but since he'd mostly kept her contained to the house, it wasn't necessary knowledge.

"You don't seem to know much." Mae tapped the knife against her lip, leaving dots of Charlie's blood shining against her red lipstick.

She met her gaze directly, and Charlie realized this had all been a game. She didn't have any answers that Mae needed. The woman was playing with her the way a cat toyed with a mouse before ripping off its head.

"I know!" Mae cocked her head to the side, her expression brightening. "Maybe it's because you're John Finch's daughter."

"What?"

Mae continued as if she hadn't spoken. "Yes, I think that's it after all. You see, your daddy is a pain in the ass of every single family-run business on the eastern seaboard. So imagine my surprise when I discover that his beloved only child is fucking Aiden O'Malley."

"I think 'beloved' child is going a bit far."

"Do you?" Mae casually drew the knife across Charlie's other thigh. "I think that John Finch is a man with no weaknesses—at least at first glance. You know what I also think?"

Charlie gritted her teeth, the pieces slowly coming

together. *This isn't about Aiden at all.* "I think you're dying to tell me."

"I think every single one of us—Eldridge, Romanov, O'Malley, and the rest—would cut off our own nose to spite John Finch." She grinned, eyes cold. "Or maybe I'll just cut off yours instead."

I should have gotten in that car that Dad sent.

She'd been so incredibly blind. So sure of her righteous rage. So sure that her dad was wrong—about Aiden and about her. "What exactly are you hoping to accomplish?"

"I'll settle with breaking John Finch's heart." She leaned forward and tapped Charlie in the chest. "When I'm done with you, I'm going to send him yours in a box. If that doesn't break him, then maybe your daddy really doesn't love you."

It was a lose-lose situation. It didn't matter if she protested, because Mae was going to do what she promised, if only to see how Charlie's dad reacted. *Would it break him?* She didn't know. Frankly, she was more concerned with getting out of this mess alive, but she didn't know how she was going to accomplish that quite yet.

She wouldn't give up.

She'd done that once before, and maybe things would have been different if she'd been more stubborn. Fought harder. *Something.*

"Aiden will come for me." The words were out before she could think better of them.

Mae laughed. "Aiden is fucking you for the same reason I have the itch to cut off that cute little nose of yours. Your world and ours don't mix. If he told you they do, he was trying to sell you something."

Wasn't that exactly what Charlie was afraid of?

He told me he wants to make a go of it. He might not have told me immediately about Romanov, but he did tell me.

It came down to who she trusted more—Mae, who was telling her everything that dark voice inside her suspected, or Aiden, who had offered her hope several times over in the last few weeks. Last time she'd been faced with this choice, she'd listened to the voice that whispered she deserved whatever she got, because she'd never be good enough no matter how hard she tried.

She wasn't listening to that voice anymore.

Charlie lifted her chin and stared the other woman in the eyes. Maybe if she could provoke Mae, the woman would offer her an opening. Or maybe the psycho would just kill her that much quicker.

"You can pretend this is about my father all you want, but we both know the truth—you're jealous because you want Aiden's cock and I'm the one who has it. He knew you were practically panting for it, and instead he tracked down me—a cop's kid—to play house." She tilted her head to the side. "Or was it Dmitri's cock you wanted? It's really difficult to keep track. No one wants you, Mae. Not even the monsters."

"Aiden chose you—"

"Because he wants *me*." Charlie tried for a saucy grin, but it hurt too much to look truly convincing. "If he really wanted to hurt my dad, he would have snatched me off the street the same way you did." She jerked her chin at the warehouse around them, and then lowered her voice. "Though, honey, seriously, he would have done the whole torture bit with more pizzazz."

"Bitch." Mae slid forward, tipping her chair onto two

legs, getting right in Charlie's face. "I'm going to send your engagement ring back to that bastard—with your finger attached."

Charlie head-butted her. It wasn't a clean hit, but she felt Mae's nose give. The woman screamed and hit the ground, blood pouring from her nose. Charlie stared at her, weaving despite being tied to the chair. *Going to have a hell of a headache if I live through this.*

She would have kicked Mae while she was down, but her ankles were zip-tied to the damn chair. She couldn't even work up the fluid to spit on the fallen woman, but she managed to say, "You talk too much."

* * *

Aiden moved through the dark, Romanov at his side. He wasn't too keen on the arrangement, but it was a necessary evil—James was liable to snap Romanov's neck if he had the opportunity. They approached the side of the north warehouse facing the water. There were two men milling near the door. The guards.

They didn't break their stride, moving almost as one. He shot the man on the left, and saw the one on the right drop at nearly the same moment. The silencers on their guns made the smallest of sounds as they delivered death. It didn't seem right. Death should be an event—something loud and impossible to ignore.

But the guards' silent slide to the ground suited his purposes. He glanced back without slowing down. Mark and his men would remove the bodies and take out their replacements, leaving Aiden and Dmitri free to search the warehouse. There was a second team coming in from the back with the same intention. At the south warehouse, James was doing the same thing. One of them would find her.

They had to.

He strode into the warehouse and froze. Charlie sat in the middle of the space, her head lolling, covered in so much blood it was a wonder she had any left in her body. He started for her, but Romanov threw out a hand and stopped him short. "Not yet."

That's when he noticed the moaning body at Charlie's feet. Mae.

Aiden shoved Romanov's hand away and stalked across the space. A movement in the hallway between two stacks of pallets morphed into a massive man who looked intent on murder. Aiden didn't give him the chance to take another step. He shot him.

He kicked the chair across from Charlie out of the way and pointed the gun at Mae.

"Wait." Charlie's voice rasped through the roaring in his ears.

He didn't look away from the woman on the ground. "This is the only way."

"Aiden, *wait*."

He kicked the knife away from Mae's side and then used the same foot to flip her over onto her back. Her nose was definitely broken, the bottom half of her face covered in blood. She blinked stupidly at him. "What are you doing here?" The words came out jumbled.

"Give me one good reason why I shouldn't shoot you."

"*Aiden*." Charlie took a shuddering breath. "Aiden, call my dad. Do this the right way. Please."

He didn't want to. Mae was a threat—even if the theoretical trial managed to come down in their favor and put her behind bars, she could orchestrate a whole lot of damage from a prison cell. "You won't be safe as long as she's alive." His finger hovered on the trigger, his need to keep Charlie safe overriding everything else.

But if he shot Mae right now in cold blood, he'd lose Charlie forever.

He took one step back, and then another. "Romanov, get something to tie her with."

"This is a mistake." But the Russian did as he asked.

Aiden grabbed the knife from the ground and moved to cut Charlie's ties. "How hurt are you?"

"I'm alive."

It was an answer and no answer at all. He kept a hand on her shoulder so she wouldn't slump out of the chair, and moved around to check her injuries. There were shallow cuts everywhere, but judging from the amount of blood that was half-dried, she wouldn't bleed out like he'd feared before they could get to safety. He glanced over to make sure Romanov had secured Mae and then back to Charlie. "Fuck, Charlie." He kissed her, quick and light, and then picked her up to cradle her against his chest. "Let's go home."

The fact that she didn't argue with his carrying her told him exactly how hurt she was. He turned to Romanov, but the Russian had a phone to his ear and a vaguely annoyed look on his face. He hung up and slipped it into his pocket. "We have to leave now."

"Cops?"

"Feds."

It figured. He didn't know if John Finch had a way to track his daughter, but if Aiden had been driven batshit crazy with the knowledge that Charlie was at Mae's mercy, surely even a stone-cold bastard like the fed would be affected.

He held Charlie closer and started for the door. "Leave Mae for them."

"Gladly." Romanov didn't follow him, though. "You may use my residence for a stopover before returning to Boston."

"Where are you going?"

"I have business to attend to."

It wasn't really an answer, but Aiden had more pressing concerns than Romanov's games—namely, getting Charlie somewhere safe so he could clean her up and figure out how badly she was injured.

So he could apologize for getting her into this mess to begin with.

He shouldered out the door and stopped short. Mark and his men were facing off with cops. All had their guns drawn and steely looks on their faces, but his attention was caught and held by the man in the center. John Finch.

Guess I didn't move fast enough.

Charlie raised her head, and the relief on her father's face was apparent for all to see. He strode forward, ignoring the standoff around them. "Charlie."

She managed a smile, which made Aiden want to hug her tighter. "Dad."

He'd never met John Finch in person, but the man looked older than in his pictures. Or maybe it was seeing his daughter in danger that had aged him in such a short time. His eyes were Charlie's eyes—though more gray than blue—seeing far too much. His gaze flicked between them, and Aiden didn't try to hide how he felt about the woman in his arms. He and Charlie had some shit to work out, but he fully intended on making this thing between them permanent.

Both he and John Finch had a lot to come to terms with as a result.

"Dad, Mae Eldridge is in the warehouse—*alive*." Charlie's voice was strong despite the circumstances. "She kidnapped and tortured me. I'll testify."

"We'll talk about that later." He looked at Aiden again and hesitated, seeming torn. Finally, he cursed. "You and I will have words later, as well, O'Malley."

Since it suited his purposes perfectly, Aiden didn't comment on the fact that Finch was more concerned with arresting Mae Eldridge than seeing his daughter to the nearest hospital. He didn't ask about her injuries, didn't show more than the barest hint of emotion, aside from walking directly to her despite the hostile men at Aiden's back.

From the way Charlie wilted, just a little, as he carried her away from the warehouse, it was clear she hadn't missed it, either. "I knew you'd come." She spoke so softly, he had to strain to hear her.

He kissed the top of her head and made his way to the waiting car. They'd stop over at Romanov's "residence" long enough to get her cleaned up, and then they'd go back to Boston. Any talk of the future could wait until them. "I'll always come for you, bright eyes. Always."

CHAPTER TWENTY-SEVEN

Dmitri left the helicopter on the roof of the building he'd purchased a little over a year ago and made it to the car waiting for him at the curb in record time. He checked his watch as the driver muscled his way through the early morning traffic. Aiden would see to his woman's health before he tried to travel back to Boston, and by that point he'd be hitting peak rush-hour traffic.

All going according to plan.

He hadn't known Mae was going to be so foolish for the second time in less than a week, but he wouldn't hesitate to take advantage of the situation. In the last few days, he'd discovered that Aiden O'Malley had attempted to pit the FBI against him. He could admire the man's genius, but he had no intention of spending the rest of his life in a prison cell—or rotting away in an unmarked grave somewhere. Once he'd realized Charlie Moreaux was none other than Charlotte Finch, it all became clear.

She would want revenge for that unfortunate business with the NYPD. It would never occur to her that he'd had nothing directly to do with it. He hadn't even known the cops on his payroll were going to strike one of their own until after the fact—though he hadn't stood in their way as they'd put together a case against her.

Dirty cops really were loathsome creatures.

It would be best for everyone if she put that all behind her and settled into a life with Aiden—and if Aiden himself did the same. Let sleeping monsters lie and all that nonsense.

But Dmitri knew people, and he knew that was a lost hope. Even if Aiden called off his vendetta, he wouldn't willingly follow through with their deal regarding Keira— a deal that had clearly been made to distract Dmitri while O'Malley got his players into place. And *that* Dmitri couldn't allow.

"We're here, boss."

"Keep the car running." He slipped out into the brisk morning air and looked up to find the first rays of sunrise lightening the sky. If Aiden had alerted the family to the emergency, it would make Dmitri's job significantly more complicated. He took his phone out as he strode down the block toward the O'Malley town house.

The phone rang several times before a sleepy voice answered. "Do you even know what time it is?"

Dmitri slowed to a stop, able to imagine Keira perfectly. Though it wasn't her bed he pictured her in—it was his. *Unforgivable.* He ignored the voice in his head, relishing the sight of her tangled with his sheets, her hair spilled out over his pillows, her eyes barely open as she murmured her question.

Sentimental. Not something he was used to being accused of, even if *he* was the one doing the accusing. "Are you still wearing my ring?"

The sounds of rustling echoed across the line. When she answered, the sleep was gone from her voice. "Yes."

It was on the tip of his tongue to offer her everything she could ever want and more, but for the first time in his life, he wasn't sure how a person would react in a given situation.

Keira might come with him, no questions asked, because she wanted him.

She might *choose* him.

He couldn't guarantee that she would.

So he went with the safer bet. "Your brother intends to break his word to me and cancel our engagement."

"*What?*"

"You can stop it, Keira. Come with me now and I'll forget that he was going to break his word."

There was movement in the window of her room. She pulled the curtains back and stared at him from behind the relative safety of the glass. "If I come with you now"—her voice hitched—"promise me there will be peace. Give me your word."

He couldn't. Dmitri never gave his word if he couldn't guarantee he could keep it. "I give my word that I will do nothing further to antagonize your brother and the situation."

"But if he comes after me, you'll finish what he started. No. I'm not signing Aiden's death warrant." She was a smart girl. She'd heard what he *wasn't* saying.

He cursed in Russian. "I will do everything in my power to broker peace *if* you come with me right this moment." The longer he stood outside the O'Malley home, the greater the chance someone would see and report it. "The clock is ticking, Keira."

She hesitated, and he could practically see the wheels in her head turning. Finally, she nodded. "Give me two minutes."

"Be quick."

Exactly one hundred twenty seconds later, the window opened and Keira climbed out. She carried a small bag, and part of him was curious as to what had been important enough for her to pack. He'd get the answer later. If she was coming with him now, it meant he had the rest of their lives to delve into her secrets.

Anticipation curled through him as she climbed down the tree with ease. After the repeated frustrations and disappointments the last few years had brought, he was walking away with the single most important piece of the game as far as he was concerned. *I win.* He touched the small of her back, because he could, and turned toward where the car was still idling down the block.

He should have known it wouldn't be that simple.

"Stop."

Dmitri looked over his shoulder to find Cillian O'Malley standing on the front step, pointing a gun at him with an unwavering grip. He almost sighed, but he had no intention of getting himself or Keira shot. "Put the gun down, Cillian."

"I don't care if you helped Aiden and Charlie, you are *not* taking my sister anywhere."

That was rich coming from the man who was currently married to *Dmitri's* half sister. Since Dmitri valued his time with Hadley—and Olivia by proxy—he couldn't draw the gun he had nestled in the shoulder holster beneath his jacket. Not to mention that Cillian showed every evidence of being a good man and had been a positive influence on both Olivia and Hadley. Shooting him would be a damn shame.

Fortunately, Cillian had already gift-wrapped for Dmitri the key to his undoing.

He kept his hand lightly resting on Keira's back, a physical reminder to her to not to move too quickly. He didn't want her idiot brother to pull the trigger by accident. Dmitri turned his attention to Cillian. "Do you remember when we called a cease-fire?"

The man glared. "You mean when you extorted that promise from Olivia that granted you access to Hadley? Yeah, I remember."

"There was another promise made that day." He didn't wait for the man to work it out. "You owe me a favor, Cillian O'Malley."

"The fuck I do."

Is there no honor left in this world? He bit back his irritation. "Break your word and our deal is null and void."

Cillian hesitated, clearly torn between the woman he loved and his youngest sister. Dmitri couldn't be sure which way Cillian would fall at the end of the internal struggle he was currently engaged in, and that aggravated him almost as much as the man threatening to break his word.

Keira put her hand on Dmitri's chest and stepped forward a little. "Cillian, please. Just let me go. I'm choosing this. I'll be okay. I promise."

Cillian relaxed, partially lowering the gun, and Dmitri almost rolled his eyes. She was lying through her teeth. She hadn't been okay in a very long time, as best he could tell. But if her brothers hadn't stepped in before now, there was no reason to expect they'd step in today.

The gun inched lower, finally aiming safely at the

concrete at Cillian's feet. "Aiden is going to come after you, Keira. You know that."

"He promised to respect my choice." Her voice was low and fierce. "If he pulls the same shit Teague pulled with Sloan, I'll shoot him myself."

Cillian's gaze flicked to where her hand was still on Dmitri's chest. "That was a different situation."

"No, it wasn't." She turned and walked away, now gripping his shirt to tow him after her. Dmitri allowed it, because if it looked like she was in control, it would assuage Cillian's guilt and maybe he'd be quiet about what had occurred for a little while longer.

It wasn't until they were in the backseat that Keira slouched against the leather and closed her eyes. "How long until we get to your place?"

"We're not going to my place." Not yet.

She opened one eye. "Then where are we going?"

"A chapel."

* * *

Aiden couldn't make himself let go of Charlie. He held her the entire car ride to the Russian's home. He carried her up the stairs to the suite that was apparently theirs for the duration. The bed was luxurious to the point of idiocy, but he was more concerned with getting Charlie cleaned up so he could see the damage.

He turned to the man who'd met them when they arrived. "We'll need medical supplies and something loose and comfortable for her to change into." The man nodded, and Aiden shut and locked the bathroom door.

Only then did Charlie speak. "I can stand on my own."

In more ways than one. "I know, bright eyes." He helped her sit on the counter and carefully took stock. The blood had dried in many places, fusing the clothes to her skin. To get them off, they were going to have to reopen the wounds. "If we get these wet, they'll be less likely to hurt you when we get them off."

"And harder to get off." She gave a halfhearted smirk. "That's what she said."

He pulled a knife from his boot and set to work cutting apart her clothes. It would make it easier to pull them away once he got her in the shower. "I'm sorry."

"For what? Saving my life?" She rested her hands on his shoulders as he worked. Her passiveness and too-wide blue eyes read shock to him. The faster he got her cleaned, patched up, and in warm, dry clothes, the better.

"You wouldn't have been in that warehouse if it wasn't for me. I pulled you into this mess."

"Because I'm John Finch's daughter."

He froze. He could lie to her. He could remind her of all the good things they'd shared that had nothing to do with whose children they were. But if he wanted a chance in hell of her staying, he couldn't dodge this truth. "You're right. I picked you because of who your father was and the fact you were burned by Romanov."

She sifted her fingers through his hair. "I know."

"Charlie, I'm sorry." He went to his knees in front of her, still holding onto her hips. "I could have found another way, and we both know it. It sounds cliché as fuck, but my motivation changed almost immediately, right around the time we ended up in bed together. I don't even know how to explain it, but you *fit*. You see me in a way that no one else does, and you're never afraid to push back when I'm being a dick."

"Which is regularly."

For once, he couldn't read a single thing on her face. Aiden didn't know if it was shock or if she had written him off right around the time Mae took her. "If I hadn't—"

"Aiden, stop. As charming as it is hearing you grovel, the truth is Mae taking me had nothing to do with you."

He went stock-still. "What are you talking about?"

"That vendetta you have against my father? You're not the only one. From the sounds of it, he's managed to piss off every single organized-crime family in a three-hundred-mile radius." The corners of her lips turned down. "He never told me. I knew his work was important—dangerous, even—but he never bothered to warn me that it might trickle down to me."

She looked so damn heartbroken that he pushed to his feet and gathered her close. "I know this isn't something I can make right, but I meant it when I said I was playing for keeps. It's too fucking soon, but if the last twelve hours have proven anything, it's that we can't take a damn thing for granted. I love you, Charlie. I love your strength and your intelligence, and your wicked sense of humor. I love that you're a survivor and it doesn't matter how hard the world knocks you down, because you come back swinging."

"Aiden." There was a wealth of information in the way she said his name, weary to the core.

He pressed a kiss to her forehead, right above one of the cuts. "It's too soon. You don't have to answer now. Or tomorrow. Or, hell, next week. You're safe, bright eyes. I'll wait as long as you need, and once you make your decision, if you tell me to get lost, I'll respect that." He checked to make sure she wouldn't keel over and then stood up to turn on the shower.

Neither of them spoke as the water heated up. Silence

continued to reign through the painful process of cleaning Charlie's wounds and bandaging her up. Aiden found two sets of clothes laid out on the bed and quickly changed into the sweats and T-shirt meant for him. He helped Charlie put on a matching set.

She looked like she'd gone through a war—and she had.

"Where do you want to go?"

"My apartment." She rattled off an address that he remembered from the file Liam had compiled when they first put the plan into motion.

Aiden nodded. "Let's go." The sooner they were out of the Romanov residence, the better. He didn't think Dmitri would go back on his word after enduring so much shit to keep them alive, but he wasn't willing to risk Charlie on an assumption.

Forty-five minutes later, Mark dropped them off in front of a run-down building six blocks from the bar Aiden had first found her in. He fought down the instinct demanding that he toss her ass back into the car and drive to a safer neighborhood. Charlie had lived here for two years without incident. She was more than capable of taking care of herself.

That didn't mean he had to like it.

He hesitated in front of the door. "Will you let me check the place out?"

"I'd like you to stay the night." She shook almost imperceptibly. "Just tonight."

"Anything you need, bright eyes."

She unlocked the door to her apartment and let them in. It was as run-down as the rest of the place, but Charlie had livened it up with bright throws on the secondhand furniture and equally bright prints on the walls. Her bedroom was more of the same, a orange and white chevron knitted blanket covering the dull gray comforter and making the whole place feel more like a home than just a location where someone slept. "I like it."

"You're already categorizing the improvements you'd make—if you wouldn't buy the whole building and condemn it outright." She carefully pulled the T-shirt off and slid the sweats down her legs. Her body was a patchwork of bruises and cuts, but she hadn't had any trouble breathing and showed no signs of internal bleeding.

"I should call Doc Jones."

"I'm fine." Charlie shook her head and then winced. "Not fine. I'm nowhere near fine. But Mae was careful enough not to do anything that would kill me, and the cuts aren't deep enough to scar. She wasn't done playing yet."

His stomach lodged in his throat. Aiden stripped quickly and pulled down the covers. "Come here."

She didn't hesitate. He settled them in her bed, her back against his front, and tucked the blankets up around them. Her little shakes didn't dissipate for the longest time, but she slowly relaxed, muscle by muscle.

"If you need to talk about it, I'm here."

"I don't want to." She pulled his arms tighter around her. "Not yet."

"Okay." There was nothing else to say. Nothing else to do. Aiden had played every card in his deck, and if he kept pushing her when she was still in shock from being tortured, then he was the worst kind of asshole. So he held her and murmured nonsense until her breathing evened out and the last of her tension melted away.

He said he'd give her time, and he would honor that. No matter how much he hated the thought of walking away from her, even for a short time. *Hopefully, a short time.*

Please, God, don't let it be forever.

* * *

Charlie woke slowly. Every part of her body hurt, but her heart most of all. She kept flashing back to the way her dad had just walked past her in pursuit of arresting Mae. To the fear written across Aiden's face, which hadn't gone away, even when he was crawling into bed with her.

She reached out, but the other side of the bed was cold. Her hand came in contact with her phone, and she pulled it to her face. Someone must have found it at the warehouse, because she distinctly remembered Mae taking it from her. It was remarkably blood-free and fully charged. She had half a dozen notifications, and she scrolled through them without unlocking her phone.

From Keira:
Where are you? Everyone is freaking out and no one will tell me anything.
Charlie, what the FUCK is going on?
Oh my god, Cillian told me. You had BETTER come home safe, goddamnit.

From Carrigan:
James is less than 30 min behind Aiden. I know you won't get this until after, but keep fighting, Charlie. They're coming for you.

The last one was from a number she didn't recognize.
Liam will live. I know you'll be happy to hear that. He wants to see you when you get a chance. —Cillian

Charlie's heart beat too hard. The O'Malleys had closed ranks around her. They might not be physically here, but she felt it all the same. *Is this what having a family is like?*

She tried very hard not to notice that there were no calls or texts from her father. After nearly thirty years, that shouldn't hurt. She should be used to it by now. Charlie had always come second to the job. Almost dying wouldn't be enough for her dad to change.

Would he have come to my funeral if I had died? Or would he have just arranged for me to be cremated, and scattered my ashes when he had a day off?

Feeling sick, she sat up. Her thumb hit the screen and accidentally swiped the wrong direction, bringing up the daily news. Charlie was about to swipe it away, but the headline caught her eye:

DIRTY COPS ARRESTED

She clicked the article. Shock grew with each line she read—with each *name* she read. Her former partner. The same trio of men who framed her and then beat the shit out of her. Someone had come forward accusing them of taking bribes from local criminals and stealing drugs from the evidence locker. "I...What...How?" She finished the article and sat there for a long moment, just thinking.

Somehow she knew that Aiden had to be behind their being arrested. *Justice.* She didn't know if it was something he'd done in the last few days to make up for Dmitri walking free or if it was something he'd set in place the moment she'd agreed to help him. It didn't really matter. What mattered was that he'd promised her justice—and he'd delivered.

Without killing anyone.

The last two weeks felt like the most surreal of her life, which was saying something. It shouldn't be possible to fall for someone that fast.

What she and Aiden had wasn't perfect, and there were still kinks to work out, but was any relationship perfect? He was willing to work with her and meet her halfway. He challenged her and forced her to be better than she'd been before. It was surprising how well she'd fit into his family.

He was still a criminal. That wouldn't change.

She stared at her phone. Could she live with that? It went against everything she'd been raised to value.

But the man who'd raised her with those values had left her in the arms of a criminal last night. He hadn't stopped to ensure that she'd get medical care or to find out what their plans were. Her dad just let them leave.

And the police department she'd spent most of her life admiring had kicked her out on her ass the second she did something they didn't like. Every single "friend" she'd had who was a cop had dropped off the map the second the news came out that branded her as dirty. The legendary loyalty she'd always believed in had dried up and left her totally and completely alone.

Was she going to throw away a real chance at happiness—and potentially doing some good in the world—because of people who obviously didn't give two fucks about her?

The criminals had shown her more compassion and loyalty than the people on the right side of the law.

They'd been more family to her than her actual family.

And Aiden…

Aiden.

He'd made her feel alive—truly alive—for the first time in as long as she could remember. Her body lit up in his presence, where she felt truly safe. It wasn't a lie. The world wasn't perfect, but with Aiden she felt like there was actually a chance she could make a difference. Somehow.

She called him.

Aiden answered immediately. "Are you okay? Is something wrong?"

"Everything is fine." Better than fine—or it would be as soon as she saw him again. "Where are you?"

"A few blocks away. I went to grab you something to eat since the only thing in your fridge is a bottle of ketchup."

Charlie smiled, though it pulled at the cut on her cheek, and settled back against her headboard. "You didn't leave."

"Fuck no. I said I'll give you time, and I will, but it'd be a dick move to disappear without making sure you were good." There were traffic sounds in the background and the rustling of paper bags. "I'll be back in five."

"Okay." She found a robe that she'd never bothered to use tucked into the back of her tiny closet, and wrapped that around herself, since getting dressed was beyond her at the moment. Then she waited for him in her tiny living room.

It felt like a small eternity before Aiden walked through her door, but it couldn't have been more than the promised five minutes. He looked tired, scruff on his jaw and shadows beneath his green eyes.

He set two bags and a drink carrier on the kitchen counter and walked over to crouch in front of her. "You okay?"

"Thanks to you."

He gave a sharp shake of his head. "We went over this last night."

"Aiden, stop." She framed his face with her hands. "Did you mean what you said?"

He didn't pretend to misunderstand. He covered her

hands with his own. There were no masks between them this time. Just the naked longing on his face and her holding her breath, waiting for his answer. "I love you, Charlie. I'll give you all the time you need, but I love the fuck out of you, and if you'd go home with me right now, it would make me the happiest man alive."

She kissed him. It was the barest brushing of lips, and he let her control every second of it. Charlie shivered and sat back. "Have you seen the news?"

"Yes." Just that. Nothing more.

She sighed. "Did you have something to do with that?"

"They hurt you." His green eyes went hard. "I'd prefer them to be at the bottom of the Atlantic, but that wouldn't clear your name. This will, eventually."

Once upon a time, that would have been the most important thing to her. It *was* important, but it had slid down the list. The only people whose opinion mattered to her now were the ones who'd stick with her through the good and the bad—who didn't jump ship at the first sign of trouble.

She stroked her thumbs along his cheekbones. "This won't be easy. We're both too stubborn for our own good, and I'm going to demand we take a page from Carrigan's book and start to balance the scales a bit."

He went so still, he might not have been breathing. "What are you saying?"

"I'm saying I love you, Aiden. I'm saying that I don't need time, because all I want is you."

He looked like he wanted to pull her into a crushing embrace, but he leaned forward and kissed her lips, her jaw, her forehead. "Fuck, Charlie, I love you, too."

"Take me home." She slapped his hands away when he went to pick her up. "I can walk this time."

"Humor me? I want to hold you for a bit, bright eyes."

She cast him a put-upon look, but she couldn't hold it, because she was grinning too hard. "How long is 'a bit'?"

"Oh, I don't know." Aiden carefully scooped her up like he had the night before, cradling her against his chest. He headed for the door. "How about the rest of our lives?"

DON'T MISS THE NEXT BOOK IN THE SIZZLING O'MALLEYS SERIES!

Read Dmitri and Keira's story in *The Bastard's Bargain*, coming in early 2018.

ABOUT THE AUTHOR

KATEE ROBERT is a *New York Times* and *USA Today* bestselling author, who learned to tell stories at her grandpa's knee. Her novel *The Marriage Contract* was a RITA finalist, and *RT Book Reviews* named it "a compulsively readable book with just the right amount of suspense and tension." When not writing sexy contemporary and romantic suspense, she spends her time playing imaginary games with her children, driving her husband batty with what-if questions, and planning for the inevitable zombie apocalypse.

Fall in Love with Forever Romance

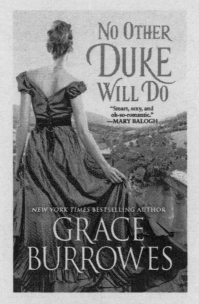

"Smart, sexy, and oh-so-romantic."
—MARY BALOGH

New York Times BESTSELLING AUTHOR
GRACE BURROWES

NO OTHER DUKE WILL DO
By Grace Burrowes

From Grace Burrowes comes the next installment in the *New York Times* bestselling Windham Brides series! It's the house party of the decade, and everyone is looking for a spouse—especially Julian St. David, Duke of Haverford. The moment he meets Elizabeth Windham, their attraction is overwhelming, unexpected...and absolutely impossible. With meddling siblings, the threat of financial ruin, and gossips lurking behind every potted palm, will they find true love or true disaster?

Fall in Love with Forever Romance

ALWAYS YOU
By Denise Grover Swank

Matt Osborn had no idea coaching his five-year-old nephew's soccer team would get him so much attention from the mothers—attention he doesn't want now that he's given up on love and having a family of his own. Yep, Matt's the last of his bachelor buddies, and plans on staying that way. That is, until he finds himself face-to-face with the woman who broke his heart. The latest from *USA Today* bestselling author Denise Grover Swank is a winner!

Fall in Love with Forever Romance

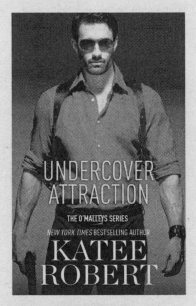

UNDERCOVER ATTRACTION
By Katee Robert

New York Times and *USA Today* bestselling author Katee Robert continues her smoking-hot O'Malleys series. Ex-cop Charlotte Finch used to think there was a clear line between right and wrong. Then her fellow officers betrayed her, and the world is no longer so black and white. Especially when it's Aiden O'Malley, one of the most dangerous men in Boston, who offers her a chance for justice. The only catch: She'll have to pretend to be his fiancée for his plan to work.

Fall in Love with Forever Romance

THE BACHELOR CONTRACT
By Rachel Van Dyken

Brant Wellington could have spent the rest of his life living under the magical spell of alcohol, women, and forgetting his problems. That is, until a certain bachelor auction forces him back on the family payroll and off to assess one of the Wellington resorts. Only no one warned him that his past would be there waiting for him... Don't miss the newest book from #1 *New York Times* bestselling author Rachel Van Dyken!

WICKED INTENTIONS
By Elizabeth Hoyt

Don't miss *Wicked Intentions*, the *New York Times* bestseller that started Elizabeth Hoyt's classic Maiden Lane series!